Cries from
the Static

Cries from the Static

Darren Speegle

Cries from the Static © 2017
by Darren Speegle

Published by Raw Dog Screaming Press
Bowie, MD

First Edition

Cover Image: PLACEHOLDER
Book Design: Kevin Kusisto

Printed in the United States of America

ISBN: 978-1-935738-61

Library of Congress Control Number: 2017958679

www.RawDogScreaming.com

Previously Published

"A Lonely Town in Alaska" previously published in *Shivers VII*, 2012

"Der Teufelobstgarten" previously published in *Brutarian*, 2005

"Hexerei" previously published in *Corpse Blossoms*, 2005

"Kiss of Chromium, Caress of Isolation" previously published in *Of Eggs and Elephants,* 2013

"Lago Di Iniquità" previously published in *The Third Alternative*, 2005

"Lauren, with the Fall of Night" previously published in *Dark Discoveries*, 2016

"Saudade" previously published in *Crimewave*, 2008

"The Horticulturist's Daughter" previously published in *Cemetery Dance*, 2008

"The Moon, a Roman Token" previously published in *Fantasy*, 2009

For Chiraphon, who keeps me in check

Contents

Introduction: Paper Hallucinations

I roomed with Darren Speegle toward the end of the *2006 World Fantasy Convention* in Austin, Texas. We were in town to shake a few hands and watch other writers take home awards. A physically strong guy, flint-eyed and barrel-chested. Tough as nails beneath an easygoing and collegial demeanor. At the time, he lived in southeast Alaska and routinely traveled across Europe. These journeys left a stamp upon him—physically and creatively. Were he to appear in a Rider-Smith-Waite tarot deck, Speegle's likeness would be that of The Hermit, wand and lantern in hand, eyes fixed upon the veil that separates this reality from whatever awaits.

Speegle's imagination is inherently sui generis, but writing is as much nurture as it is nature, and so I'm grateful his adventures in far-flung regions from Juneau to Iraq have inflected his ever-growing corpus. In 2006, I'd read his two early collections—*Gothic Wine* and the follow-up, *A Dirge for the Temporal.* Both were published in 2004, the former by *Aardwolf Press* and latter by *Raw Dog Screaming Press.* Yet, digging into the bibliographical provenance of the various stories, there's a seismic shift from his earliest work around the turn of the millennium (albeit trippy and complex, it cleaves to more traditional horror tropes) to material produced even a couple of years later, which segues into weirdness worthy of Robert Aickman and Jorge Luis Borges.

Speegle found his bearings in short order and for the past dozen years he's steadily compiled a catalogue of fiction that overlaps the boundaries of horror, occult, and psychosexually-charged mystery. His writing is imbued with dark wisdom, perhaps borne of cynicism, and if not cynicism, definitely hard-knocks experience. He uses weird fiction as a lens to examine our eternal preoccupation with the strange territory of humanity's inner life, which is but a microcosm of the strange territory of the greater universe. He sharpens that focus with brilliant intensity upon the subcategories of betrayal, fraught romance, and sudden, inevitable death. His specialty is a naturalist's eye for a certain subspecies of expat. The doomed kind.

It's an oft-abused habit to describe authors and their work by comparing and contrasting to other writers. That said, the field is broad, and its soil is rich. There is value in contrast and comparison. The contemporary author who reminds me of Speegle in a significant respect is Don Tumasonis, whose slim, but potent, oeuvre includes "Prospect Cards" and "What Goes Down," two of the finest examples of weird fiction published since the last century.

I briefly referenced this connection (during a broader appreciation of Speegle's work) nearly a decade ago. Quoting from my essay:

*Tumasonis and Speegle share certain qualities and explore similar themes—strangers in strange lands, the uncertainty and mutability of relationships, geography as a mirror for the mind, an extension of dream state. Both produce work I find grandly elliptical and consummately dark. Fellow author, Gary Braunbeck, once referred to Speegle's stories as "Hallucinations on paper." My reaction to a concentrated dose of **Gothic Wine** and **A Dirge for the Temporal** in a brief period was one of profound cognitive dislocation. Speegle's tales frequently approximate lucid dreams, his protagonists often interchangeable with the author, if not the reader. Seldom has the unreliable narrator been so smoothly accomplished. As is the hallmark of much heavyweight literature, immersion in this guy's world may affect one's own dream state. The elliptical nature of Speegle's prose, its elegance and simplicity is striking as evidenced by this passage from his short story "Lago di Inquita":*

"We did Florence, Venice, and Verona, in that order, during the first three full days of our seven-day vacation. In the presence of Michelangelo's *David* one reassessed one's opinions about the nature of things; all the superlatives, no matter how soulfully or originally uttered, became instant cliché. Lovers' Venice, with its watery streets and sighing bridges, was a much easier distraction. As was Verona, which ensnared one in Roman history rather than the elusive and delicate Renaissance. Somewhere in the middle lay the dark ages, my real reason for being in Europe again."

Speegle has lived in Europe, spent a significant amount of time exploring the landscapes, the cultures. These influences are unmistakable, indeed, inseparable from the fiction itself. His horrors, the intrinsic darkness of his themes, derive from the angst of the American as outsider, the barriers of language, custom, the very weight of history no process of naturalization is likely to ever fully breach.

Ten years on, the superlatives readers, authors, and editors heap upon Speegle continue to stand—continue to stand and continue to accrue. The example above exhibits the airtight craftsmanship you'll find whatever page, paragraph or line you might flip to at random in this collection. If anything, he's improved. Enthusiastic pursuit of a stainless-steel polish has given way to a rawer, edgier finish. The closing number, *American Kisses* demonstrates a tonal shift, a welding of homage (Peter Straub's M.O. Dengler and Speegle's Hinterlove tread similar benighted hunting trails) to 1980s literary horror/noir and latter day realities of instant communication and instant disinformation. The approach complex, dizzying, and ultimately, effective.

The tales included in *Cries from the Static* cover Speegle's aforementioned fascination with the corruption of romantic love and an affinity with the lost and the fated among us. He's a nimble and accomplished stylist; he shifts from the lush informality of "Lago di Inquita" to the mannered impeccability of "Hexerai," and makes it look much easier than the reality, which is that this control is the product of a strong work ethic and rare talent. Recent years have seen him travel to Afghanistan and Iraq, and while I possess no special insight regarding his experiences, Speegle's newer work (such as *American Kisses*) seems to be influenced by what he's seen in the Middle East. His narrative voice, his techniques and thematic concerns are mutating on a profound scale. Smoke, ghosts, and psychic screams fill the margins with commentary on this modern iteration of an ancient, savage world.

A cut from *American Kisses* to emphasize the point:

"Hinterlove didn't wait until his senses returned to him. He was on top of the kid in a flash, securing him with his knees before bashing in his teeth with the butt of his weapon. Inserting the gun's barrel into the jagged and bloody hole, he blew the back of his skull into the desert floor. Regarding the end product satisfactorily, he then stood, undid his fatigues, and in an action that received more shock than support from the contingent of men that had rushed in behind their fallen comrades, pissed on the boy's face."

This is brutal and unflinching, and within the context of the narrative, slides hooks into the reader and makes them complicit to the unfolding atrocities. *American Kisses* serves as a not-so-gentle reminder that we're *all*, to one degree or another, complicit in the violence perpetrated in our name. We should thank him for that.

Gary Braunbeck indeed captured the essence of it when he referred to Darren Speegle's prose as "hallucinations on paper." Braunbeck's perfect description has stuck in my mind, wedded to the complementary notion that a rarified literary style, a rarified literary composition, activates the brain in a manner similar to classical music. *Cries from the Static* is certainly rarified; a beautiful and arresting dark symphony resulting from the maturation and refinement of one of our best. The highest compliment I can pay the man, is to say it could have been written by none other than Darren Speegle.

Now, permit me to step back into the shadows and cede the auditorium to the maestro.

—Laird Barron
Stone Ridge, NY
December 31, 2016

Lago Di Iniquita

"This is the most beautiful place I've ever seen," came the inevitable words from Lily's mouth. She was posed like the lover she was against the balcony's decorative railing, blouse revealing her midriff, the caressive June air as Italian as it was Alpine.

Her exact sentiment must have been expressed thousands of times, in a variety of different languages, from the balconies and terraces of the mountainside on which the village of Tignale had been built. The words nonetheless sounded recited to me, as if she had consulted my late wife's journal, or ghost, or my own nightmares prior to our departure from the States. I had the brief inexplicable urge to press my palm against the tanned arch of her back, to cause her to have a flutter of doubt about my intentions as I forced her to look at the stone building below.

How had we ended up here, in an apartment so close to the one I had stayed in with my family five years before? Of course there had been that risk when I selected a Tignale location out of the *Tui* vacation rental catalog, but what were the chances we would be within eyesight—indeed practically on top of—the *Rustico Spagnol?* Perhaps subconsciously I had remembered the name of our current spot, *Cottage Mediterraneo*, from the sign on the winding rutted road that led up from the lake. I dared not discuss these thoughts with Lily, for she would call it destiny, a flavor that did not linger well on my tongue.

"I told you you would like it," I said. Past the moment of danger, I placed my hand on the naked skin of her back, rubbing, consciously ignoring that her thong underwear was visible above the low-cut waist of her fashionable pants. In many ways I got along with her *in spite of* her attractive features and figure.

She turned to me, putting her sleeveless arms around my neck. "Yes, you did. Now I'm wondering how you're going to drag me away from here to see Florence and Venice."

It had that effect, the northern part of the Gardasee. Across the lake from us the lushly green slope, punctuated with granite bluffs and medieval church steeples, merely provided the foreground for the snow-capped peaks beyond. Lake Garda itself painted a blue-green glassy serenity, playground to sailing vessels and dinner boats, and the promise of an aesthetically-oriented God.

Lily was further evidence towards that promise, as amazing to my touch and awareness now as she had been the day I found her deliberating over her studies outside my evening philosophy class. I had been more than willing to help her with the question about which she had been waiting to consult Dr. Jessie (whose nickname spoke to an uncanny resemblance to the actress Jessica Lange), though I discovered for my efforts that my younger peer grasped its core meaning better than I did. Her reason for haunting the university after dinnertime was the textbook one; mine, on the other hand, had more to do with loneliness than education.

In a sense, I thought as I smelled Lily's hair, felt the years that separated us against my rough cheek, this trip was like that.

In other ways it was vastly different.

*   *   *

We did Florence, Venice, and Verona, in that order, during the first three full days of our seven-day vacation. In the presence of Michelangelo's *David* one reassessed one's opinions about the nature of things; all the superlatives, no matter how soulfully or originally uttered, became instant cliché. Lovers' Venice, with its watery streets and sighing bridges, was a much easier distraction. As was Verona, which ensnared one in Roman history rather than the elusive and delicate Renaissance.

Somewhere in the middle lay the dark ages, my real reason for being in Europe again. It wasn't Caesar or da Vinci who'd called me, but a medieval saint named Laguaro, of whom the world at large knew nothing: a wandering monk who had wept tears of olive oil into a secluded Alpine lake in what he termed a *"valle di iniquità"*— valley of iniquity. If he had attained any renown, it was among sinners like myself—us and our victims, our wives and our sons and daughters, wherever they had gone.

While Lily and I didn't often converse about these topics, she knew that demons were in the cards and elected to accompany me anyway. It might have been easier to think she wanted a free trip to Europe, the mildly satisfying company of a widower with a portfolio and a phobia for deeper attachments.

But we had grown more than compatible over the last year and a half, such that the strange words had been floating around for months: life, marriage, baby. She had even been crude enough to suggest that this trip was a honeymoon. My soul, my conscience had the same idea, though with peace as the bride.

After hanging out by the pool and doing nothing on the fourth day, I invited Lily to ride up into the Dolomites with me on the fifth. She was duly surprised when I told her I wanted to spend the night in an Alpine village not more than an hour's drive north of the lake. To her credit, when I explained that I had always wanted to do an overnight in the mountains, she pretended to take me at face value.

We took our time, breakfasting on the balcony as we watched the low mist reluctantly give way to the windsurfers and sailors. Although the sky overhead looked promising, I suggested we carry both cool and warm attire. Aside from the fact that Garda created its own weather patterns, we were heading to higher elevations, where I had been surprised before.

Lily kissed me as we squeezed into the rental Fiesta. "You look sexy today, Tim." She always knew when to say what, pulling a smile out of the most subdued expression.

"We're going to need to stop and fill up," I told her as I let the engine idle, warming up the cool interior. "We don't want to be up there without petrol."

Had they had a station in Laguaro? I couldn't remember such details.

* * *

"You've been thinking about Kris and the kids a lot since we've been here," Lily said as we cruised along the narrow shore road, passing in and out of tunnels cut directly out of the rock, cowering from campers and buses compensating over the faded solid line. The occasional vineyards and lemon groves—their stone walls and winter housings often dating to Roman times—passed too quickly for contemplation.

"So I have," I said, keeping my eyes on the wily road.

"It's okay, you know…to talk."

"Truly, Lily, I'm not sure what there is to say." I pulled into a service station that sported a coat of arms logo and not even the pretense of a competitive fuel price.

"Say it pisses you off to pay these outrageous prices for gas," Lily said.

"It does, I assure you."

"Say it pisses you off that I ask questions."

"That too."

"Yet you invited me along."

"Yeah." I got out, only to find it was a full service, which I'd somehow missed.

Lily stepped out of the car, immediately engaging the guy in an argument over who was responsible for cleaning the windshield. I didn't care nearly as much as she did as I watched her storm away in the direction of the WC. If I couldn't expect to fill a Fiesta's fuel tank for less than sixty euro—which was seventy plus dollars at the current exchange rate—I certainly shouldn't expect service.

She reemerged in record time, perhaps in an even more incensed mood than when she'd entered. I suspected she had found one of the hole-in-the-floor toilets she so despised, and was about to issue consolatory words when I saw a shape emerge from the men's bathroom behind her.

My heart forgot its cadence as his eyes met mine for a familiar moment before his weathered mustached features dissolved beneath the shadowy brim of his hat. The afterimage remained, like a flash from a dream: the vineyards worker looking forward to (or returning from—it made no difference) another stooped day in the sun. Indeed I *had* dreamed of the stranger, in photographs snapped from around sudden corners, or as he became visible from between rows of luxuriant vines. I had dreamed of that partially detailed face ever since my Italian vacation of five years before, when I had brought my wife and my children.

Then the attendant was asking for my money. Asking for my money at that exact moment, an eventuality so terribly typical of this recurrent experience. When I turned from stuffing the twenty notes in his greasy fist, the other man had vanished into reality—the driver's seat of a car, the restaurant next door, the pedestrian tunnel that led to the other side of the street. I looked in every direction, but he was nowhere to be seen.

As Lily stepped into my sphere I sensed that the change that visited her was to do with my change, that the stupor, the disorientation had reached out to her like a contagion.

"I hate those fucking toilets," she said, following my eyes around the place. "Goddamn piss splashed up on my legs and there were no towels."

"I'm sorry," I said.

"Next time I'll go outside."

Up in the mountains you can do that. For some, the fluids fall from their bodies as olive oil.

*　　*　　*

I tried to explain the tradition to Lily as we drove the twisting roads up into the Dolomites, but my words made little sense even to me.

"Santo Laguaro said that his tears represented the sins of the iniquitous village he had found in the mountain valley. As olive oil can be removed from water without compromising its purity, so can our sins be removed from us. The custom is to pour a drop of olive oil into the *Lago di Iniquità* and reflect on a personal sin."

"And that's actually the name of the lake? They actually gave it that name because of a medieval monk's reference to a 'valley of iniquity?'"

"You'll find it on the map in your door sleeve."

"That's bizarre."

"Nonetheless."

"So why was the village given its Sodom status? What separated it from any other village?"

"I don't think that's ever explained. Maybe it was plague. Isolation. Excessive wine. Who knows."

"What does this have to do with your family, Tim?"

There it was, in fire, the present tense speaking either to the violence involved or to my refusal to let go the memories after a half decade. The question, in all its nakedness, asked: How does any of this figure into a random threesome dying at the hands of a random psychopath, across the Atlantic in America?

To which I have never been able to give a convincing answer, even to myself, with my vineyards worker peeking 'randomly' over my shoulder at my sins. My silence did not disillusion her. She knew innately that to go into the mountains seeking specific answers, rather than simple validation, was folly. The mountains were about answers in the same way that they were not about them; they filled one's body with desire at the second, with cold at the minute. Lily accepted this truth with a wisdom that was greater than me.

As the lake came into view there were no more questions. Shining waterfalls fed down from the peaks rising above the opposite shore, barely disturbing the tranquil surface as they united with the Alpine pool. Like the last time I had driven this road, the structures that came into view at the far end of the oblong body of water seemed out of place. As pristine a picture as they painted, they still seemed an annoyance on the face of nature.

For once in my life I didn't care about money, selecting the hotel with the best view. We unloaded from a street that was like an incision in its meager width, and parked the Fiesta in a pocket of our future memory of the place. Our balcony looked over the sea of my nightmares, with an empty cruet on the table, and a complimentary bottle of wine that might have been a deterrent, or an element of ease.

* * *

We had the restaurant's terrace to ourselves as we lunched afternoon-style on cheese and bread and red wine. When I ended up having to ask the waiter for the oil, he was perturbed, as though by some magic the tradition in which the village was so steeped had evaporated during the last five years. I didn't understand, and demanded to know why there were empty cruets on all the tables then. He forgot English suddenly, looking down on us from aloft before primly striding away. Lily didn't know what to make of his behavior any more than I did.

Though she had questions.

"Did you reflect over a sin back then, Tim? Is that what we're doing here?"

"Yes." The wine was like the mountains in its potentiality. "Yes, I reflected over a sin."

"Do you want to explain?" She sipped, and I saw the grape reds on her face, reflections of her European experience, its unsolicited mysteries.

The sun blazed out of a cloudless sky, counteracting the briskness off the lake. From behind my darkly tinted sunglasses I pondered the strangeness of Lily's presence. Her lips pouted her fashion of sobriety in my lenses, and I wished suddenly that I had not brought her here with me. Why had I? Was it fear? The need to fall back on someone?

"You've accused me," I said, "of being torn up with guilt about something I had no control over. Well, I may not have had control but I do have responsibility. You see, my sin…"

"Yes?"

"It had to do with my family."

"Go on." Lily said.

"Garan and Debs were always fighting. They were always being disrespectful to Kris and me. Particularly Debs, who was eleven at the time and felt the world revolved around her. She would hurt Kris with words, with disobedience, with actual physical bullying. Yet when I tried to punish her or her brother, Kris would come to their defense with the tears and blood running down her face. The family credo was dysfunction. I never understood what Kris and I did wrong aside from our differing parenting styles. I guess that was enough."

"Sounds like any middle-class family to me," Lily said, watching herself in my shades. Her wisdom had a flavor about it that reminded me, not fondly, of Kris.

"The morning we'd planned to drive up into the Alps," I continued, "we started fighting, all four of us, *loudly*. God knows what the people staying in the neighboring apartments must have thought. In the end Kris did this thing she had a habit of doing, waving her arms in the air like so and telling me I should just go on without them. *Without* them, mind you. We are in the middle of our European vacation, having planned to take a drive into the Alps to hike and picnic and enjoy the scenery, and suddenly I'm going without them.

"I should have waited till everybody cooled, but I didn't. Basically I said fuck the bunch of you, I will go by myself and I will fucking enjoy it."

I paused to drink from my wineglass.

"Still," said Lily. "I've heard worse stories from my mother about my childhood."

I lifted my sunglasses so that she could see my eyes.

"I didn't mean to trivialize, Tim. Really."

"As I drove up the same roads you and I drove this morning, I had thoughts. It wasn't the first time I'd had them. I had thoughts about what it might be like to be alone."

"I'm not sure we haven't all—"

"I thought about what life would look like if my wife and children happened to meet a truck on their way to the supermarket in Tignale. I thought about freedom from burdens."

She grew quiet now, casting a sideways glance at the waiter as he arrived with the small pitcher of olive oil, which he set rudely on the table. As he walked away again, glancing back as if for any conclusion to this apocalyptic inconvenience, Lily said quietly, "And that was the sin you reflected on."

"The waiter," I said. "How old do you think he is?"

"What? I don't know, early thirties."

"I think he waited on me before."

"Didn't you say that you wouldn't normally pay for a place as expensive as this?"

"It was just me the last time I was here. And I hadn't necessarily intended to stay longer than it took to drink a beer."

"But the legend of Saint Laguaro inspired you?"

"Yeah."

"Why is it that I see no legend, no tradition, nothing but your empty cruets?"

"Lily." My voice sounded like the one I had reserved for scolding Garan and Debs.

"Why, Tim?"

I stuck my finger in the only direction it could go. "Ask him."

To my surprise she turned and called: "Excuse me, waiter!"

He stopped in his tracks, stiffening before turning with a slight bow of his head. His face was admirably calm as he approached, but I could taste the steam nonetheless.

"Signora," he said to Lily as he arrived.

"My fiancé here,"—she dared me under her brow to contradict her—"tells me that your village has a custom that has to do with the lake. Can you tell me about it?"

What was the purpose of this? I wondered. I wasn't quite sure why she required convincing. Did she think me a lunatic? A *rendered* man searching for reason in the wake—a five-year-long wake—of his family's death?

"Yes, signora," said the waiter. "The custom involves pouring a drop of olive oil from a vessel such as this into the lake, and to *muse*—this is the word?—about a past sin."

"And what is the purpose of doing this?"

"Surely, your *fiancé* has explained this to you."

"Why would you think so? Do you know my fiancé?"

"He has been here previously, yes." The waiter seemed uncomfortable in the lenses of my glasses.

"And what makes Tim so memorable to you after five years?"

The waiter turned a quarter turn so that he faced me directly. "He was drunk and loud, signora. When he returned from the lake he wished us to fill his bottle again. This is not okay, to pour *all* of the bottle's contents into the lake. When we did not honor his request, he became…angry. We asked him to leave the restaurant, but he refused. Santo Laguaro, he said, belonged to more than our little village. He was correct to say so, but he was bold to assume that Laguaro was his personal saint."

"What do you mean?" Lily said.

Yes, what do you mean, Leonardo?

"Perhaps, signora, you should ask your fiancé."

She looked at me.

"I don't remember," I said, in all my eloquence.

"You do not remember smashing the empty vessel against these tiles that I am now standing on?" said the waiter. "You do not remember telling the guests at another table to look at the shattered glass, to look at 'your family' on the floor?"

"I don't," I said quietly. "I don't."

And yet his words conjured images, thoughts, helped to separate the oil from the water. He had indeed been my waiter, and there had been an empty cruet on my table. That's where it had begun—not at the tourist office or in a brochure. It had started with a question.

Why is there an empty vase on each of the tables?

From there the tradition sprang, as if for only those customers tortured enough to ask. There had been no advertisements, no volunteered information, only the empty cruet—a bottle, a prop as clear and perceptive as Lily, who knew me better than *I* knew me, better than *Kris* knew me, almost better than *guilt* knew me.

"I'm sorry," I offered the waiter.

He shrugged slightly.

"I'm sorry for assuming Laguaro was my personal saint."

"Was he?" he said.

"More than you know."

* * *

We took the cruet down to the lakeside, Lily holding it like a funeral candle while I wondered why I hadn't brought my jacket like she had. The sun still hung superior over the mountains to our right, but the lake shimmered with an icy brilliance. As we stood on the pebbled shore, I turned to Lily.

"'Fiancé?'" I said.

"Yeah, why not? Could you ever hope for better than me?"

I thought about it as I took the glass candle from her. "Not in multiple lifetimes."

The waves lapped in, cold, clear, snow-born. I sat on the beach, tempting the water with the bottle for a couple minutes until at last I let the drop fall. My eyes closed as the foreign substance struck the water, and I forgot about Lily and Laguaro and the Alps for a while. Forgot about confessions in favor of the therapeutic breathing of a five o'clock am jog.

Without my mornings I never would have been able to cope with dadhood, nor discovered the meaning of being human. In addition to its skyscrapers and its CNN, Atlanta had its parks and birds, which provided the setting for my regular loop. That morning was no different than any other pleasant spring morning—a diversion, an aviary and a botanical garden to my senses. I thought nothing of the fact that Lily hadn't been in bed beside me when I woke. She often slept on the couch where the darkness of her nightmares somehow couldn't reach.

Then I saw the leg protruding from between the bushes, and the cap that Garan always wore, lying by his ankle. The wish that had remained so well submerged now surfacing in blood, the blood of more than a sacrificial boy, for in there with him were his sacrificial sister and his sacrificial mother—and my jogging clothes convenient because of the wiping, the wiping and the strange thin streams from my glands as I dropped among my family and should have died there, there at nowhere. Nowhere in a pool of my graceless fantasies.

As I looked up again from my memories Kris spoke from her eye, the tear like the drop of oil falling from its glass container into the pure melted snow. We both lay back on the pebbled recession as the waning afternoon sun fawned over us as though we were worth it. In my sun dreams I saw Kris but I couldn't see Debs because she was never there. I could see Garan, but not his wrecker sister Debs, whom he clutched in his shadow as if he had known bad times were coming.

And then the day began to die.

*　*　*

"No, I'm going to stay and enjoy this room, thank you." As I looked at Lily's lopsided expression, I knew a serenity, if a cautious one, that I had not known in a long time. Santo Laguaro had knelt with me in prayer, and I almost forgave him because of it.

"Are you *sure?*" she said. But her smile told it all.

We made love and slept in each other's arms, the window open to the gathering chill. Sometime during the night I got up to close off the outside air, and stopped by the balcony window. On the breast of the lake a boat seemed to drip with the light from its lamps, to coalesce with the figures on its deck. I forgot about the chill, making myself comfortable on the balcony, drinking the house wine, smoking one of Lily's cigarettes, then actually sleeping on the chair until the four o'clock came to claim me.

As I pulled back the cover to check on her, I thought I heard a whisper from somewhere. But it was only the vineyards worker, staring back at me from chaos.

"Lily!" I hissed as I covered his face.

She obliged, laughing lightly.

"I'm sorry to have brought you here," I said.

"Don't be. I've my own sins to reflect over."

As she removed the cover completely, revealing her jarring nakedness, I thought that easily could be true. Meanwhile, the vineyards worker had other tales to tend to, other iniquities to reap. We were alone in the room, as we were in the world, lovers among strangers. We clung to each other, sweating and searching for breath, until the light peeped through the cracks in the blinds, and then we talked from faces slashed by dawn about the skewed reality of being.

"You really adored Debs, didn't you?" she said at some point.

"You couldn't imagine what a monster she was. Yeah. I did adore her. I adored them both." With those words I let it come, the anticlimactic flood of tears, no less than *all* of the bottle's contents as Lily held me in her arms and whispered words of meaninglessness and salvation. I drifted off wondering what I was going to do now that I had no more missions to fulfill and no load to cast off my shoulders.

"Coffee," Lily said, holding a cup as she smiled down at me. Where she had gotten it I didn't know. But her smile was the color of my freedom.

*   *   *

The Fiesta purred to life under an Alpine blue sky, Lily looking like the goddess she was. There was a lightness about the world that made it subject to the caprice of the wind and weather, the mountains, the man and woman who visited its wonders. And yet, suddenly nothing was shallow to me, not Lily's perfection, nor her company, nor my own fathomless self-absorption that so defined me as a human being.

As we started out of the parking lot, Leonardo our waiter stopped us, presenting an empty vessel to take with us.

"*Grazie*," I told him as I handed the cruet to Lily.

But the face under the brim of the hat, offering a certain *ciao*, wasn't the waiter's.

As I sped away Lily wanted to know why. But I couldn't say why. We were wrong to invade the mountains, I was wrong to have brought her to Laguaro. I didn't know truth from sanity as I simply wanted to be out of there, down the winding roads to Lake Garda again. We managed to coexist without words as the kilometers coiled up to escort us in our descent. I knew that she wondered about my stability because of her calm…

Yet over the next hour or so we managed to find our way along the tunneled paths of the Gardasee to our *Cottage Mediterraneo*, the sun still shining as brightly as it had tomorrow and the next day. The pool would be a welcome diversion, a solvent of sorts for my still shedding layers. Lily went ahead without me, asking me to bring a wine cooler when I was finished in the bathroom. It took a while but eventually I vomited, the confusion as intertwined with my metabolism as Santo Laguaro's oil.

Outside, the sun transformed the lake into a mirror; the warmth felt good on my face as I found assurance in the exoticism of the property's cypress trees, in its palms spilling over walls of stone. But there was no assurance for what I found when I walked onto the pool's deck. The blood trailing along the concrete towards the reclining chair said only for the raw fact of it.

And Lily's eyes still locked upon her visitor peeking from beneath his hat before slipping away to his fields.

Lauren, With the Fall of Night

1: Glimpses

June 2013

We were still fighting when the bouncers, clutching the backs of our shirts, opened the door and threw us out into the wet cobblestone street. It was late, even by German standards, and Trier's Old City was quiet, with not a soul around to see this senseless display of barbarism. Or so I thought when I finally ended the thing by punching my attacker in the throat as he pounced on me where I'd fallen trying to escape his latest flurry of blows.

He sat on his ass now, clutching his throat with one hand and waving me off with the other. All the fury he'd displayed inside the club had been replaced by genuine fear for his well-being as he gasped and gulped for air. Suited him right, I thought, fucking with someone with a bum leg. What had we been fighting about anyway? Some woman? His woman? Had he thought I was hitting on her? Who knew, maybe I had been. I was pretty drunk. Easily drunk enough to fail to recognize who was with whom on the wild dance floor that had nonetheless accepted a cripple like me.

My attention was diverted by an abrupt blast of the music coming from within the club. The face of one of the bouncers appeared again at the entrance, shouting, "*Raus hier!* Go home or we call the Polizei!"

I was turning back to the German in the street to call it a truce when I saw her. She was standing just at the edge of the halo of light surrounding one of the streetlamps, the swirling rain obscuring her features within the frame of her matted dark hair. She was more than a silhouette though; I could see enough to tell that she was a young woman, probably in her mid-twenties. Moreover, it was evident to me that she was watching us, or more specifically, *me*, where I'd risen, in spite of the pain in my bad leg, to a standing position above the still recovering German. A protracted moment to let the certainty sink in that we had made mutual contact across this drizzly void and then she was backing up, now turning and moving away briskly into the darkness.

How like the Trier night to produce such oddities, I thought. And extended a helping hand to my fallen opponent. Which, to my slight surprise, he accepted in the proper spirit.

*   *   *

"Hell of a way to start a vacation," I said to the taxi driver as he deposited me at the steps of the footbridge that crossed the narrow Kyll River to my residence. Perhaps a bit unsettled by my appearance, that and the alcoholic stench I must have given off, he'd waited until we were almost to our destination before inquiring about my injuries.

"You're vacationing at home? Not going anywhere special?" he said politely, taking the euro notes from me.

"Special? Look at the place where I live, man." I motioned across the river to the watermill silhouetted in the dawn's early light against the backdrop of the valley's fir-covered slope. "For me, this is like a fairy tale."

"Yes," he smiled. "Yes, I see what you mean. Enjoy yourself, friend. Here's my card, should you find yourself needing a cab again."

I thanked him and, acutely aware of my aching leg, climbed the steps to the bridge. Halfway across, I stopped and leaned against the wooden railing, admiring the picturesque valley of the winding river. Indeed the setting *was* like something out of a book, particularly now, deep into spring's foliage-rich reign. It had been by pure luck that I'd walked into the Housing Office on the very morning they'd posted the rental. Like many of the U.S. installations in Germany, Spangdahlem Air Base was rural and depended on available rentals in the small surrounding villages to house its personnel. While there seemed to be a reasonable number of such properties, they also seemed to be regularly snatched up almost immediately. I knew this from my first stint in Germany, when I worked as a contractor shipping vehicles back to the States. This time around it had been wonderfully easy compared to what I had gone through then, when I was on such a tight budget after my divorce that Lady Luck couldn't have intervened if she'd wanted to.

Not that I hadn't earned my current favors. Having spent six years in Iraq and Afghanistan as a defense contractor, often living in a tent and *always* working twelve hours a day, seven days a week, I felt I deserved whatever glimmer of a smile came my way. I'd of course been paid handsomely for my civilian services in the logistics arena, but I'd also given a lot of my soul in the process. When you whore yourself out to the highest bidder for wars—particularly one of them—with which you do not morally agree, that's how it feels. Like you're selling your very essence. And what's worse is that you're doing it under the watchful eyes of the real casualties, the soldiers, who are neither paid handsomely nor have a choice in the matter, but who do their diligent duty without complaint.

A balance to strike, for sure, as I now tried to strike a match against the canyon's breeze. Failing once, then again, I returned the cigarette to the crumpled pack. Shoving the pack in my pocket, I left my thoughts to drift with the rising, silvery breath of the Kyll River and continued the limp to my abandoned flour mill, stuff of drunken songs.

While I wasn't singing as I descended the steps at the end of the bridge, I was drunker maybe than I'd realized. I slipped on the wet wood and would have crashed against the steps behind me had I not managed to grab the rail for support. When I'd corrected myself, I saw something. Saw and heard it simultaneously. Movement in the boughs of the trees above the mill's roof. And not a minor disturbance as a squirrel or a bird might cause, but a significant one, as though a monkey was shuffling around up there.

The shuffling turned to passage as the source now moved from limb to limb between the trees, offering the merest glimpses of itself as it put distance between us. That I was the cause of its retreat, I didn't doubt. The flashes of...fabric? human hair...were a little harder to swallow. But I was sure, as it disappeared into the forest, that a human form was exactly what I'd seen. A lithe, wet-haired woman of a form. An almost revenant sort of form. The sort of form a concussion might conjure up out of lamplit cobblestone streets.

I rushed, as far as my leg would allow, to my front door, fumbling with the key as I tried to fit it in the lock. But there was nothing to be afraid of, finally, as I was back inside my house and the Grimm monsters relented to the fairer fairy tales. I tried to sleep, and when that didn't happen in a timely fashion, I wrote. I did that when I wasn't serving the cause. I wrote short stories and novels and sometimes slept with them.

* * *

I woke tasting old liquor and a sourer something from my dreams. My face ached almost as much as my leg, which itself vied with the place inside my skull for the honors. Recovering the memories gradually, I touched the swellings around my mouth and eye. Fuck. Had she done this to me? No, that wasn't right. It was the dude in the club—what was the name of the place? Something subterranean... *The Vault*. Yes, that was it. A place you had to use a spiral set of stairs to exit while some cat with a woman problem tried to beat your face in even as the bulls were escorting you out.

Jesus. Had I been a part of that? A thirty-two-year-old man acting like a member of the university set thronging the fire hazard of a place? But as my head continued to clear, I knew that yes, I had indeed been a part of that. That and more if you let your nightmares creep in. If you let yourself try to reconcile what you thought you had seen with what had actually occurred. Had there been a woman in the street watching you when you were thrown out of the club? Entirely likely. Trier had its indigents, its crazies, its voyeurs, like all cities of any size. Had this same woman been in the trees above your house? Now who was crazy.

I went to the bathroom and splashed water on my face before looking at myself in the mirror. When I did, I nearly recoiled from my reflection. The lump on the side of my head was bigger than a golf ball, while my upper lip sagged puffily over the bottom of my mouth. My cheekbone had been split open, and a wide swath of blood had dried on that side of my face, joining the blood around my nostrils and mouth in a grim mosaic. Finally, the eye on the opposite side of my head from the lump was bruised and bloodshot. I was a living, breathing grotesquerie, something fit for Trier's torture museum.

Oh fucking well was about all I could say as I treated the wounds to the best of my ability, washing off the blood, applying Band-Aids where needed, butterflying the cut on the cheekbone, placing ice on the lump around my temple. I sipped coffee and Goodies for breakfast, rice soup for lunch, then slurped buttered noodles for dinner. Watched a lot of CNN and BBC, slept some, watched some more TV, called the guys from work to tell them I wouldn't be breaking all the known protocol of the universe by spending a segment of my vacation with their sorry asses after all, and then zonked out for the long haul on the sofa with the TV buzzing in the background.

I woke sometime around midnight to find her sitting there in the armchair adjacent to the couch, images from the flat screen flashing across her watchful face.

* * *

It took a while, some seconds anyway as the shock tried to wear off, before she finally spoke. I'd been able to manage only the obligatory "Who are you?" during the strange interim. It was that question she seemed to be circuitously responding to now.

"Lauren. French father, German mother. Heidelberg. Do you remember her, Roderick? Is it Roderick still? Or have you reverted to Rod?"

I swallowed. "Rod will do."

"Yes. And I suppose it's always done. I supposed it then, when she shared the experience of you with me, and I suppose it now looking at those fading dreams on your face. Roderick, you told her, would better serve the writer you aspired to be. Readers wouldn't take to Rod. It wasn't intellectual enough. Write down to earth, you said. But be above it. Have command. It's the way you saw your reader seeing you. Isn't that so?"

"I suppose."

"But that never played out, did it, Roderick? The reviews of your small press releases criticized you as being too above your work. There was too great a distance between yourself and your readers, the critics said. Oh, it was dazzling prose, mesmerizing even, but you put your reader too far away from what was going on. They couldn't relate. Couldn't participate. Couldn't empathize. Didn't care really beyond the poetic lines, the hallucinatory images, the disturbing nature of the content as revealed by your fabulous words. Style over substance, isn't that what it was, your attempt at writing? No story. No real experience as it came to other people's experiences. For you not only wrote above the salad you were treating them to. You lived above it. You always have. You have always witnessed your world from aloft, haven't you? It's your way of dealing with the mundaneness, the frivolity of it all. Are we together on this?"

As I looked at her, searching for any answer but the truthful one, my shock had turned to despair. For there were no answers. Whoever had sent her, whatever they were up to, their grasp of me was as perfect as anyone could achieve in a pool of strangers.

"I don't know what you mean...I don't know you. I don't know how you can know me."

"But that's just it, Rod. I *do* know you. I am the one person in the world who has lived aloft with you. Who has understood your way of seeing things. It's why I am here. It's true that I had never experienced you until Lauren. But I have now. You come with the highest recommendation from her. Are you aware that she died with you? That she gave the blood of her heart to you?"

"I have no idea what you're talking about. Who is Lauren? Who are *you?*"

As she leaned forward, it seemed her face finally came out of its shroud of mist. Her eyes were large and bright, with irises of the deepest brown. This face, with its otherwise delicate though unafraid features, touched something in me. Something from another time. Some other history. "We know you, Roderick Lachance. You partied with us, when we were all so young. We lit each other up in our drug-induced euphoria. Ah, to be young again, right?"

It was coming to me. At least to that suggestive part of me. This woman had power. She created where perhaps there was nothing. "When did I know her? Know you? I get that it was in Heidelberg, but when specifically?"

"When you were reeling, Rod. When you were reeling from your divorce. When you returned to the place you had lived in your youth when your father was in the service. When you returned to Germany and went to Amsterdam every other weekend, supplying yourself with drugs for the long sleepless nights. Do you begin to remember now?"

"I could remember a lot better if you hadn't broken into my house."

"I didn't have to break in. You left it open."

"That's impossible. The door locks automatically."

"There are many ways to enter a house besides the front door."

I looked at her. "If you're you, you mean."

She smiled. "Then you do begin to remember."

I sighed. "If you'll just give me a spark…anything…"

"Branden Apartments. 2007. You lived there for a time, surrounded by Heidelberg University students. Lauren, a graduate student, lived next door to you. She invited you to a party at a place off the Walkplatz. A pre-party, actually, for the real attraction—the Vampire Ball at the Heidelberg Castle. You were high when you answered the door, and you'd remain that way for a week. Think on it, Roderick. And when you're ready, call for me. I'm never too far away."

With that, she rose and with what might have been a slight bow, was out of the room and gone.

2: Recurrances

February 2007

The knock comes just as I am lying back on the bed in my shorts, amazed by this transformation a little magic dust has inspired. The cat in Amsterdam called it a substitute for the real thing, but I think he lied for the sake of the sale. I'm not the type, he must have recognized when I asked for ecstasy, a drug of a wholly different ilk. At least I think that's what I did. Who knows now, with the door seeming so far away, the knock so inconsequential.

But whoever it is, they're persistent. A woman's voice has joined the rap of knuckles. *Rod,* she calls. *Rod, are you home?*

It's Roderick, I want to say, but haven't the inclination. Easier just to get up and go there now that she's added this layer to it. Truly, my body floats, while the idea of speech seems cumbersome. It's the least of two evils simply answering the door.

"Yes," I manage in spite of myself as I hold the door open and try to get a fix on her. I've met her once or twice, it seems to me. But I can't recall when or why. I can't recall circumstances at all except as they pertain to my current state.

"Hi, Rod. Are you okay?"

"Adjusting," I say, feeling freer even as I do. What's it been, five or six minutes since I snorted the stuff? Yes, I'm beginning to cope a little better now, thank you.

"It's Lauren. You remember me, right? I mean we don't talk much, but we live right next door to each other. I feel like we should know each other."

"It's a pool of strangers," I say.

"What is?"

"Humankind, of course. Never mind, come in. I'm just lazing about the place, wondering when someone will knock."

It's a trick of words. "Pool of strangers." "Lazing about the place." My own, previously used words. Something to hold on to as I continue to come into it.

"Nice place," she says as she enters the studio and I close the door behind her. "The art makes it different than my apartment. Smaller...and yet, less cramped somehow. Does that make any sense?" She turns to look at me.

"You wouldn't believe how much," I reply. I'm feeling I can command my situation now. With every moment that passes, my high and I are coming to better terms with each other. It isn't a matter of whether it controls me or I control it. It's a harmony thing. Balance. Is this how Keith Richards, Lou Reed, Iggy Pop, Kurt Cobain felt?

"This is a da Vinci print, isn't it? Wow, I'd not have guessed you could incorporate it into a student's décor. The matting is fantastic."

"Actually, I'm not a student. Though I do happen to do some part-time work at a picture framing shop to make ends meet. It's what we call French matting. The strips of marble paper, the gold outlines. The small frame inside the matte is called a fillet. The cut-outs in the corners I do with a cheap little device with a blade that cuts at a bevel. Learned it in the States, where I bought art for a chain of shops."

She shakes her head. "The more you talk about it, the more interesting it becomes. Where are you from in the States? When we talked in the hall a week or so ago, you said you were from America, but I don't think you said where."

"No?" Did we talk, actually, or are you in a dream like I'm in? "Louisiana. Mardi Gras land."

Her smile grows. "That's an amazing coincidence. I'm actually here to ask you if you'd like to go to a Fasching party."

"And what makes you think I know what Fasching is?" I say in a teasing, though genuinely curious way.

"Um, let's see…you wrote about it in your story *Fasnacht for the Damned?*"

It settles on me now. She read the article in *The Heidelberg American*, which provided links to a couple of my online publications. A fan. How strange, considering I can count on one hand how many of those I have. And here is a German one.

"I'm delighted to hear my work has reached a wider audience," I say for lack of anything better.

"You're pretty good, you know," she smiles. "And now that I hear you're from Louisiana…that's just a bonus for a half-French girl."

"Yeah?"

"My father's from Nice."

"But you knew my name was Lachance if you read my work…"

"Yes. But most Americans have European names. Made no connection."

"So you're half French and, I'm assuming, half-German. Where does this perfect command of English fit in?"

"Both home and school. My father taught English and insisted I speak it at home. And I, myself, am an English major."

"You make me feel ashamed that I haven't yet fully cracked Deutsch."

"Don't. German is so throaty it would drive anyone crazy."

I smile. I like the girl and I'm on my game now. A Fasching party sounds like something I can embrace. But…

"Costume?" I say.

"It's not obligatory at the party. But if you're coming with us to the Vampire Ball at the castle afterward, you might at least put on a monk's robe or something."

"Like with sandals? It's kind of cold outside for that, isn't it?"

"Don't worry. We'll fix you up."

Will you indeed, I say to myself.

"Can do now if you like? My friend Gabe's been part-timing at a costume shop."

I chuckle. "You have this all planned out, do you?"

She smiles in turn. "Really, I hadn't thought that far ahead. I'm a little surprised you don't already have plans."

"What? I'm Captain Carnival because of a story I wrote? Give me a few minutes to shower and put on some clothes."

*　　*　　*

I can't remember her face as I knock on her door. It's been at most a half hour, yet I can't visualize her. Can't feel the what of her. It's like I'm wound up in a mystery, and everything outside me constitutes the mysterious. I've never even considered attending Heidelberg's Vampire Ball for that very fact—that it is a costume party, an affair for non-identities. Too close to home for me normally. But now, because of the drug, I revel in the notion.

Is she aware that I'm high? Does she care? I wonder as I wait for her to answer. Does it at all matter?

No, I decide as the door comes open and there is that face I couldn't recall. Behind its smile it seems something I should remember for the future. But I know I won't. I pass through this life as a shadow even when I'm straight. The props, the comers and goers, they are even less solid than me. Being among them is like being among one's toy cars as a child. They have features, color, they are distinct, but it's the world you create of them that is real, not the objects themselves. I don't know, perhaps that's the writer talking, I think as I follow her into her austere environs.

Gabe's here, and he's obviously gay. There would be some relief in that if I needed any. That I don't says nothing for his having found himself in the wilderness. He is still a magnificent specimen in the pool of strangers. He still commands his road in a way that the rest of us, save for those of us on our substances, cannot. I resist the temptation to kiss his hand, knowing it would not be normal. That it would be unbecoming of an invitee.

"Let's just take a look at *you*," he says, admiring something in me, perhaps my lazy build. "Yes, yes, I think Lauren is right. You will do best in the simplest garment. A monk it is for you then. Sandals for your cold feet, I'm afraid. Don't worry, we'll rub your feet for you if need be, isn't that right, Lauren?"

She blushes. "Gabe, it's not necessary to tell him I told *you* about our conversation."

"No worries," I say. "I like the idea of a foot massage."

As we laugh, Gabe says, "*Do* you now?"

"Back off, tiger," Lauren says. And winks at me.

They put me in my robe, and it is a great feeling being in a single article of clothing, with only my underwear beneath. I forget that it is February, don't even bother wondering why they didn't cover the garb I had on. Maybe she does know the state I'm in. Maybe they both do, bless them.

As I ponder that and the nothing it represents, Gabe, as if in my mind, produces a tray on which rests a powder very similar to the one that has freed me tonight. I'm tempted to call it cocaine, just of a slightly different hue, but I know it is not. They've come for me full-throttle, whether knowing what I've been up to or not. To our collective credit, we merely snort it as I did before, no more. It's a secret and secrets are kept without marks. When it is done, when the full effect has taken hold, Gabe slips into his outfit, a vampire's. Lauren applies his makeup. And then he, hers. When he's finished I ask her what she's trying to be—for she still wears the black tube dress she was wearing before.

"A whore, of course."

"Of course," I say, letting it all float out there in front of me.

"Let's to it then," she says. "Maybe you'll find fodder for your next story tonight."

* * *

The pre-party is in a school-lunchroom-sized common area as opposed to the private apartment or suite I envisioned. "The old Paracelsus Music Hall," Gabe tells me. "The building's owner rents the place out now for smaller events." And a small event it is, with a few dozen people occupying a space that could easily accommodate a few hundred. We are mixing with them almost upon the moment of our arrival, Lauren or Gabe introducing me to people whose faces I will not remember, but whose costumes I sense will continue to flash on my retinas as the night progresses.

"Welcome, my American friend," says one of them, ghost-kissing my cheeks in the European way. "Rod? Isn't that short for Roderick, a Germanic name?"

"Is it?" I say. Any previous knowledge is overshadowed by the use of my name in its long form. The authorial form. But I won't get into that. I won't be the conversation piece that perhaps Lauren wants me to be.

But Lauren needs no help impressing as she sweeps among the small crowd, playing a game she seems at once to love and to despise playing. She seems pale to me, almost ghostly in her contrasting black dress, her severe makeup. As though playing the part of the whore must involve a self-sacrifice of blood. Gabe, meanwhile, is almost absurd in his depiction of the vampire. While it's no doubt intended, it's hard not to feel as though one is on the Nosferatu set with him, in his abrupt and dramatic visuals. Indeed, where do these light effects come from in so open a space? But now I see Master Phantasmagoria up there in his booth above. It's Halloween here at the old Paracelsus Music Hall.

"Come, let's get a drink," Lauren says.

"Is that wise?" I ask.

"Oh? Is this your first time on smack? Could have fooled me."

Indeed.

We pass through bodies, occasionally offering something of ourselves to the curious or polite soul who inquires. The more I watch her, the more I realize Lauren is not a social butterfly. The part she plays is either expected of her or is for some other's benefit. Let that someone, I think, not be me.

The drink is strange to my tongue, but I have no reaction otherwise to it and so continue to sip as we float deeper into the mix. It occurs to me that Gabe is no longer with us and I ask Lauren where he has flown off to. "Wherever they do," she smiles. Which sets as strangely on me as the flavor of my drink on my taste buds.

"Is there more to this thing than drifting?" I ask. "Shouldn't we be participating in some activity?"

"Like what?" she asks, turning to me. There is a weird, almost dangerous something in her eyes.

"Hey, cool down, sister. It's dancing I had in my mind."

"Is it?"

"Yeah," I say hesitantly. "I think so."

She puckers her lips, scanning the group that's congregated here. None of them are dancing. Nor, it hits me, would the somewhat eerie music that seems to come from Master Phantasmagoria up there be conducive to such. Says Lauren: "I haven't danced in at least a year. I lost interest somewhere along the way. It just seems so..."

But suddenly she is doing just that—dancing to the strange vibe permeating the place. It starts with a slow, rolling motion of her arms, then extends to her hips and legs as she calls up some sinewy, erotic thing out of herself—the only thing that can possibly meld to the sound that now finds its way into focus at the expense of the surrounding conversations, the pattings and the kissings of the hall's anonyms. A moment to absorb and now I am there with her, feeling it out with my body, with the blood that flows through it, the ghost that inhabits it. Conjuring the snake out of myself, slithering in the naked air.

"Christ, you two," comes Gabe's voice from out on the skirts of it. But I ignore him. I'm performing the serpents' ballet with her. It's more than a dance; it's a story, some ancient story that only twain, synchronous bodies can tell.

"Enough," comes his voice again. Now more forcefully: "Lauren, behave yourself!"

Though my eyes are closed, I feel her obey. And as she does, so do I, dissolving into a puddle on this random floor in this place that is fit for neither of us.

As I look up at him out of the melt, I see something resembling wrath in his eyes.

He disguises it with a grin. "There will be plenty of opportunities, Roderick, at the Vampire Ball."

"Opportunities?"

"To lose yourself."

I exhale. "As though it's any of your fucking business."

"Someone must take an interest," he says, gesturing to the rear corner of the hall, where I'm almost sure I see her fall from some higher place before slipping into the passage that, according to the sign above the doorway, leads to the toilet.

* * *

Being a Louisianan, I have been to many parties in my life. Mardi Gras. The New Orleans Jazz Festival. Wild impromptu beach affairs in Daytona, Fort Lauderdale, Panama City, Florida. And that's just my younger years. Add in the raves in Amsterdam, the Love Parades in Berlin, the Rock am Rings in Nuerburg, and I'm a grizzled veteran of such experiences. What can one Vampire Ball in admittedly one of the most imposing castles in this land of imposing castles give to such a body of memories? That remains to be seen as we present our tickets and are admitted into the fray.

I'm feeling unnerved now, but in a pleasant way—if that's possible. Something happened in the Paracelsus Hall that I cannot quite reconcile in my borderline delirium. It was to do with physics, of that I think I'm sure.

Physics or reality, if the two can be separated. Lauren became a slithering, then a falling thing. Gabe became the thing that keeps the dangerous defier of physics, of reality, in check. Or was it all an opium dream? Something devised by Morpheus to keep his own reality in question. I like to think it's that. That the heroin takes care of itself and we just play in the little pools it spills.

The Vampire Ball is a wondrous thing in this historical place. In my right mind I might find discrepancies between the eras, but what are the eras really? Medieval this, ancient that. What do such terms matter when you're talking in the present day about fortresses and monsters? If I happen to remember anything about this night it will be the adjectives that spring to a writer's mind—garish, loud, surreal, absurd, affected, false, fantastic.

I consider this in less than a moment's time before tossing myself into the wonder.

If Lauren's still with me, I don't know it as I work my way to the nearest bar and order something gassy.

"Gin and tonic?" the Lady of the Lake says.

"That will do!"

"Or did you mean bubbly, like champagne? Come to think of it, maybe you want a beer and a Jager. You'll have plenty of gas in the morning."

"The gin and tonic will do, thanks."

Why something gassy? Does the stomach revolt against this heathen display? I laugh.

No one's to answer. Or to ask the question. Gabe and Lauren have gone off to wherever they've gone, leaving me alone with the vampires. As I look around at the costumes, I wonder for a moment what it would be like to be the real thing. Would you attend these parties to laugh at the mortals? Indeed, why wouldn't you? It would be a great cover. *Withered body found at the foot of one of the guard towers with puncture marks on neck. Culprit believed to be a delusional psychotic among Vampire Ball attendees.* Yes, it would be too, too easy.

I let my thoughts go as one of the fanged faces appears before me, slowly sticking out its tongue. I see the tablet on it but am reluctant to accept the invite after what I've read recently about the local authorities wanting to stem the drugs coming in to such public events. It's only a moment, enough time to ask myself, *What the fuck are you talking about, Rod?* Then I'm sucking it out of her mouth, not caring what it is, though suspecting it's what I went to Amsterdam for in the first place—X.

Will they mix, the X and the H? Who the fuck knows? Vampire Balls only come around once a year. Enjoy them while you can!

"Come, cowboy," I hear behind me. "Let's go home and pretend to make love."

I turn and it's Lauren, but it can't be her, the party's only just begun.

"You don't like our little gathering?" I say.

"Just want to know more about you, that's all."

"What's to know? I live, I hurt, I fear, I write about it all."

"Exactly."

I don't know what to make of it as I follow her to the exit, where suddenly Gabe is there, something of the look I saw earlier in his features. As he glares at me, he speaks to her. "I told you, Lauren, it's to stay in house."

"I don't know what that *means*!" she hisses.

"It means," he says as he continues to stare at me, "that this man can't help you. None of them can help you. Now get your ass back inside. That or leave with me. Those are your only options."

"Or *what*? What will you do, Gabriel? Who the fuck do you even think you are? I didn't ask for this shit."

"Didn't you," he says on a breath, shifting his eyes to her at last. "Didn't you, with all your questions during my myth lit class?"

I know it best not to enter into this, but can't help myself somehow. "So you're an instructor at the university, Gabe? I'd never have guessed, as young as you look."

Seems he can't help himself either as he turns to me, snapping, "I'm older than you could possibly realize."

"*Gabe!*" fires Lauren.

They stare at each other, during which strange, ticktocking moment he seems to lose his thunder, to slowly, painstakingly resign himself to the futility of it. "Very well then, Lauren," he says. "You're on your own now. Don't come to me again with your mortal angst. I'm finished."

But it isn't over. His words have softened her. "Gabe…please. I must have a life. I cannot be under your wing forever."

"Where there is shadow," he says, "there is safety. Remember that as you cavort with your memories of yourself. Goodbye, Lauren." To me, he nods. "Take care of her, writer."

It seems he will be on his way with those words, but at the last moment he pauses, looking me directly in the eyes: "Take care of *yourself.*"

Until this moment, as the gaze we share lingers, it has been merely weird. Alarming to some part of me, yes, but mostly amusingly dramatic. But there is something in his eyes, in their penetrating quality, that chills me through my opiate insulation.

"Just let him be," Lauren says. "Let us both be."
He nods again and is gone.

*   *   *

Outside it is cold. Wonderfully cold to my lightly clad body. Lauren shivers, but it might be a memory, the passage of a ghost across her person. The lights of the Neckar River, on whose slopes the castle sprawls, enchant and disillusion at the same time. On the opposite side of the river, closer to town, Lauren unnecessarily tells me, is the *Philosophenweg*, where Heidelberg's philosophers and professors have traditionally walked with their thoughts or the company of their fellows. What that has to do with this side of the river, with the here and now, I don't know. Lauren has grown philosophical. Melancholy.

She guides me down a narrow road to a path that leads to a parapet. The parapet is not connected to the main castle, but is rather an extension, like the property's outlying towers. It rests atop an earthen rampart of some fifteen feet in height, one of several tiers ascending to the fortress. The view afforded is made grander by the knowledge that I stand upon a piece of history. Gazing out from the brick structure, I think I should like to take off from it as from a cliff.

As if answering this unintended call, a shadow suddenly descends on us from the right. I hear Lauren scream, see her lifted up as if into the crook of a wing as I'm falling, gasping, splintering upon the ground below.

3: Scars

October 2014

I was on a cruise on the Mosel River when I saw her again. Summer was over, the wine fests were finished, and it was harvesting time for the vineyards on the steep slopes of the larger body of water into which my own beloved Kyll River, a stream really, emptied.

It was a dinner boat, with all the perks, and I was alone on the upper deck enjoying a random finger delicacy and watching the evening scenery when she seemed to simply appear beside me at the rail. I didn't say anything at first, and neither did she, but when one of us finally did speak, it penetrated.

"Now do you know who I am, Roderick?"

"Yes, for the love of God."

"When did you come to realize?"

"I don't know? When I was dreaming about seeing the bones stick out of my leg? Why does it matter?"

"Why does it matter that we spent the most mysterious and revealing nights of our lives together?"

"Yeah, okay, why does it matter that we did that, Lauren? It was seven years ago."

"Have you found someone in the meantime?"

I glared at her, "How could I ever find someone after what you did to me?"

"Did to you? As I recall, it was just the opposite. I did *not* do what you wanted me to."

I looked at the lights of Bernkastel on the far bank and mumbled, "Whatever makes you right."

She joined me in surveying the scenery. "After a week of it, you wanted to die. Gabe *commanded* me to kill you. But I could never have done it. Not after that week…"

"*Why*? What do I have left? My mortality? Please."

"You don't understand, Roderick. You didn't understand then and you don't understand now. How could I know you would become so…involved. After Gabe's doctor friend set the broken bones, we were supposed to be living again. Remember?"

"I really don't care, Lauren. Whatever they were, they were never games for me, don't you get it? I'm from Timbuktu, Louisiana. I'm a country boy at heart."

She looked at me hard. "You know that's not true."

I sighed. "Go away, Lauren. I asked for it once. I won't ask again."

"What if I told you I'm ready to give it to you? That Gabe's dead? That I myself killed him?"

Though something stirred in me, I didn't let it outwardly known. "I would say you are lying. You're the slave now that you were then. What do you want from me?"

Our gazes met, and I could have sworn I saw a tear form in her eye, though I knew it was not possible. "To be with you," she said softly. "That's all."

"You are a lying, fucking *bitch*, Lauren. You wanted a child, that's all. You admitted it to me in your heroin delirium that last day. Where is that child, Lauren? It's been more than a year since I last saw you. Why are you fucking *here*?"

"Rod, I was young then. Just a one-year-old baby. I didn't understand. I thought I still had that much humanity left. I'm so much wiser now. You have to believe me."

I smirked. "So you're alone, without a baby. Gabe's gone. And you've now come back to me to give me the gift you wouldn't give me before. How very pat *if you live in a goddamn fantasy.* I wanted that fantasy once. Now I don't care. I just don't give a shit. You should have killed me while the two of you were bleeding me for your pleasure."

She looked away but then immediately snapped her head back again. "Don't pretend you didn't like it. That you didn't get off on it."

"And that changes something?"

"It does. I mean…it *must*. I know there is a connection between us, Roderick."

"Yeah, the edge of a blade." I turned my back to her and lifted up my shirt. "Remember?"

"Oh, Rod."

"Oh, Rod. Oh, fuck you. Kill me now or go the fuck away."

"I won't kill you. But I will…"

"I won't ask for it. Never again. I won't give you an invitation."

"I don't need one," she said.

I saw it in her eyes, felt the thirst emanating from her, and held up my hands to ward her off. "Stay back, Lauren. You can't want anything but the pleasure now, you sadistic bitch. There are plenty of others on this boat you can feed on."

Breathing heavily, she drew back, looking off at the lights of the random German town that served as the harbor for this equally random boat. The shadow of loss, regret passed across her features. But I wouldn't feel sorry for her. I would never give her what she had failed to give me.

Composed again, she said, "It was Gabe. You can't imagine the power they have over you."

"They?"

"The ones who make us. Our masters."

"Because he made you what you are, he was your master? It seems to me you could have run, hidden, become invisible—"

"Ha! There's no hiding from them. There's nowhere to go after they've given you…"

"Given you what? Say it, Lauren. After they've given you *immortality?*"

"Don't be crude."

I laughed. "Crude. Now that's a fucking irony. Almost as ironic as the fact that none of us ever said the words, as though they were so unreal they might destroy the whole contagious fantasy. Drink your blood like you mean it, Lauren. You didn't have any problem feeding me my own."

To my surprise she seemed shaken by that. "No," she said. "No, that's not how it was."

I'd no idea what to make of this reaction, so simply waited silently.

"He...Gabe, I mean...he said it was *his* blood, that he was contributing his power to the conception. That I could later come back to finish the job if I wanted. But not then, not while we were trying to make a baby."

I shook my head. "Did it never occur to you, Lauren, that all of this was to some purpose other than your own? That while you were looking for a baby, he was looking for something else through what was obviously a ritual of some kind?"

Her lips parted, began to quiver. "You mean...you mean *Kawa*?"

"Kawa? Are you kidding me? What the fuck is Kawa? Are you on drugs now, Lauren?"

"It's...it's just—" she stammered. "Just something that came up occasionally."

"And? What the hell is it?"

"You won't believe me if I—"

"*What the hell is it, Lauren?*"

She pulled back from me, uttering the words as though they were the unholiest of unholies: "Kawa is a rite of communion with Aerthryr."

"And what is this air-whatever?"

It was a whisper now: "Demon."

My mouth fell open. "Oh my *God*, Lauren. You *are* out of your mind."

"It's our world, Roderick. It's the world you practically begged to be a part of."

"I was a fool," I said.

"Because you don't believe in monsters?"

"Because I do, Lauren! I believe in the possibility of physiological aberrations. Hell, I'll even give you a whole physical species that's been roaming this earth, hidden to mortal eyes, since God knows when. But this. This notion of some spirit world is a lot harder to swallow than—"

"Blood? Than blood, Roderick? I'm finished talking. Be with us now."

Before I could react, she was upon me. As her fangs sank into my flesh, all I could think was, *Oh Jesus, this can't be happening, this can't be happening, this*

can't be happening...
And it wasn't.

*   *   *

I woke abruptly. In a cold sweat and confused. A moment to get my bearings, to realize it had only been a dream, and then I was mumbling a prayer to the gods on the off chance that there did indeed exist spirit realms. How real it had seemed. But no, *thank the gods, no!,* it had never happened. That week of being high, it was in the hospital, not in the hands of those monsters. My heroin had been rawer morphine for my wrecked leg.

Which led me to wonder, had the incident at the castle even happened in the way I thought it had? It wasn't until weeks after the strange woman had visited me at the mill that the details had begun to emerge. I'd thought my leg had been mangled in a freak accident involving drugs and alcohol. Mightn't her suggestions have shaped later memories? And even if they hadn't, mightn't I as easily have slipped reality at the scene and fallen on my own?

Yet she'd been there at my house that night. And she'd also taken me to the Vampire Ball years before. Of that I was reasonably certain, as those memories had begun to come back even before she'd left me in my lonely millhouse to contemplate my existence. Then again, how could I be sure of anything in this world? One moment, you're a guy with a bad leg and some regrets; the next, you're part of some supernatural or hallucinatory universe. What was there really to think about when nothing, in the end, could be known?

I went to the medicine cabinet and popped two of my pain pills and returned to bed. Don't let me back in there, into that dream again, I gently implored the gods. And within a few moments was out again.

*   *   *

"Rod? Baby? Can you hear me?"

I woke standing in front of a mirror, this girl from some past there to guide me.

"See these marks on your throat, Roderick? They will forever remain with you. Scars of what you were. Scars of what you are now. They are neither to be admired nor regretted. They are what they are. What you make of the change they represent is all that matters. These were the words Gabe shared with me, and for all his faults, they are meaningful words. Ponder them as you undergo the last of your transformation. They're all I have for you. All anyone could expect, considering—though I remain here for you throughout the process. No, not your master. Your friend and lover. Together, we'll mold our world. We'll change what it means to be immortal."

I heard her words, clear as a bell . But my eyes were looking beyond her through the mirror, to the chair on which Gabe sat, mouth open, eyes staring into nothing, the short end of a large wooden crucifix protruding from his blood-stained chest. To my suddenly awakened senses, it was a perfect sort of symbolism. A Euro Christian-mythos kind of kiss to anyone who cared. I hadn't believed in that aspect of it before, and I didn't now, even through these awakened eyes.

"Get rid of him," I said. "What's wrong with you?"

"So you're coming 'round?"

"Enough to know we're lying to ourselves just like mortals do."

"And if the picture isn't what it seems?" came a masculine voice.

I turned to the tableau of which he was the centerpiece and for reasons an immortal can't explain, was not struck dumb by his resurrection.

"Gabe," I nodded, casting a glance Lauren's way.

"Are you tired?" he said. "You've barely been able to move, much less speak, these last few days."

"Days? Has it been that long?"

"We had to carry you off the boat, with a little help from a member of the crew."

"Where are we now?"

"Why, Trier of course. That's where you live, isn't it?"

"This…" I looked around me. "This isn't my place."

"No," he smiled. "We weren't that bold. We're in my rental on the Ehrang side. It's not much, but it's done okay so far. So how do you feel, soldier? Are you swinging from the trees yet?"

"I…I don't know. Getting there maybe."

"Good, good. We want you to feel as comfortable as possible, of course."

I didn't know what to say to that, so shifted to the rational angle. "Aren't you dead?"

"Have been for a good while."

"And all the stuff before? Was that intended to help me along somehow?"

"One could logically assume that, yes."

I felt alive and disoriented at the same time. "Which means?"

"Which means you're asking too many questions. Wondering too much. Here, let Lauren provide you with another drink and we'll explore it later."

And on and on and on it went until finally the morning light spilled into my bedroom and I found myself not burning in it, but merely waking to another, otherwise normal day, with my leg aching and my heart beating regularly, mortally, in my chest.

4: Toxins

November 2014

The mobile rang as I was rushing to finish the day's work, the major having given the entire 52nd Services Squadron the Wednesday afternoon off before the long Thanksgiving holiday weekend. I ignored it at first, but after hearing one too many rings, finally picked up.

"Hello?"

"Rod?"

"Yes?"

"It's Valerie Rousseau."

It didn't click immediately.

"Don't tell me you've forgotten your former mother-in-law."

"No, of course not, Val. Sorry, my mind was on my work. How are you?"

"Well, I've been better. Which is why I'm calling. Danielle's been hospitalized. A snake bite, if you can believe that. She's been in the hospital for several days now, and they're not sure what's going on. Some kind of reaction to the venom. The snake wasn't identified—hell, she didn't even know she'd been bitten until after she got back from a camping trip with her boyfriend and his kids—so they used something they call a polyvalent antivenom. Doctor says there's no cause for alarm at this point, that weird reactions occur from time to time and just need to be treated carefully. But I thought I should make you aware of the situation."

She had my full attention now. "Yes, thank you so much for calling, Val. How is she doing? Is she okay?" *Why are you calling me, Valerie, what is this? Is this serious or are you on the booze again?*

"She's weak. And has a rash around her neck, where the snake bit her—"

"Her *neck*? How does one get bitten in the neck and not know it?" I could feel my heart missing beats.

"I don't know, Rod. Knowing this boyfriend of hers, they were probably drunk or stoned and she was passed out. She says that wasn't the case, but how else to explain it? I know she's been taking tranquilizers lately. Valium, I think. It kills me how they prescribe those things like they're candy. But apparently her antidepressants hadn't been doing the trick, so they decided in their great apathetic wisdom to just numb her."

"Valerie, this is a bit much to take. Since when has Danielle been on antidepressants?"

"Do I really need to tell you that, Rod? Since you divorced her, of course."

"Jesus. I've told you before, she divorced *herself* when she had an affair. Look, let's not get into this. Will you please let me know if her condition worsens? Better yet, are you at the hospital now? Can I talk to her?"

"I'm in the car."

"Well, what's her cell number? Is it the same one she had before? I assume she's okay to talk on the phone?"

"Goodness, yes. It's not *that* bad. Here's the number. Ready?"

Ready being a relative term? I took the number and clicked off. Tried not to think of the implications, if there even were any, as I finished up my work and drove home to the rental I'd moved into in Trier after my landlord at the watermill had decided to let his granddaughter and her husband have my fairy tale.

The place was spacious, more than comfortable enough for me, myself, and I. The owner lived on the ground floor of the typically large German house; I occupied the second floor. Often he would ask me when I was going to get married so he could stop feeling guilty about taking the generous cost of living allowance I got from the government. Had I no shame, he said, using almost all that I was allowed as a single person? (How he knew how much I was and wasn't allowed, I didn't know, unless he'd gleaned it out of a former American tenant.) My standard answer to his question in all its permutations was, *I may live in Germany, Herr Orenstein, but as a federal employee I'm still an American taxpayer. This is my money, and I won't feel ashamed using it. Besides, what do you care? You'd rather have a brood of hellion children running around tearing up the place? Or worse yet, some party animal with friends?* He always smiled at that, teaser that he was.

I sometimes wondered what Lauren would have thought of this residence, where the pictures I'd framed in Heidelberg so much better fit the furnishings that had come with the place, courtesy of Frau Orenstein and her fine touch. Would she have been amazed by how the sepia in the mottled hues of the couch complemented the French-matted da Vinci that hung above it, centerpiece of the living room? Would she have marveled at how the Klimpt so matched the golden-brown Italian marble tiles? Though I'd not seen her since—when was it? at the watermill? the parapet at the castle?—I found myself, illogically, missing her at times. This afternoon was such a time as I ate a sandwich and watched some news before calling Danielle.

She answered on the third ring. "Hellooo."

It was more an aimless drawl than a greeting. Which naturally concerned me as I let the volume down on the TV, focusing in on this woman with whom I hadn't spoken in years.

"Danielle? It's Rod."

"Hi Rod." She sounded sleepy. Weak, as her mother had said. "I haven't heard from you in soooo long. How're you, baby. Are you coming to rescue me from the snakes?"

Baby? Was she drugged now?

"Your mom called and told me what happened. Are you okay? How are you feeling?"

What might have been an attempt at a laugh came through. "Feeeeling? Feeling a little woused, that's how. I don't know what it put in my body, but it feels wicious. You going to come and give me the good medicine, Wod, like y'used to?"

"Jesus, Danielle. What have they got you on? And why? For a snake bite?"

"Snake bite. Yeah, that's what it was. A little boy snake with loooong teeth."

"What do you mean, Danielle?" Her words, along with the way in which they were delivered, chilled me, though I could not have said exactly why. "Where are you? What hospital? Are you still in Baton Rouge?"

"I'm here baby. Come and give me the medicine. I miiiiiss you. Shhh! Don't tell Chris."

"Just give me the name of the hospital, okay?"

"Nurse. What's the name of this place?"

"The hospital? Our Lady of the Lake," I heard in the background. "Get that, Rod?" Danielle said. "King Arthur like. Come soon with the medicine, 'k?"

"Okay, Danielle. Can I speak to the nurse?"

But she'd closed the connection. Come give me the medicine, bye.

*   *   *

The medicine was sex. She'd used to playfully refer to it as that. Which probably took some of the sacredness out of making love. But it was just a flirt, a form of foreplay. Talking about sex in advance made her horny. This suited me just fine for a time. After a couple years of marriage, there was no sacredness left anyway. Eventually, however. my tolerance for her flirts wore thin, which is likely why she looked elsewhere for her medicine.

Strangely, hearing her talk that way to me again stimulated me. I ignored the sensation at first, dismissed it as perverse, unfair to her and unworthy of me, considering her situation. But the more I thought about her, the more aroused I became, and in the end I went into the bathroom and relieved myself of all the frustration, picturing her in her most decadent position while releasing tensions that otherwise had nothing to do with her.

Afterward, I thought about how long it had been since I'd had sex, or even masturbated. Who wanted me now after all, gimp that I was? But I knew that wasn't it, not really. I could perform; nothing had changed in that department. And on my good days I could almost entirely disguise my limp. Which made me, I suppose, an on-again, off-again cripple. One without the power to flip the switch.

Never mind, I thought as I got a beer from the refrigerator and turned on the TV. I found myself only half listening to the CNN story, however, as my thoughts drifted from Danielle and her circumstances to whether I should go out this afternoon or stay home and try to write (either of which would mark the first time in a while). I had plans for the holiday weekend. Tomorrow, after talking to family in the States, I was going to get in the Jeep and do a tour of the Mosel River valley and the Rhine Gorge. One-way, the trip from Trier to Bingen—by way of Koblenz, where the Mosel emptied into the Rhine— was only a couple hundred kilometers. But I'd be locating at inns along the way, spending the afternoons visiting castles and other attractions or just lazing on the river bank with a cold beer or a bottle of Mosel wine. The vineyards wouldn't be sporting that vibrant green color they did before the grapes were harvested, when their foliage literally carpeted the slopes, but there would still be the scent on the air.

But that was tomorrow. Today—if I could get up off my ass—would have the flavor of spontaneity, once a very close friend of mine. Yup, let's do it, I decided. And no use waiting. Anytime was a good time to walk around Trier's Old Town, nibbling on those greasy potato patties before settling in at a nice

German restaurant for some *Jagerschnitzel* and Bitburgers.

Anytime was a good time to get away from the toxins of the nightmares and snake bites for a while.

*　*　*

As it turned out, freeing my mind wasn't a simple matter of finding diversions for myself. From the moment I arrived at the town center, the unwanted thoughts nagged at me. As I stood before the *Porta Nigra*, the massive, weather-blackened gate that served as the entrance to the Walkplatz and Square, I wasn't thinking about the ancient Romans who built the structure, but of a hospitalized woman with wounds in her neck—the neck I used to kiss. As I toured St. Peter's cathedral, it wasn't the lofty ceilings of its baroque interiors I considered, but what I should do if Danielle's condition worsened.

I'd experienced a foreboding when Valerie informed me of the situation, and the unease had never really left. Certainly not after talking to Danielle, though that conversation had disquieted me in a different way. A part of me said I was overreacting, that my fears were to do with past experiences, not present ones; and that Danielle was clearly not in any serious danger, her lethargic speech notwithstanding. However tempting it was to find meaning, to see *motifs* in the coincidences, they were still just a set of coincidences.

Rationally, I believed this. The trouble was containing the more fanciful thoughts, the ones that ran with perceived feelings that something lay underneath it all; and that the only way I might be able to get close to that something would be to take leave from work and fly to America to question Danielle, to look with my own eyes at those marks on her neck. What had that other French girl, the half-French, half-German one, done to me? Would she forever haunt me? Wasn't it enough that I carried her memory in my leg?

To my credit, I did manage to get a grip whenever my thoughts strayed too far, and was eventually able to go about my afternoon with a minimum of unpleasantness. I stopped for dinner at a place off the Square called *Der Schwarzwalder*, ordering *Jagerschnitzel mit Pommes und Salat*, my favorite German meal. Dipping the thick fries in the richly dark mushroom sauce and washing them down with a fine German *Pils* was the best experience in the world as far as I was concerned. When the waitress came around for my plate, I asked her to pass along my compliments to the kitchen, and ordered another beer. As I was resting back in my seat to watch the evening passersby through the window, my phone rang.

Had I been less relaxed, the foreboding might have returned before I actually heard the voice at the other end.

"It's Valerie again, Rod. The doctor wants to talk to you. I told him you had nothing to do with this, that you were in Germany for godsakes. But he's insisting. They've discovered Valerie's been taking Valium while in their care—I'm guessing now that that asshole Chris gave the pills to her—and they're none too pleased. She's gotten worse just in the hours since you spoke to her. When asked why she would risk her health that way while under medical treatment, she told the doctor to ask you. Kept murmuring some nonsense about you telling her to do it to 'make the transformation easier.' I tried to tell them that you hadn't spoken to her in years before that call, but—"

Another voice, its owner apparently having taken the phone from her, replaced hers. "Mr. Lachance? Yes, I'm Doctor Allen. I'm caring for your ex-wife. Mrs. Rousseau has explained the gist of it to you. I just need to ask you a couple of questions."

It took a moment to get my reply out because I was so stunned, I couldn't think. "Yes, of course. Whatever you need."

"Before this morning, when was the last time you spoke to Danielle?"

"Jesus. I can't even remember, it's been so long."

"Do you have a son, Mr. Lachance?"

"A son? What—" My heart was suddenly drumming. "No, I have no son."

"I ask because Danielle has this notion that your kindergarten-aged son visited her at the campground where she was staying when she was bitten—"

"What?" came Val's voice in the background. The rest was faint, but it sounded like, "You didn't tell me she said *that*?"

"Please, Mrs. Rousseau." Then: "Mr. Lachance?"

"I'm here."

Was I? Or was I remembering a drugged voice talking about *a little boy snake with loooong teeth*?

"Do you have any idea what Danielle could be talking about? I'm by no means ruling out that she's delusional, but she was pretty specific when she described the boy telling her he was there camping with his uncle Gabe."

Oh Christ. Oh Jesus, this can't be happening.

"Sir? Are you there?"

"Are you her medical doctor or a psychiatrist? What does any of this have to do with treating her for a snake bite?"

"Mr. Lachance, I'm only trying to ascertain whether we should be worried about more than a snake bite."

What? What could he be saying?

"If she has other problems, we have to take that into account when treating her. The Valium's caused enough problems on its own. Given that it could be interacting adversely with other chemicals in her body, I've never known a tranquilizer to produce these kinds of delusions. Tranquilizers shut the body down. They don't wake up the imagination like this. Particularly when a person's been taking the dosage she has. Which leads me to the main point of this conversation. Did you in any way, either personally or through another party, influence Danielle to take these drugs?"

"No, goddamnit."

"Very well. Thank you for your time—"

"Wait. I need to know if she's going to be all right."

"I can't answer that at this point."

A wail from Valerie in the background. I was surprised she'd kept it in that long, considering the content of the side of the conversation she could hear.

"Nurse, please take her out of the room."

"What room?" I said. "Are you in Danielle's room now? May I speak to her?"

"Hold a minute." A second or two passed before he continued. "Okay, we're alone now. Mr. Lachance, you cannot speak to Danielle. We haven't yet told Mrs. Rousseau, but Danielle is in a state of unconsciousness that very soon will be labeled a coma if she continues to fail to respond to stimuli. We considered gastric lavage—pumping her stomach—after locating the empty prescription bottle. But results from lab tests run earlier, when the nurse alerted me to her increasingly slurred speech, indicated that this would be a futile—and already risky in her condition—path to take. She'd been ingesting the tranquilizers, probably in increasing amounts, for days. To be honest, we're left wondering what previous diagnoses can now be attributed to what. It is a strange and difficult case, but we're doing everything we can for her, I assure you."

"I understand. But why haven't you told Mrs. Rousseau yet? She seemed more concerned about me than her daughter before you got on the phone."

"It is not that we have intentionally withheld anything from her. We cannot term it a coma until a certain amount of time has passed. Nor have we concluded definitively—if you can ever get that in medicine—that Danielle's state of unconsciousness is due strictly to an overdose. As far as Mrs. Rousseau is concerned, we're running tests—which we most certainly are, on an ongoing basis. I'd like to keep it that way for at least a little while longer. If we understand each other, Mr. Lachance…?"

I sighed. "Thank you for being forthright with me. Now let me ask you—is it time for me to start thinking about buying a plane ticket to the States?"

"That entirely depends on you, Mr. Lachance. You don't seem to have maintained a relationship with Danielle, yet I can see that you —"

"I'm asking you, Doctor, if there's the possibility that she will die."

"There is that possibility, yes," he said gravely.

"Likelihood?"

"Let me continue to be frank. We don't know what's wrong with her. We didn't know before. We know little more now. In my personal opinion, when considering the body of symptoms, Valium is a secondary player."

"And in your professional opinion?"

"Unfortunately, this is one of those rare cases where I'm forced to admit I've failed to establish one."

"Let me have your number. I'm getting on a plane as soon as I can."

5: Pools

Black Friday 2014

As I sleep on the transatlantic flight, I am walking in the forested wetlands in which the campground is nestled. There are willows, cypresses, water elms, and hickories surrounding me. Cattails and alligatorweed and a thousand other plants in the freshwater bayou. I've been here before, or to some place very much like it, but names escape me. Is it a state park? A refuge? There are so many in Louisiana, who can remember every one they've visited?

This one is different, though. This one is home to the campground where my uncle…Gabe, was it?…used to take me. Yes, I do know this place better than the others, in spite of my memory lapse. There's nothing random or nameless about it after all, I realize. Its map is built into my constitution. It is a part of me, my childhood as a pre-schooler. How else could I be so easily following its trails through the marshes. I'm looking for something. A particular pool, it seems to me, among the many pools that occur around the inlets and outlets of the river that flows through here. Yes, there's something I must see at that pool, as I did as a child.

As I recall, it has a surface like a mirror. Captures the branches and leaves of the trees exquisitely. It might be a child's fantasy, true, but why am I here if not to prove the fantasy real? We've little enough time to dream in our adult lives. Why spend any of it trying to qualify what we've yet to discover again? As I pick through the small bodies of water I remember a feature of a book I read in middle school. Read again as a teen, and then watched in motion picture form as an adult. The Mirror of Galadriel, the author named it, after its keeper. A basin filled with water in which one might see the past, present, or future. Yes, this pool's like that one, though the boy who looked into it had never heard of Tolkien or his trilogy.

I sense it is near now. My uncle has led me here without actually taking my hand, as he will lead me to where the woman my father was once married to sleeps, sedated, on a hammock between the trunks of two live oaks. Is it now or then—who knows when you're the victim of your memories, for a pleasant change, instead of your experiences. Or is it the other way around as I step out of a thicket and finally see the pool shining like glass in the sunlight spilling through the canopy?

What is on offer, Galadriel? Can you at least guide me if you cannot, yourself, predict what I will see? She does not answer. For this is not her pool, it is mine and mine alone. An answer lies here. An answer to questions from another world. If it is not forthcoming, I shall conjure it up out of the depths of the glass. Invoke it, as Uncle Gabe has said he invokes. *Whisper his name once for every year of your former life. Five is a magic number. It was the number he chose for you when he allowed your virgin mother to bear you.*

"Virgin, Uncle? What does that mean?"

Among them it can mean unwed, undefiled, or innocent, the latter of which can be interpreted in different ways, depending on your patience and your interpretations of their tiresome morals and scripts. Among us it is less complicated. It simply means forever barren.

"What is barren?" Boy and man, man and boy.

Unable to bear children.

"I don't understand."

Nor are you supposed to. Being a virgin yourself, you are to come into it like a cherub. Go now, to the pool and call him forth. We've work to do, young man. Remember his name. Pronounce it correctly lest we be deemed disrespectful.

I look upon the surface of the pool now, and I imagine I see him waiting. *Oh, glass, produce our master Aerthryr. Come forth. Aerthryr. Guide us, Aerthryr. Be among us, Aerthryr, as we do your duty. Aerthryr, we call thee, Aerthryr, come forth out of the depths that we may serve thee.*

I'm an adult, but I've had fangs since I was young. Young as I am now, Lauren. Wherever you are.

*   *   *

Danielle was dead when I arrived, on Black Friday. As I left the airport, the first person I called was Doctor Allen, who delivered the news to me, adding that the body had already been moved to the funeral home. I tried Valerie, but apparently she was too exhausted with grief and incoming calls to answer. I could imagine her husband, a deeply religious man, saying Danielle was in God's hands now. But for her, it would be traumatic. She'd been a terror of love to her daughter when we were married. It couldn't have changed much since then.

Regardless, I had to go pay respects before I did what I knew I had to do, which was to visit the park where she'd been camping. The doctor hadn't had an answer to that. He'd learned from Danielle or her mother only that it was a state park. The boyfriend had conveniently never been around when the doctor was, apparently delivering the goods to Danielle at night, before visiting hours ended. Hopefully Valerie could at least point me in his direction. Maybe, just maybe, I could convince him to take me there. If he even gave a shit.

I did my diligent duty at the funeral home, inquiring as to when the body would be available for view and wrapping both parents in my embrace, feeling guilty for so many things, not least seeking information from them while they were here to take care of the details.

"Don't contact him," Valerie tearily said. "What good will it serve? You see he's not here now. He just doesn't care. Let it be."

"I'm not concerned about him or his feelings, Val. I just want to go to the campground. I want to be where she was when it happened."

"Valerie," said her husband. "Give him the number or address, whatever you have. He's a right to remember her however he wants. Roderick, at least, was good to her."

She gave me both, and with kisses to the both of them, I left.

He didn't answer my call as I sat in the rental car, prepared to pursue the thing to its conclusion right now, though I was lagging from the flight, with night fast approaching. I tried a second time on the phone I'd bought at the airport. This time there was an answer.

"Hello." It was a male child's voice.

"Hello, yes, is your father home?" I remembered the name at the last moment. "Chris. I'm looking for Chris."

"He's not available right now."

"Well, is he at home?"

"I'm sorry, I can't talk to strangers." And he clicked off.

You may not talk to me, I thought as I turned the key in the ignition. *But someone will, I swear it.*

I drove the fifteen miles to the rural address I'd put into the rental's GPS and waited for a couple of minutes in the dark gravel area in which an old Ford truck was parked while I planned my approach. If he was the loser I envisioned, then God help him; I already had the tire iron at the ready and would gladly use it on him if he refused to take me to the site of the incident. If he half convinced me he wasn't the guy I thought he was, then I'd give him the option of putting his kids into safe hands before forcing him to accompany me. Thank God neither scenario played out.

When no one answered my knock, I turned the knob. The door was unlocked, which I supposed was no big surprise out here in the boonies, whether they were home or not. "Hello," I called as I entered cluttered interiors that reminded me of the house my grandmother had lived in all of her adult life before she died of pneumonia. "Anyone home?"

No one answered. Nor, now that I thought about it, had the Ford truck seemed other than a worthless relic where it sat outside listening to the nightly song of the crickets. Convinced that no one was home, I took the liberty of rummaging around, looking for anything that might be of use to me. I of course expected to find nothing. Who kept state park literature after the fact? But after a few minutes of digging through piles of bills and other miscellany, that's exactly what I found—a leaflet for what had to be the place I sought: Hickory Chip State Park. On the back of the brochure there was a small map showing the park's location. It was some thirty miles west of here, off the same state road that had led me to this house.

I stuffed the brochure in my back pocket and went to the car. As I was about to open the door, lights appeared through the trees that surrounded the long drive, which wound around a boggy area on its way to the house. A moment later the car itself appeared, blinding me with its brights before the driver, obviously seeing me, dimmed and then completely shut off the headlights while still rolling to a stop.

The only light to be had now was the porch light, which merely served its immediate vicinity. While I couldn't have identified the make of the hatchback as my eyes readjusted to the dark, it was evident to me that its windows were tinted. For when the driver turned on what must have been the overhead interior light after shutting off the engine, I saw only a faint, concealed glow. Some seconds passed—time enough for me to calculate how long it would take me to get to the tire iron lying under the front seat of my rental—before the driver's door came open. Why I felt danger was uncertain to me as a tall, thin man unfolded out of the vehicle, closing the door behind him. Perhaps because I, myself, had brought it?

"Hello," I said. "You must be wondering who this stranger in your driveway is?"

"We get them from time to time," he said. "What do you want?"

Cozy greeting, I thought as I decided not to scramble for excuses, but to put it out there exactly as it was. "My name is Roderick Lachance. I was married to—"

"I asked you what you want, not who you are. Spill it or get off my property."

I held the anger in check, but at the same time refused to mince words. "I want to know where you and Danielle were when she was bitten by the snake."

As he responded, the interior light came on again in the car. "Who is Danielle and what are you talking about?"

I wasn't sure which of the two instances to be more alarmed by—the light coming on or his denial of knowing Danielle. It was natural that he'd have his children with him, but the finality with which he'd closed the door had left the car vacant to my senses. As to his not knowing Danielle, well, that was another matter.

"I'm not in a very good mood, Chris. I've had a long flight and—"

"How do you know my name? Are you one of those asshole thieves from over at the Cranston place? Coming 'round introducing yourself to get a lay of the land? I'll fillet your ass like you do the game you poach."

The passenger door came open, and out stepped a woman whose face was turned from me as she folded her seat to let one, two, now three children out of the car. There was something disturbingly familiar about her as she closed the door behind the last child, a young boy who now stood staring at me while his siblings ran off toward the front door. I barely heard Chris's next words as her face finally came into view.

"I think it's time you climbed back in your car, stranger, and got your ass out of here."

"Never mind, Chris," said Lauren. "I know this man. Don't I, Roderick?"

I had no words. It must be another dream. That could be the only explanation

56

for it.

"Cat got your tongue?" said the boy, displaying a smile in which I imagined I saw the flash of *two looong snake teeth.*

"Meet my son, Paul," Lauren said. "He was once Saul, before the conversion."

"Is—is he *mine?*" I stammered. Knowing the years didn't match up, but remembering the world they ostensibly existed in.

She looked at Chris, who was now staring across the hood at the boy.

"Chris has two children. I have one. Together, we form an episode of—"

"You never told me Paul had a *father,*" Chris said.

"Why of course he does, darling. What did you think? He materialized out of thin air?"

"You said he was a test tube baby."

"And so he was," she said pertly. "Test tube babies aren't immaculate conceptions in a bottle, love. But admittedly, I might have misled you a little. There was no fluid medium. I myself am the test tube."

"*What the fuck is going on here?*" I released. "What did you do to Danielle?"

"Judging by your concern, and if I in fact knew a Danielle, I'd say she's probably gone on to a better place."

Before I could absorb it, much less react, Chris came in again: "And this guy standing here right now—*he's* Paul's father?"

"I didn't say that," Lauren said. "Though you might say he was a…*facilitator.* Wouldn't you agree, Roderick?"

I'm going to wake up any second. Any instant now. This isn't happening. None of it ever happened. I carry histories into dreams with me, and none of it, neither past nor present, is real.

"What about the future?" Lauren said to me. "Have you thought about that?"

She's not in my head. Except in the sense that I've created her. My mind conjured all of them up on a heroin-substitute trip gone bad. Yes, that's what happened. I was lying back on my bed in that student apartment in Heidelberg, a knock came, and then phoof! Existence as I knew it ceased to be.

"And yet, Danielle remains dead, doesn't she?" It was the little boy, flashing white again.

Shouldn't he still have baby teeth at his age, even in a dream?

"Who, for fuck's sake, is *Danielle?*" Chris demanded.

"Do you remember, Chris, when we watched *The Last Temptation of Christ?*" Lauren said. "Remember what the last temptation was? A trick of Satan's where Christ was offered the life of a mortal instead of dying on the cross as God's son and the savior of man? Do you remember the contradicting realities?"

He was clearly confused. "I guess. I mean I think so. I might have been high that night."

"Well, this *isn't* like that."

Upon which she turned and stared me directly, penetratingly, in the eyes.

"*Is* it, O Roderick, Keeper of Even Scarier Flames? In this story there are no contradicting realities, are there? You were offered the fruit and chose instead to father the serpent that did the offering."

"I *chose* nothing."

"Didn't you, you fiend? Didn't you call upon Aerthryr, himself, to assist?"

"Gabe did that! Not me."

"*Gabriel?* Ha! Who do you think you are if not that God-despising archangel? You were tired of delivering His messages to the mortals, so you decided to deliver a different one, with help from the other side. You made me, and then, with that high demon Aerthryr's assistance, you made our hybrid. That all of creation might laugh in His face. I know you, angel. It took some time, but I know you now. Flaunting yourself in your vampire outfit. Imagining that you, too, can be at least affiliated with mortality, if only in some vague, viperine way."

"Enough!" came a voice from behind me. I whirled, and there, in the flesh, stood Gabe. "We've toyed with him enough," he said. "Will you finish the job, Lauren, or shall I?"

"You do it, Gabriel. You've always done it best."

I'd turned back to her as she spoke, but I couldn't tell whether she was looking at him or me.

It didn't matter. I was in the car and driving again now, and it was only Gabe beside me.

* * *

We walked along the park's dark paths, lost in the cacophony of insects and frogs. I didn't know what I felt. How to feel. Who or what I was. I knew only that, whatever came next, I had already been transformed. I had tasted the fruit of the branch and been introduced to worlds without end. Did vampires exist? Did gods? Did angels and devils? I didn't know. But I did know this: I was here, now, my senses alive to my environment. I knew that I was being led by a figure whose pale skin seemed to glow from some internal source in the darkness. I knew that he called himself Gabe and I called myself Roderick. And that we were headed toward a pool I had visited previously, and yet never in my lifetime. I knew that these lifetimes were ephemeral and strange, if they occurred at all. I knew sensation, finally. Or the perception of it. And perhaps that, in the end, was what it was all about.

As my thoughts broke up, dissipated among the flying insects, my guide suddenly turned to me, an earnest look on his face. "Let's have sex," he said. "Here and now, before it can never be known between us again."

"You feel that way about me?" I asked.

"I know you're straight. I know you're what most of your kind are. But you are a part of me, don't you see? Or soon will be. I saw how you made Lauren feel. I want to feel that way again, before it's too late. If you like I can come to you as a woman. It's within my power…"

"Do that, yes. Be a woman to me and I will be a man to you."

"Do you want me to be Lauren?"

"Yes! God yes!! Be Lauren, delivering herself to me with the fall of night."

"I did, you know." Becoming her even as he spoke. "I came to you, with the fall of night. And you partook of me even though you knew what I was. You gave yourself to me and I gave myself in return. And the rest of it—what's real and what's not, what's right and what's not—can any of it really matter in the embrace of such magic?"

"It doesn't," I whispered, accepting her mouth, her tongue, all the liberties of her as I flung her to the ground, ripping her pants off and turning her so that her ass was to me, and mounted her, freed animal that I was amongst the wild chorus of the bayou. I gave her all that she asked for and more as the juices of the fruit of the Tree of Mortality and Immortality flowed down my legs, my face, my very soul in this its last dance.

When it was finished, when we'd cum a half-dozen times between us, I felt empty, as I had as the masturbating pubescent. But the feeling would soon go, along with the guilt and all the other mortal concerns. We didn't speak about it as we continued along the trail. There was nothing to say that her now absolutely luminous flesh didn't already say. We'd paired in some interim between worlds, and that was the first and the middle and the last of it. Story, among the endless stories, told. Now was to find the next one among the dusty texts. Now, for me, was to find the secret that made our union such a thrilling, wondrous mystery.

And at last we have arrived. The surface of the pool, as the three of us gather around it, is as luminous as Lauren's skin. What must we call out of it to validate what has already been validated? The demon? The snake that bit Danielle? God Himself?

But no, as Lauren murmurs her invocations, I suspect it is something less crude than that. Something...fairer. Like the home I once lived it on the banks of the Kyll River. Like the home I once had with a wife who later learned she could not bear children and changed her view of the world as a nurturing thing to one of an indiscriminately punishing existence. I mourned her as I stood here awaiting my fate. She'd been something to me once, in my own failures as a human being.

Lauren, finished with her prayers, now turned to me. "You'll have to recite the name, of course. One time for as many years as you've been alive as a mortal. Thirty-three is a magic number. Wasn't it Jesus's age when he was tempted on the cross? All you've to do is welcome him, by name, up into your world."

"What name?"

"What name?" she said, frowning and smiling at the same time. "I'd have thought that obvious by now."

"Is it Aerthryr?"

"Aerthryr? Are you really talking about Aerthryr? The way is with you, Roderick, not myths and monsters."

"What name, Lauren? Let's have it done."

"Look into the mirror of the pool and you'll find it."

I did, and all I saw was my own reflection. Superimposed upon itself that many times.

"Don't waste it," she said as she sank her teeth into my neck. "It's what will speak for you when Judgment Day comes."

Epilogue

August 2004

You look for the tomorrows, but somehow they never arrive as soon as you'd like. You've tried to talk to her, to reason with her, but there's no reasoning with a woman who treats sex as a pastime, a sport, and then finds herself devastated when she learns she can't conceive a child. You've told her it's okay, there are other ways, but she hasn't spoken to you since starting on the half-liter bottle of vodka that has put her in the state she's in now as she sleeps beside you, oblivious to your own restlessness.

"Danielle," you say aloud. "What is it you want from me?"

Though she is a rock where she lies, you can hear her saying, as she's done so many times before, "I want you to acknowledge that your writing gets you, gets us, nowhere. Find a real job, Rod. Be what a man's supposed to be."

It seems strange to you, mixing the two marital problems. But didn't she in fact, during tonight's hellish backlash, blame her barrenness on your writing? *If you put as much into the act of sex as you did your writing, maybe we wouldn't be having this discussion.* That she corrected herself almost immediately after making the statement did nothing to mitigate its effect. Indeed, the next words were worse: *God! And all along I thought it was you with the problem, with your forever limp dick.*

She's a sexual creature, your wife. You've always known it. You even enjoyed it in the early days. Yet lately you seem to only be able to forgive her for it. The two of you parted company some time ago—if not in practice then in spirit. Life came again when she started talking about having a baby. Though you were skeptical, you entertained the notion that maybe, just maybe, better tomorrows were on the horizon. What a fool you were to think so. Her cold heart is her barrenness. There's nothing external about it. You suspected it the day she brought home the Viagra. You know it with certainty now. You cannot please her. She's dead to your kind of emotion; it's her nature.

So you toss and turn while she sleeps. Wondering what's next in this wasted union…

*   *   *

"Lauren, sweetheart," I said as I got up out of bed and went to the bathroom to relieve myself. "You're going to be late for work." It seemed a strangely normal thing to say after yesterday's news and the unpleasant evening that ensued.

I heard her turn, probably checking the clock. A moment passed before she spoke. When she did, it was completely devoid of warmth: "Wait, what did you say? Lauren? Who the hell's Lauren?"

"What? I didn't say that."

"Yes you did."

"Just a minute, babe." I flushed the toilet and washed my hands and face. When I stepped into the room, she was in a sitting position on the bed, looking at me darkly.

"Baby, stop," I said. "I must have been dreaming, that's all."

"I don't bring names back from dreams with me."

No, you just bring the eroticisms, I didn't say.

"Well?" she persisted.

"Well what, Lauren? You're making something out of—"

She threw the covers off her lap, leaped out of bed, and literally attacked me.

"I don't know what I'm saying, Danielle, I swear," I said as I warded off her blows. "It's last night. I had nightmares. I must still be fucked up over it."

"That's the lamest goddamn thing I've ever heard!" she screamed, still pummeling me. "Now I know why you can't perform. It's because you have someone on the side!"

"Baby, *please*. I swear to God I don't know any Lauren."

It took some time, but eventually she relented. I didn't kid myself into thinking it was because she believed me. On the contrary. She'd probably decided, yeah, okay, now I'm *really* free to pursue other interests. But where *had* that name come from, I wondered as she went into the bathroom, presumably to get ready for work. They still have to do that, don't they, after they find out they're barren? Get ready for work?

I didn't want to think about it as I went downstairs to make breakfast. Cooking was one of my jobs since I'd gone to full-time writing for the second time in our marriage. God knew, writing was no job. It couldn't come close to taxing the brain like her big-firm marketing bit did. Christ, with those two-hour lunches, it was no wonder she came home with bloodshot eyes and her hair in a tangle.

If only that were true, I thought as I placed the strips of bacon in the pan, waiting for the comforting sizzle and smell of this normalcy. Even if she was fucking somebody, she'd never overlook her hair, her makeup, her prim investment in her world. It was against her nature, this embodiment of perfection that was my dear wife. Life, for her, was a sort of controlled carnival of the senses to be indulged in on her terms. I'd always liked that about her, I truly had, until it had come to me one day that her free-spiritedness was just a decoy for her compulsions, of which I was a necessary object, being her husband and all. In the end all of her props were just playthings, and vice versa. The only question was, what did I actually do for her other than cook? I was an emasculated thing for my failed writing, for my inability to be stimulated by her anymore. Why did she stay? Had it always been for that amorphous thing, "a baby"? Surely not. The first time she'd mentioned it was a few months ago, after another failed encounter in bed.

Fuck her for trying to be human, I thought as I flipped the bacon. She was more a sore than an open wound, and I detested her for it.

I cooked the eggs in the bacon grease, as we both liked. Considered toasting potato patties but opted instead on sandwiches, which I preferred. I was just placing hers on her plate when I heard her descending the stairs.

"Rod," she said as she appeared in the kitchen doorway in a towel. "Could you get my gray slacks out of the dryer so I can iron them? I'm sorry, by the way, about earlier."

They were the words of a snake, but I did as bidden, humble servant that I was.

"Maybe we should take a weekend and go camping?" she said as I delivered her pants to her. "Would you like that? It's been at least a year..."

"Yeah, sure. Breakfast is going to get cold."

"Down in ten," she said, and fled back up the stairs.

*   *   *

"What's the name of the park again?" she asked me as we pitched the tent.

"I don't know, Danielle. Hickory something. I'd never heard of it until you brought the literature home from work."

"Hickory Chip. That's it. What a weird name, huh?"

"I guess so."

When we'd hammered the last stake in, I asked her where she wanted the hammock. "Between these two trees okay?"

"Marvelous. God, it's so good to be out in nature again, what with all the troubles we've had lately."

I agreed that it was as I took the roped mess out of its bag. "Can you help me, Danielle? It's gotten tangled up."

"Sure," she said. And within moments at least that puzzle had been solved. We pulled the hammock tight and tied the ends around the trunks of the opposing trees, knowing there would be give when we actually occupied our outdoor napping bed.

"Ready for a cold one?" she said, heading to the cooler.

"Do me up, lady."

"I like when you call me that," she said as she handed me the beer, kissing me on the neck. "Maybe you can give me the medicine later." She motioned suggestively to the hammock behind me.

"Maybe I can at that," I smiled.

"Don't do that," she said.

"What?"

"Flash those canines of yours like that. It's unnerving."

"What, you don't like the idea? Never mind, I'll come to you silently in your sleep."

She stuck out her tongue, and I reciprocated.

Maybe she wasn't such a cold heart after all as I took her in my arms and smelled her throat for its always present, never less than provocative perfume.

A Carnival of Events

Sapphire could see that the world was breaking down. The endless wars and the orbital conflicts they inevitably spawned. The monstrous weather systems and the not so bewildering phenomena they produced. The overconsumption. The overpopulation. The over-poisoning. The relentless characterization of the planet's state as a cyclical reoccurrence, just of a more modern brand.

Sapphire saw this in her sapphire eyes, and she saw how the people doing the characterizing quite relished the wonderful freak show they hadn't had to buy tickets for. Attuned to it all, Sapphire didn't care for being the antenna and decided to do something about her world.

So she put on her boots and she went out into the Vegas morning, earlier than she normally would have after doing a night's show. She practically skipped around the corner to have some simple black and white flyers made on the fly, so to speak—and to put in an order for glossy color affairs for later. The guy gave her an odd look when she described what she wanted, but he did them up for her on the spot. Carrying the stack in her hand, she went to the first residential door she saw, and knocked. No answer here, but at the next one she was greeted by a shirtless man looking dazed as he scratched his package and raised a brow at her.

"Sorry to bother you so early, sir. But have you masturbated to world events yet this morning? You really should do your part in the way of fuel, you know. There have been signs of a letting up."

"What? Who are you? Did Jamie send you over here to mess with me?"

"No, I suspect Jamie is already up with his or her coffee and watching the news. We all have to contribute. Here, have a flyer."

The man took it, looked at it, muttering as he read the words.

FEED WORLD EVENTS. THEY NEED YOU.

He flipped it over.

HUMAN CATASTROPHE. DON'T LET IT DIE OUT!

YOU'LL NEVER FIND ANOTHER CHANNEL AS SATISFYING AS THAT ONE.

He looked at her. "What in god's name is this? Are you for real, sugar?"

"Sugar and cream, that's it. Go get yourself a cup and do your duty to the human race. Thanks, and have a pleasant day!" As she trotted away, waving a little finger wave.

She spent a couple hours at it, sparing a little extra time for a few people. In one case because the lady was aging and had some things to say about the state of affairs. In another because the two female companions and a male friend had gathered around the thing as though studying a historic artifact. In yet another because the guy had such a cool question.

"What event are you advertising for? Looks awesome, whatever it is."

"The Event of Events! It's going to be the bomb!"

"I like the clever way it's done. Looks like you're promoting chaos."

"You have it right, my good soldier. Now go thee forth and photocopy the truth you hold in your hand and send the copies out to all your friends and tell them to repeat the process. Spread the word!"

"Might do, sister. Great conversation piece. But listen, you really ought to do these things up in color, with some design, give it the professional look. Easier to buy into that way. Of course, if the austerity was intended…yeah, come to think of it, I can see that too."

"Later, trooper. I'll stop back in a week to check on you."

"Do that, gal. And bring those sapphire eyes back with you."

She did her finger wave and headed back to her apartment. The fire was still there, but she had other things to do today. Tomorrow she'd stand on the Strip and pass them out, but today she was busy. Rehearsal this afternoon, a show later. Tonight's might be her last one. She'd been thinking about it. Vegas wasn't the carnival for her anymore. She enjoyed the masquerade— was like everyone else in that regard—but too much of it and you began to believe the lie.

So she went about her day, sometimes humming the show's finale number without consciously realizing she was doing so. After rehearsal she went out to the Devil's for some Mexican, a thing she didn't ordinarily do before a show, even in a conscientious and selective way. No Green Thumb Deli salad for her today! Not today, with so many exciting things going on in the world.

The night arrived, sucking her into its bosom, and she put on her little outfit in the private dressing room before joining the other girls backstage. She could see the eager faces out there beyond the curtain and was quite enamored of them. Who could blame them for wanting to get away from their laptops and mobiles and TVs for a while? They needed this diversion.

So she stepped out there and she did her song and dance with the other girls. Time flew by, and before she knew it the chorus line was wrapping up the final number, doing the bows, and heading off stage. Sapphire taking her time, eyeing the microphone before picking it up on her way by to say to the whole audience:

"Feed world events, guys! Do your duty and champion human catastrophe that it may live on until it has fully baptized us all in its great glory!"

She knew the audience wouldn't remember her precise words, would probably think they'd misheard. But the critics in attendance would. They'd remember her words right into their reviews in the print and electronic newspapers!

Saudade

There are things we do in this life, crimes we may or may not have committed, that no amount of reflection can shed light upon. Intention can neither be confirmed nor denied. Circumstances cannot be placed back in their proper order. We think we remember what we thought at the time, but can any perspective ever truly be revisited? Can any motive ever truly be known, much less reknown? If not, then regret, remorse, guilt can never truly be applied. We are what we are at any given moment, we do what we do, and the rest is an unsatisfactory record, an analysis without worth, a drive among back roads that deposit us wherever they will.

One such road, a narrow, zigzagging affair that leads up to Tignale above Lago di Garda in Italy, makes no pretenses about its capriciousness. At one turn it might leave you gasping at the beauty of its rugged, foliage-rich setting; at another, hanging in midair over a grove of cypresses or skidding toward the wall of one of the tunnels cut out of the mountain. Where it left me was at the foot of a tiered collection of columned stone structures that vaguely recalled Roman temple pavilions, but whose actual function was lost on the uninformed observer. Particularly one, on that July afternoon, whose preoccupations didn't end with the Opel finally cashing it in after the troubled three-hour trip from Milan.

For a few minutes I just sat there watching the dashboard lights surrender what chi they had left, not bothering to try the ignition, not wondering again whether it was the battery or the alternator, just sitting there thinking about how this situation so coincided with my own journey, my own battle to will it out. Indeed, the car might as well have been me as it merely occupied space in the pull-off, powerless, dead except in the stories of its bones, a fresh relic among the fossils of Lake Garda.

A movement distracted me from rising away out of my body to ride the currents of the surrounding mountains, eternally ashamed of my failure of will but comforted to be done trying. I looked across the road to a point above the pale columns where a woman was descending a set of stairs into the remnants. For a moment her manner and shape were familiar to me, recalling a scene from the first days of my vacation. But

I reminded myself that images, like links in the knotted chain of fate, were not to be trusted, and the moment passed—for the short term.

Across the distance of a hundred feet or so she saw me looking, and waved. I reciprocated, knowing that was all I had to offer, a salute, an acknowledgment that we survived in the same world, that our skeletons would mingle when dust had claimed us, and the winds would sing with our unintelligible recollections.

It wasn't until I was out of the car and moving toward her silhouette framed by the sun burning over the slope that the memory returned, though again only for a salvaged moment in time.

I'd been riding a bike along the Neckar River in Neckargemund, Germany, the sun gone down and the moon, that Renaissance token, risen, saving me from spoiling the shadowy beauty surrounding me with my headlight. My friend Donny was back at the tent, reading by lantern, fearing a resurgence of the rain that had plagued us for the past two days. I didn't care. In the Nevadan desert rain is a rarity, and when it does fall, it awakens you, doesn't put you inside reading some egoist's blather. I read, yes, but not as an alternative to experiencing, not as a retreat. I read to know the author. I read to know how the mind works. A fiction author is the best case study around. That's my game as a psychologist, to know the where as to the what. That's why they keep me on the police payroll in Reno, why they recruited a skilled gambler to their ranks. In criminal justice it's the dealer—whether that be the captain or the killer—that takes the final fall, not the player, and that's why we're a perfect match, me and the PD. I was never very good at finishing, and that's what they like, the capitalizing on another's subjectivity.

But tonight, as the bridge came into view, the woman's lifted voice reached my ear, I suppose I was reading. Who would be strolling along a footbridge singing her lungs out at this hour? Would the next page tell? Would she be carved out of the night or was she the carver, her tongue the blade? Would I remember her in the future? Was she that lucky or unlucky a hand? I confess to mixing metaphors, but is the page not a card distributed by a crazy, egotistical god? Are lyric and meter not expressions like everything else? This noise of hers was poetry as surely as was a flush at the beshadowed end of the table. As surely as the encoded messages from captain and killer alike. A tease, a promise of something great.

To this day I don't know why when her silhouette came into view, hand carrying the sandals that had at some point in time been carrying her, too heavily, I didn't muster the courage to call up to her, interrupt her song, demand to know if she was simply drunk or if she was enlightened. That she cared not who heard her voice echoing among the bridge's walls only heightened the fascination, to the degree that, yes, she did live on and wasn't that her, there among the Romanesque columns, dark in comparison to the pallid stone, mined out of shadow as opposed to Garda's stony slopes. If the woman who approached me now lifted her head in song, I would return to the lemon Donny had let me borrow and simply mold into its husk, and that would be both all and enough. She didn't, and maybe that, too, was enough.

"*Buongiorno, signora.*"

"*Buongiorno.*"

"Do you speak English?"

"Enough, yes." See? "Are you having car trouble?" She gestured to the broken little scar on the scenery.

"I am."

"Yes, I saw you from the balcony of my hotel. I recognized frustration when you struck the steering wheel with your fists."

"Did I? I thought I just died."

She laughed. Her eyes were the color of her hair, both the perfect complement to her only slightly less dark skin. She wore a skirt about her slim waist, as Italian women tend to do in summer, and a tank top. Her feet were sandaled, her left wrist braceleted. The straps of her bra were visibly transparent. There might have been a shade of blush, a tinge of mascara, earlier, but the heat of the day had worn cosmetics away. We were two people, that was all, joined by the thing that had disrupted our beats.

"Do you have a handy?" she said. I didn't have time to process the European word for cell phone before she added, "No matter, I can call a service for you. Should you end up needing a room, there are two hotels there above the lemon houses. Mine is a nice one. Restaurant, wine, private bath, internet…"

"Are you a spokesperson for the company?" I said, hoping she got the joke.

"Didn't you see my commercial?"

"I wish I had. TV's boring these days. But am I so obviously a tourist or passer through that you'd be prompted to suggest a hotel?"

"You have German plates on your car and are speaking English. You could be a businessman, I suppose." She looked at my attire of sleeveless shirt and surf shorts dubiously.

"That's me," I said. "Corporate car and all."

She smiled. A perfect Italian thing among her slightly prominent nose, wondering eyes, suited-to-whatever-expression-emerged mouth. The bones were the only fixed thing about her countenance, supporting her face well, as her frame in general did her undersized breasts, her oversized muscular legs. Her voice, I thought as she issued her next words, had its own infrastructure from which to petal and flesh out with intonations that grazed softly but rippled powerfully.

"Do you recognize me from somewhere?" she said.

"Should I?" Hearing the song carry fully between bridge walls.

"No, but you look like you do."

"Ever been to Baden-Württemberg, Germany?"

"Not that I recall. But I half-wish I had, to inspire such a look."

I don't know why I said it, particularly in this situation, needing help not a date. "You're inspiration enough as you are."

"Yeah," she smiled. "What sort?"

I vacillated between many poles, finally settling on:

"The only sort."

She didn't say anything, but was not turned away, God forgive me my forwardness.

"So," I said, "You have a phone."

"In my room. You're welcome to use it…" She seemed to want to wrap up the sentence, but then abandoned the knot. *I think.* I imagined that's what she'd been thinking.

"Thank you, Miss…"

"Elena," she said, offering her hand.

"Darrin."

Now if I could only dredge up the funds the car's fix would require and see her naïve faith in me through. That ability, as we ascended the stairs she had come down, hinged on the severity of the problem. I made just enough at my Reno PD gig to pay the bills, which included $500 in child support. If it was the battery, I might be able to cover the cost without resorting to my emergency 18%-interest credit card. If it was the alternator, on the other hand, the problem grew more complex. Aside from the expense, how many days would it take to get a part out of Verona or Milan for a fifteen-year-old shitbox a friend had lent me? Two days? Four?

"You have ADAC, I assume," she said over her shoulder.

"Yes. That's why I didn't politely reject my friend Donny's beater when I got a firsthand look at the 'functional car' he'd offered me the use of before I flew over. Said they'd be available to fix whatever needed fixing, that I wouldn't be stuck until the car died. And no sweat if the car did just that. He was tired of having it around anyway. So I guess you could say he just gave it to me to finish off while he finishes up a dissertation over the next couple weeks."

"So you're doing a bit of touring. Been to Italy before?"

"Rome, Pompeii, a few years back."

"Where are you from?"

"Originally, Colorado. Now I'm in Nevada."

"What do you do there?"

"Criminal profiling. I'm a psychologist." I waited for the inevitable "how fascinating" or "like on TV" but neither came. Maybe television was as boring for her as it was for me. Maybe her silence was contempt for psychology. Or the law. Whatever the case, she was not obliged to reply.

"And yourself?" I said as we paused for a breath at the top of the stairs.

"Ticino, Switzerland. My mother's Italian, my father Swiss. I—is something wrong?"

She'd recalled another memory, a fresher one, one I wasn't keen to revisit.

"I know someone in Lugano," I said. "She says she's half-Swiss, half-Italian. Her husband, a friend of mine, says she's made up the Swiss part to fit in in Switzerland."

"Maybe I'm making up the Swiss part, too. Maybe you're not really a criminal profiler."

"Why would either of us lie?"

"Maybe we're not lying. Maybe we're deluded."

"Deluded? Your English doesn't want at all, does it?"

"I dreamed of moving to America. Put myself to learning all I could."

"Dreamed? Past tense?"

"I don't see myself getting there now. The hotel's a big responsibility, and I can't really see it in anyone else's hands."

"When you said, 'my hotel,' I assumed you meant you were staying there."

"Well...I am."

As we resumed walking, I thought about her "deluded" remark. What had it meant? Was it obscure Italian humor? I was about to ask, but she beat me to it.

"You want to know what I meant by saying that maybe we are lying to ourselves. Well, we tend to see ourselves as the mirror depicts us, yes? The left eye is the right eye, so forth. What we really are is quite different from what we think we are. We are always guests at the balls we host. I may think I entertain my patrons, but my patrons in fact entertain me. You may think you have insight into the criminal mind, but the criminal mind actually has insight into you. These lemon houses below us, for instance –"

I'd stopped, gripping my skull, the memory of Lugano a lemon ripened beyond its branch's capacity to support.

"That's very Nietzsche of you," I said between the heels of my palms. "How much are your rooms? You do have soft pillows…"

"Sixty euro per night. And yes, of course."

"Consider me booked."

* * *

I woke the next morning from dreams of philosophers in summer skirts. I ignored the ringing phone on the stand beside me, as I'd ignored my own cell phone for the past two days. Had she not offered me her telephone to call the garage, I'm not sure I could have brought myself to use my own, for fear of who might be waiting in the interim. I didn't want to know who was calling, I didn't want to know anything. When it quit, I turned over, thrusting the pillow over my face. Sleep. There was never enough of it. Not anymore.

A knock at the door. Could I let that go too? Could I muffle the persistence of a call involving so little distance? That's what it was all about, wasn't it? Proximity? The more distance I put between myself and Lugano, the shorter the fall. Now the brink beckoned again, and if I accepted its invitation, maybe it would finally be over.

I didn't bother donning my shorts. I didn't care that I was in my underwear, only that I opened the way upon the depths. And yet, as the door swung open, I found myself surprised to find the space beyond as vacant as advertised. Not even a hand to help pull me down. I stood there looking at the opposite wall of the corridor, perplexed.

"Darrin?" I heard from the vacuum. Then she appeared in the doorway, one hand mussing her hair.

"Sorry to wake you, but the garage called. It's the alternator belt. An easy fix, they said. You can pick up the car anytime."

I adjusted. Wiped sleep from my eyes. "What time is it?"

"Nearly nine. Did you not enjoy your dinner?" It seemed a non-sequitar until she pointed beyond me to the tray of half-eaten lasagna, bread, salad.

I readjusted, wiped sleep, sleep from my eyes. "It was good. I was just too tired…"

"Well, breakfast is still being served downstairs. But you'd better hurry. Nine o' clock they clear the buffet."

I nodded. "Do I have time to brush my teeth?"

"And put on clothes?" She smiled. "I'll make sure they hold at least some toast and coffee for you."

"Thanks."

When I got downstairs, the buffet was still laid out, though the dining area was empty except for Elena at a table on which rested a small pot of coffee. I loaded my plate with eggs, salami, bread, and yogurt, and sat at the offered chair opposite her. She poured my coffee, offered milk and sugar, sat back watching my half-delirious "mmm" before I put the mug down to spread butter and marmalade over my bread.

"Join me?" I said as I partook.

"Thanks. I've had mine."

I chewed, suddenly conscious of her gaze, of the fact that I was eating alone, and yet flattered in some weird way by her attention.

"I appreciate your help," I said, wiping my mouth. "Lucky for me a benevolent soul like yourself was on hand."

"We help each other," she shrugged. "That's what this business of life is about, right?"

I paused at my attempt to extract a soft-boiled egg from its shell, then resumed the effort, tapping the hard cocoon too sharply with my spoon. I let the spoon clatter on my plate, said, "I suppose."

"You suppose?"

My next words sounded bizarre even to my own ears. "Are you a friend of Sophia's, is that it? Did Nick call you from Lugano, ask you to look out for me? It was his suggestion, when he learned I wanted to visit Lake Garda after my stay with them, that I find lodging in Tignale, with a mountain view of the lake. Funny you happening to be here..."

I could see the shadow bleed into her eyes. "What are you talking about? Who are these people, Sophia and Nick?"

I looked at her, seconds ticking by. "Friends. Never mind."

"What are you running from?"

"Life. Death. If I told you..."

"Aren't we all? Running? Tell me."

"I can't. I'm—I mean, I'm sorry." I stood, pulled a fifty-euro bill, the last of my easily accessible money, out of my pocket, dropped it on the table. "That should cover room and breakfast. Thanks for your help."

"It's included."

"What?"

"Breakfast. A taxi to the garage can be too, if you'll just mellow a moment."

"I...yes, I could use a taxi."

"Finish your breakfast, have a shower—you look like you need it—and I'll meet you in front of the hotel with my car. You don't mind that sort of taxi, do you? The concerned kind?"

Her hospitality was surreal. "You haven't grown wary of me yet?"

She just looked at me, frowning.

* * *

As we passed the lemon houses she informed me that they had been erected almost four centuries ago, were located variously around the Gardasee, having been part of a productive industry. "I like to think of them," she said, "as four-dimensional photographs. Have you ever heard of the Portuguese word, *Saudade*? It is a nostalgia for something never personally experienced. That's how I feel about the lemon houses. When among them I can smell, taste what they once contained."

I thought about that. I thought about it for a long time. Then we were at the garage and Elena hanging around while they insisted on showing me the old battered belt before letting me pay for the new one. I wasn't sure why she stayed, but I was glad to have her. I was glad to see her embarrassed looks as I caught her glancing at me from outside the garage, was glad to feel my own embarrassment for catching her catching me. Maybe she wasn't here to remind me after all. Maybe she would offer another night's escape, this time in her arms. It was hard not to think such thoughts as we stood by her car again, Elena asking where I would go next, me replying maybe Venice or Florence, I didn't know. When the words came from her lips, they were terribly welcome, like a demon temptress's breath.

"Stay here one more night."

"I would love that—"

"But only if you'll tell me."

"I will," I said, brushing her hair with my lips. The strands in the sunshine smelled of lemon.

* * *

We lay together in her bed, legs entwined, enjoying the afterglow. The guilt I felt for making love to her under false pretenses, for not having told her what I really was, was real, but the moment was even more real, a steady light in the darkest of tunnels. She didn't have to tell me it was time, that what we'd just shared was a sealing of trust, a forging that went beyond animal pleasure. I considered the notion that the philosopher in her had found a specimen in me, a sample of human mystery to probe, to profile, and that she had been willing to pay with her body for my secrets. But I knew this wasn't so. Some deeper part of her had imprinted itself on some deeper part of me. The music of our union had not spent itself in its crescendo, but lingered lazily, not an echo but a protracted chord, a clear vibration going inerrantly on in a vacuum.

Once I started, I was at the mercy of my confession. The words were their own engine, fueled by a necessity of the soul. "I came here on a dime. Before I was a profiler, I was a gambler, an uncannily good one except when it came to the killing stroke, where I failed time and again, accruing a huge amount of debt that I've not even begun to put a dent in. When friends invited me to Europe for some time away, I told them I didn't think it wise to take on the expense. But both my buddy Donny in Germany and Nick in Switzerland insisted, saying they would provide lodging—and in Donny's case, even a set of wheels to get around in. It didn't take much convincing. I've been through a lot over the past couple years, including two rough sociopath cases in succession, and to experience Europe again—it's been ten years—seemed worth the cost of a paycheck or two.

"The trip was going well until I got to Lugano and the house of my friend Nick and his wife Sophia. I've known them both for several years, but I'm not really sure I ever thought of her as a friend except by extension. But it soon became apparent that since I'd last seen them—how long had it been? A year and a half since they visited me in the States?—that she'd thought *a lot* about me. At first I passed her flirtations off as just that, innocent amusements, minor sport, whatever, but then I began to realize she was seriously attracted to me. Whether Nick noticed anything, I couldn't say, as a lot of it went on behind his back, an intimation over salad chopping in the kitchen, a touch here or there, suggestive remarks. None of it blatant enough to justify a stern response on my part, but enough to make me very uncomfortable. There was no way I was going to betray a friend with his wife, particularly not Nick, who's helped me out of more than one spot in the past. After a couple days of this…embarrassment, I begged out of a planned weekend in Lauterbrunnen with them, fabricating a story about having heard from a friend at Como who'd managed to postpone a work engagement in Brazil that would have prevented him from seeing me while I was in Europe. I told them I'd return in a couple days. It was a reasonable story. I do have a number of friends abroad, acquired mainly through the gambling circles. Nick knew this—in fact, that's where I met him. As to Sophia, I hoped she'd take the hint and be cooled off by the time I returned. But things were not to go as devised—not by a long shot. Nick had taken time off work for my visit, but on Friday morning he got a call on some urgent out-of-town business. I was immediately suspicious. For all I knew Sophia had phoned in a favor from somebody, knowing I wasn't planning to be on the road until about noon."

Elena gently interrupted me at this point, moving her calf against mine. "Friday, three days ago? The day before we met?"

"Yeah, the day before we met," I said, enjoying the glide of her skin, wondering just how much contact she'd want to have fifteen minutes from now when the tale was told. "So, as I'm sure you've guessed, Sophia seized the opportunity. Oh, she was casual enough about it at first, remarking that Lake Como was less than a two-hour drive from Lugano and I might as well hang out at the pool for a bit now that we had a clear day for a change. We could even go for a sail. Yeah, a sail. Did I mention Nick's a finisher? Has the killing stroke? Yeah, he owns a lot of toys, hell, Sophia's probably one of them. Anyway, she wanted me there, and after some resistance on my part, had no scruples about pulling her best card. Her exact words: 'We both know Como's a farce. You don't like me, that's okay, but you owe me.' 'Yeah? How so?' I said, growing angry. She said, 'For convincing Nick to offer you accommodation in this sparkling new house of his. Don't think because we paid you a visit in the States you're his last best pal. Come on! You live in Reno, for God's sake. Nick would as soon entertain his mother as a—and this is his word—*loser* like you.' My reply to that was disgustingly feeble: 'If that were so, why would he have bothered inviting? Why take two weeks out of his life, offer his home to a fucking loser like me?' She laughed. 'Because I asked him to, for the love of Christ! What do you think this thing is, Darrin? Where do you think he's gone today? Probably the golf club! I want what I want, he wants what he does, and we don't stand in each other's way. Do you really think he's so dense that our flirtations flitted right by him?' '*Your* flirtations,' I corrected, in a last-ditch effort to stop the bleeding.' She wasn't relenting. 'Delude yourself, cowboy, but you were right there with me all the way. You may have been embarrassed. You may have been ashamed. But what you haven't been is unflattered and untempted. Look at me! Look at yourself. Fucking Christ.'

"The 'look at yourself' hit hard, but not nearly so hard as the notion that I may have been receptive to, may have encouraged her flirtations all along. Hadn't I, in fact? If only by letting it go on? I needed a drink, which she fetched like a maid instead of the class-A bitch she was. She wasn't too good to dirty work it, that's for sure. She poured a second vodka on ice for herself, and as the liquor took effect it seemed to temper the air—momentarily.

"'Look,' she said. 'Let's just hang out. You know you're a player, so what's to lose? If you leave me in a puddle of tears, you're a winner. If you leave me in a puddle of something more…viscous—' she grinned like a lascivious old man at the playground—'we're both winners. Whattaya say?' 'I say you're a whore,' I said, and stood up to walk out. As I reached the door, not caring about my suitcase, not caring about anything but putting the serpentess behind me, she said something that brought my retreat to a halt.

"Once, at a party, a half-drunk friend of a friend, someone I didn't personally know, made a homophobic joke at my expense, an unclever response to something I'd said. I was alert enough to turn the tables on him, telling him that would have been funny if I weren't gay. Sophia used exactly the same tact. 'That would have been funny,' she said, 'if it weren't true.' I realize now, and probably did then, that it was a designed thing, a sympathy play. Why I fell into it, I can't say, unless it was simply a matter of my having succeeded in insulting her, in penetrating her spheres deeper than she had mine. All I could come up with by way of response, and this with my back to her, was, 'You've such a low opinion of yourself?' The worst of all mistakes, this acknowledgment. I was hers then, for the morning, the afternoon, wherever the day took us. I cursed her, I cursed myself, but that didn't stop me from sucking down the next vodka, and the next. I admit I was charmed by her raw edge, even stimulated, but the game had taken a different turn now and damned if I wasn't going to prove she couldn't make me succumb to her. Short-term surrenders, sure. But long term? She would be paying for her presumption. One way or another.'"

I realized the weight of my words even as I said them. But honesty was at the heart of our game and I wasn't going to shrink because her body had stopped moving.

"That's scary," she said.

The hairs on my arms stirred at the words in spite of my conviction. But I told on, because that's what had to be done. "Sophia and I swam, we sailed, we parasailed, never with more than brief touches. It was like a dance toward delirium. It was like you and me, but without the sense of destiny. The experience would be retrievable after it was finished, but only in the most cursory sense—a sort of landmark between unremembered fucks. Evening brought sekt, champagne, some erotic French short film, reminders of what she considered a determined path. To cap it, this wondrous day, she suggested a place on top of the mountain. We ate strawberries there, ice cream, drank more sekt, but it wasn't until we were heading down again that it all reached the head she was looking for.

"'I want you to stop the car and fuck me,' she told me. We were in her car, not the lemon Donny lent me. Her car, me driving, as if Porsches had always been my choice of transport.

"'When we get back,' I said. 'It's only a—'

"'Now!' she demanded.

"'You won't like it if it's now, Sophia. I promise you you won't.'

"'Then again, maybe I will.'

"'Fuck you,' I said.

"'Fuck me? *Fuck me*? I get the words, is that all!' Then she began hitting me, in the shoulder, the chest, the head, screaming, 'Let me out of this fucking car! Let me fucking *out!*'

"And you know what? I did. Tired of the whole fucking bash, I did. I stepped around the front of her Porsche, jerked the door open and *let* her out by her hair. She laughed. She laughed and she laughed, and I dropped her there on the shoulder of one of Lugano's steep slopes like so much unwanted baggage and sped away in her sports car wishing only for another sekt to bring it all back into focus.

"But when I hit the road that led to the Italian border, forced to think about my passport and all that, I also thought of the whore I'd left on the edge of a drop-off, and I'd no choice but to go back. I can't tell you how many twists I had to navigate back up that mountain, but they were many, and the prize at the end an anti-prize, a projection of my own being. I wasn't sure where I'd abandoned her exactly, but figured I'd find her staggering along the shoulder, nursing her no doubt significant wounds. I was drunk and the country outside my headlights a foggy one. If she'd decided just to sit where I left her, I might easily miss her. So I tried to keep it slow. I say 'tried' because the Porsche was a steed beneath me and I had a mission, though I couldn't really say what that mission was. To fulfill some human obligation? Some devotion to Nick? My own sense of decency? No, none of these, I'm sure. I simply wanted to put the pieces back together, to not leave a wreck behind me that might haunt me later. Yes, that selfish. How I would accomplish the task, I wasn't sure, but I knew I needed to retrieve her from the possibility of falling victim to some other drunk on the road, or a misstep that would land her at the bottom of a cliff. Eventually I decided I must have missed her along the way, and turned around. My feet were angry on the pedals by then. I screeched out of my turnaround, was in the process of rounding a sharp bend when there she was, on my side of the road, facing me. She had no doubt seen me pass and was waiting for me. The sudden sight of her caused me to overcompensate, sending the car into a skid. It was enough. The *thunk* as the car struck her was solid, impressive. I somehow managed to correct the car, braking to a stop before the next turn. I sat there surrounded by blackness, heart pounding, thoughts gone haywire. Minutes I sat there, unsure what to do. Eventually one certain course of action emerged. I had to see what had become of her.

"I turned the car around and slowly approached the point of impact. At this pace I was able to see just how narrow the shoulder, how empty the region beyond it, and I knew she'd gone over the edge. I considered leaving then, saving myself the image that I knew would haunt me for the rest of my days. But I had to see. Call it morbidity. Call it the need for even the feeblest measure of closure, but I had to know. I thought of the smallest things then. Assuming she was visible, how would she appear? Graceful? Broken? Would the headlights glaring out into the vacancy be a detriment or an aid to the onlooker? They proved to be both, taking away my night vision while at the same time providing the glow that divined her silhouette from the darkness of the tree branches among which she sprawled twenty feet or so below. That's the tableau I carry with me, this shadow of a descending bird of prey, wings spread, trapped in leaves. She landed gracefully, I think, as gracefully as one could expect of such a creature."

I let my confession end there, as if to lend it value, validity by a poetic strain. Neither of us said anything for a while. In the silence, the warmth of her leg, her flesh against mine was a dull, awkward pain, one which I knew I could alleviate by repositioning myself, but which I did not want to lose for fear of the cold that would replace it. When at last words came, they came from both of us, simultaneously—

"But the thing is—" Me.

"What did you do then—" Elena.

"Sorry," I muttered. "Go ahead."

"No...tell me, what is the thing?"

"Well, maybe it will be better explained if I tell you what I did next. I drove the car back to Nick and Sophie's house, parking it in the garage, rear end to the wall as it had been before we left. I checked the side of the car thoroughly and, finding no damage, no *evidence* of what I had done, I located a vacuum cleaner and thoroughly cleaned the seats and floors, wiped down the steering wheel, the dashboard, the door handles and panels with a cloth, then went upstairs and checked the answering machine to see if Nick had called to say he'd be coming in early—he'd said he didn't expect to return until late yesterday. Then I got my bag, threw it in Donny's car and left. All very mechanical. All very calculated toward fitting those pieces, that wreck back together. Nick's is a secluded house so I doubted anyone had seen the coming and going. As to people who might have observed us together, or with the car, at the lake, well there was nothing I could do about that and so didn't let it be a distraction from what I *did* have to do. That's where the 'thing' comes in."

I paused to give her the chance to extricate herself from me. When that didn't happen, I wet my lips, preparing to recall to her the comment she'd made about people seeing themselves one way, but actually being another thing entirely. But I couldn't make the words apply, couldn't make sense where there was none, and ended up letting out a terribly succinct, "I think I may be a murderer."

She moved her leg now, a stroke that shocked my nerves then immediately quelled them, the warmth merely having been conveyed to a different spot. "Yesterday," she said, "you romanticized remarks I made by associating them with Nietzsche. I am no philosopher, Darrin, just a lost soul like you. I'm not even sure what I meant at the time. Nietzsche, I can tell you, has nothing to do with anything. I was talking about *me*. About my own deluded course. I don't know who or what I am any more than you know who or what you are. I suspect the same goes for Nietzsche, and, hell, God Himself! We all just hover over the current."

She might have been apologizing for not having the answer I sought, but I sensed more than that. I sensed I wasn't the only one harboring mighty, unanswerable questions. But still we ask them:

"What does that mean, you who are not a philosopher?"

"It means what it does. Nothing. No matter which angle you look at yourself, your life, your dreams from, it's a lie."

"There is no such creature as truth, then?"

"Truth? If you return to the site of the alleged crime, see the bird again by the broad light of day, will that be truth? Will you be suddenly bound to a greater purpose? No, I don't think even Sophia has found truth."

"I didn't say anything about returning to the site."

"Didn't you? You said she was a shadow. That's where we all return. That's where I'll return when your headlights find the next vacancy. You think your story is profound? You should hear mine. Replace sekt with heroin, your whore with my john, your calculated cleaning up with my madness, and then we'll talk about Nietzsche."

But you have a hotel, I wanted to say, a phone to lend, the scent of lemon in your hair. But her response was already there, a perpetual echo in the hovel of her bedchamber. I remembered her description of *saudade*, a nostalgia for something never experienced. Wasn't that what existence was all about? Wanting more? Remembering more? Maybe it is enough just to want, to remember, the solidity of the thing having nothing to do with true value.

I was surprised when she kissed me on my chin, whispered alrights into my stubble. "We'll go," she breathed. "We'll go together."

* * *

We set out the next morning, after soft-boiled eggs and Italian bread and yogurt. As we went we basked in the lemony splash of the sun, not unlike the afterglow of our night's secrets, secrets that now seemed to have absorbed the confessions that followed them. Her hand on my leg was a minor truth in spite of her, and the road in front of us, whizzing with Italian maniacs, not a path to the site of the alleged crime, but a ripple finding its way back to the drop of rain that had created it. What difference, really, our destination, when it is founded in illusion, delusion, glorious madness? And yet, the spell was not without imperfections as we left the *autostrade* for the narrower road that would take us into Switzerland. Each rock face, every bluff and cliff seemed to flash a more arcane band of the spectrum, in turn igniting more primal emotions, ones I might have confused with anxiety, apprehension had Elena not been there to soothe them as they came. That she displayed no such emotions neither encouraged nor discouraged my acceptance of the terms of her universe. She traveled with me as freely as I did with her, and our onuses our own to bear. Still, the thing that lurked beneath it all gradually unfurled petals of the scent of fear, and the oases of companionship and mutual acquiescence began to dissolve.

It was when the first sign for Lugano appeared that I relinquished the fantasy of falsity to fear. I tried to hide it—from myself? Elena?—as we found the road Sophie and I (had I ever called her Sophie while she was alive?) had taken, but it would not be unvoiced. The twisting road up the mountain was very much a path to the site of my alleged crime. As the tableau came into full mental view, an alarm went off in my nerves, a terrible screeching recurrence that forced me to pull off the highway into the no zone as I finally gathered in Elena's suggestion that I "answer it."

It was my cell. Yes, too long ignored. Whoever it was, Nick, the police, it was past time I confronted the situation.

"Hello."

"Darrin? It's me, Sophia. Listen, I'm sorry about the way I behaved—"

I let the phone drop.

"Darrin?" Elena said. "Who…"

As if answers, suddenly, were so easy.

I pulled onto the road again, my foot heavier on the pedal than it should have been, a weight to rival the silence that had descended over the car. As I rounded the next bend a figure appeared along the left rim of the road, back to me, in the same area, my sense told me, that Sophie—whoever I'd hit—had been. I passed, looking first over my shoulder, then in the rearview, in hopes of seeing her face. But a glare, the curve of the road, would not allow it. Before the next bend I turned around, now finding my tongue again, babbling at Elena beside me, who offered no insights, no consolations, letting me through it alone. The sun was in front of me now, but disappearing behind trees. The face came into view, its hair and eyes darker than its deeply colored skin, its aspect otherwise befogged—though somewhere in there I saw a warmth, a smile of memory, of nostalgia for things never experienced. I braked hard, reaching an arm over to protect Elena. The emptiness beside me was the vacancy out beyond the drop-off. Out there, in headlight-illuminated oblivion.

I got out of the car, went to the brink and looked down into the abyss. She was still there, the shape in the branches, though her position seemed to have changed, assumed the image of closed wings, as though the bird had not swept down, but crashed. As though the shadow imprinted on my eyes had been lying all along. I found footholds and handholds, roots and irregularities enough to make my way down. The trees were smaller than my memory had them. A smell wafted up from them, a sweet yet sunny smell, a tinge, yellowy, fruity. I reached a ledge and stretched out to touch her back, walk my fingers to her hair, pulling gently. "Wake up," I said. "You've had rougher falls. This is nothing, just a couple day's rest from the pain, the places you care not to remember. Open your eyes and maybe the world will have changed. Maybe we can find that other land, that land that *saudade* speaks of." I couldn't be certain in the rippling sunlight, the intoxicating aroma, but I thought I saw the leaves stir.

Somehow, over the course of hours, it seemed, I managed to haul her up to the road. On my shoulder the body made no movements that I could discern, but its flesh was warm against mine. When I reached the car, I lay her gingerly in the seat beside me, squeezing in behind the wheel, starting the engine, uncertain where I was going but knowing it required urgency.

As I accelerated I heard a horn and a rush of wind as a truck scraped by, its tailgate flinging open in the driver's attempt to right it. Its cargo poured out of the back, causing me to brake into a skid amid the yellow specimens, angling toward the brink. The thought of going there with her, becoming one with her shadow calmed me as the question of survival hung just so elegantly in front of me. Then, in that instant that is less than an instant, we'd come to a stop, shy of the edge, the woman beside me turning, her lips forming words.

"Where...oh yes, I remember...someplace pleasant..."

Three Towns, One Migrant

1.

Juneau, Alaska

It was the silt, not the nettles, that burned me as I crouched in the vegetation behind the gravel parking lot of the Silver Salmon Tavern. As I'd learned to do in war, I'd anesthetized myself in advance against the foreseeable environmental factors. Except for my face and hands, I was clothed head to foot in plastic against both the underbrush and the constant rain that fell on Juneau in the fall. What I hadn't prepared for was what would happen when I raised my hands, after wiping them on my jacket, to remove the rain from my eyes. The gritty Alaskan soil, as I should have known after living here beneath the mountains for three months, would always find its way into the equation. Not so the sands I'd earned my combat wages on. In Iraq it had been almost reflexive, immunizing oneself against the elements. When raindrops were bullets, nettles fragmenting shells, the grains ceased to exist.

I checked my watch. Two-twenty in the morning. It had been nearly thirty minutes since the last customer had come out of the tavern. The handful of vehicles left in the lot made me consider for a moment the possibility that the bar had closed up for a private after-party. But I quickly dismissed the idea. The girl, for one, wasn't a regular. Previous reconnaissance also eliminated the driver of the red four-wheel-drive pickup, whose "1 4 AK" vanity plate, dimly illuminated by the lamp at the opposite corner of the lot, was not fifteen feet from my location. Besides, the owner and operator of the place—Burly, as the locals called him—wasn't one to deviate from course. I didn't always like them like that, but tonight I just wanted to get on with the mission. Captain Ferrer had her reports to fill out, after all.

Speak of the devil. In all her regalia, here she came now, begging me, pleading with me to do it. This uniform, that uniform, how were they different?

She'd touched my blood. I knew exactly what she was when she reached out and fingered the seeping essence of myself. "You'll survive," she'd smiled. "When your brothers in arms are dead, you'll still be standing. Some of us are invincible." As though, by virtue of her former tours as a lieutenant in the field, she could cloak the raw fact of herself against eyes like mine. No, we who survive do so by the shedding of it, not by the taste of it. I know you, Princess. I know you too well.

She was singing the song that was playing in the tavern. The door had opened with a blast of sickeningly typical classic rock, and now she carried the music along like a drunken ambassador. And no mistaking what it was she was drunk on, our good captain. I relived that smell every time I shaved. Every time I looked at the blade, wondering if the scent came from the metal or the ghost of the last cut. But if confirmation was needed, then I had to look no further than the owner of the red pickup as he came stumbling after her a moment later, accusing her of the obvious. "Baby, another bar? You're sucking me dry."

"The Dive's open in the Valley."

"The Dive? Christ, I wouldn't go there if my—"

He wouldn't have to. Nor did his life depend on it. That score had been settled when the girl's interest in remaining in his company was revealed to me. Whether that eventuality would have played out or not, we would never know. I had already pounced, sending her to the ground with a specifically placed blow before descending on him. Having allowed for this scenario and a dozen others, I spotted him no reaction time. Before he could get his cry out, I'd performed my ridiculously basic maneuver on him and sliced his throat from ear to ear.

I could hear the bubbling of his failed call as I pulled the keys out of the pocket of his jeans, replaced my rain jacket with his camouflage affair, and tossed his body into the back of his pickup. The girl, I placed in the cab with me, propping her upright against my shoulder as her lolling head muttered her love for Credence Clearwater Revival. I made it out of the lot without the bar's door opening again, though that situation was covered, too, by the weak lighting surrounding the exit.

It wasn't the A plan, but neither had it called for too much improvisation. The truck would go to a predetermined spot. The girl would go, by four-wheeler at first, then by foot, to the cabin with me.

* * *

I don't like messy. After four, count 'em, *four* tours in the desert, I'd long since had my fill of messy. Which was why the scalpel had come to be my redeemer of choice. I'd tried the straight razor, I'd tried the fine filament wire, but it just wasn't the same. As uninventive as it may sound, the scalpel, in addition to providing the clean efficiency one expected of one's instrument, had a certain aesthetic quality to it. When held up to the light, when placed in silhouette, when put to its intended purpose of neatly opening flesh, it literally sang. For me the scalpel was more than the perfect tool; it was a natural appendage from which life and beauty dripped. I'd go so far as to use a penis metaphor if the imagination could sap a cock of unspilt blood and alchemize the withered result into honed titanium.

Never let them see it. That was the first thing. While the vision of the device obviously carried tremendous power, its noon shadow carried even more. I'd learned the value of invisibility in nearby Chi Bay, Alaska—a much easier playground than well-lit Juneau—when I first began playing with the idea of redemption. If they saw it, then both the effect and the integrity of the thing were polluted. Which made me no better than the animal I'd been in combat. What is combat, after all, but a demonstration of arms? Yes, it might also be a demonstration of effect, but at heart it's a brandishing, a vanity that has less to do with politics or ideals than it has its own ego, as realized by the combatant. This is not to say that redemption is without its own conceits. Only that one may progress, by the quality of one's *art brut*, along the same paths that would otherwise constitute regression. There must be discovery in the process. The method of rendering it is a method that serves both the surgeon and the patient. Let them know an operation is to occur, but never by what device. Like perfume, expectation has different aromas. The correct manipulation of suspense is the difference between a $10 bottle and a $100 bottle.

Do I write an instruction manual? No. If anything, this is a gospel for the patient. For it's you, in the end, who are available. The vampire, invincible bitch that she was, died before I could get back to her. Thus it isn't to her body that I redeem myself, but to her spirit. Which lives in every vile thing that I so designate. Label me what you will, but remember the truth when I come calling. One man's psychosis is another man's self-identity. Let that sink in while I steal up behind your bound naked body and sink something else in. I will paint murals of you, and it will be your soul, not your blood, that smears the elegant shapes on the canvas.

I'd but four words to say to my aromatic princess between the tavern and immortality. I let them trickle over her at the very end, when we were inside the cabin and I'd opened a clean path to her spine:

"Touch me now, Captain."

The shiver that overtook her as she sought to catch up with what was happening was the finest bouquet I could have asked for. "Please," she pleaded. "I have money. Anything you want. Take my body. Anything but *thiiiis…*"

Okay, ten words if you included those uttered when the veil whispered with, but had not yet fallen behind, her passage:

"I'll meet you over there, Princess."

2.

Neckarsteinach, Germany

It was the insulation, not the snow, that got to me as I crouched behind the wall of the castle ruin, shifting every couple minutes or so to relieve some part of my body from the nagging clutch of the skins I wore. Preparing for a wintry day in Hesse, Germany wasn't the same as preparing for it in Southeast Alaska, where the extra layers were more often than not going to be needed in an outdoor work setting. Imagining myself in wait in the strange German weather couldn't be translated to participating in one of the postcards depicting a Christmas-white Hinterburg, the second of Neckarsteinach's castle ruins as one hiked in by the trail off the road from Heidelberg. My association with the elements remained the least complete thing about myself in my relationship with the job at hand. I'd improved, there was no question about that; I'd corrected the imperfections of too many variable-ridden ambushes, all but *becoming* the shadow that so complemented the blade. But climate, accursed climate, continued to escape me after years of trying to peacefully mate with it in its various incarnations. On this backwards-ass Thursday when predicted storms had thus far turned out to be no more than a lazy opportunity to commune with nature, I was warm to the point of squirming at my post. Add to that the growing prospect that a family with children might decide to get out for an afternoon of exploring the forest-setting sites of Hinterburg and the Swallow's Nest and I was beginning to consider abandoning the mission for the first time in as long as I could remember.

Until I saw the hiker emerge from the trees.

That the young man would come had never been in question. They always do when there's at least the threat of inconvenient weather. In the guise of sportsmen, adventurers, they must prove their manhood to something older and less superficial than society. Just like the detective in Juneau who made the four-hour trek up the mountain to the cabin (which couldn't be readily accessed by helicopter) like it was his divine calling. I'd been off my game then—in the botched job I'd done of it by hiding the pickup so close to the trailhead; in squatting at the cabin while I made the girl's remnants my channel to the other side; in assuming witnesses were always visible in a place like Alaska. So much had been learned since then. I'd come to terms with being a god in a nebula of gods. Or at least accepted my temporary limitations.

What I'd thought was art had turned out to be the vestiges of my claim to humanity. For a god, art was its own entity. It needed no assistance. What was accomplished was accomplished on the merits of the deed, not the doing. The result took its own inevitable form—which did not include redemption, a decidedly personal exercise. Still, to achieve absolute superiority one had to include oneself in the painting, at the painting's own discretion. Discomfort, then, became proper order. Worming around in my suit and misgivings merely preluded the fact that he was here now, ready to finally be translated. Liberating, it was, knowing the game inside and out. They didn't have to *be* anything for me anymore—not a captain, not a detective, not the uncle who'd so hungrily raised me—they merely had to shrug themselves into their own templates. Redemption, really, had become an afterthought. Art had its own impenetrable requirements.

Not least the coats I had to work my way through as I secured the knife behind my wrist and fell from the wall in his path.

Something gave as I landed. A something that could not be distinguished between bone and flesh as I escaped the tangle I'd made of myself and began limping forward, feeling the blood run in hot streams down my pierced forearm.

"What the fuck, old man?" the hiker said. His eyes gleamed in the light that wasn't supposed to have reflected off the snow today. "What are you supposed to be? A highwayman or something? I could have used you as the raw example back when I did my midterm in literature."

I wanted to answer in some satisfactory way for the both of us before I rendered him subject. But the eyes, that sparkle of...what? Being there with me? Did he dare?

With a sudden look into the sky by way of distracting him, I ripped his face, diagonally, in half.

"We wur wooking od…" he warped while the shock was still arriving, "… onteenth-century wawwessness…"

I rendered him unconscious before he could succumb to the agonies that awaited.

*　　*　　*

When I'd first arrived at the castle ruin, I'd lashed a stretcher together out of fallen branches and two sturdy limbs that served as the main frame. I used the remaining twine to affix the young man's body to the makeshift structure. The winter had stripped the forest of much of its underbrush, leaving me an easy path to the spot I'd previously scouted out. I was no great physical specimen, but I outweighed my passenger by a good thirty pounds and much of that, muscle, thanks to the dedication I'd shown the gym during my military days. Factor in the adrenaline generated by being in the thing again after a month's hiatus—the same hormone that had appeared to have cured the pain in my ankle—and it was almost without effort that I hauled my load up the hill. With luck, the weather would yet turn in favor of the prognosticators, or at least provide enough flurries to cover my tracks. But as with every mission, I *depended* on nothing. If you did, you could not rely on yourself when that one odd day that every undertaking fears came along.

Today happened to be that day.

At the top of the hill I had to cross a wide main trail used by hikers and cyclists. While I of course knew this and took all the necessary precautions before crossing—which included walking some distance along the path in each direction before returning to where I'd dropped the stretcher—I failed to anticipate the mountain biker coming like hell's own fury around a near bend in the road.

She didn't appear until I was halfway across the eight-foot expanse, leaving her no room to divert her course even if that had been an option. She literally ran directly into the stretcher, letting out this strange, halting cry as she went over her handlebars, hanging in space for a protracted moment before crashing into a tree at the edge of the trail. Meanwhile the bike had taken its own un-advantageous angle, clipping my arm hard as it sailed its way. I dropped the stretcher as the next two bikers appeared, looking as if they were enmeshed in some lunatic race.

The leader, by a neck, jerked up his front wheel and ran right over my passenger, somehow remaining upright through the stunt, while the other's reflexive action involved the use of his hand brakes, which resulted in his unhelmeted head striking the ground with such force that I could hear the impact.

I'm quick at the draw when it comes to my own reflexes. So quick, according to one former comrade, that it was a wonder my reactions didn't find themselves competing against each other. Well, they did now as I had to contend with the prospect of the next biker as well as the fact that I was as exposed as I'd ever been in combat. With one eye on the bend and the other on the biker who had made it through the chaos and was now skidding to a stop in the shallow snow, I somehow managed to find my trusty scalpel. Or rather it did me, as it seemed to leap out of my coat pocket into my palm. As three, four, five seconds passed without the appearance of another bike, I turned to face the cyclist who'd declined to participate in the wreckage, my blade nudged up against the wound it had left before ascent began. Though war had also taught me ambidexterity, I left it there, thriving on the pain.

"Danielle," the biker said, pulling up and dismounting next to the girl, who'd managed to rise to a sitting position. The rest was an exchange in German which, while I couldn't understand it, effectively rendered her a functioning threat to my mission. The third biker was another matter as the one attending to the girl left her to see after him.

I'd already come up with a story should such be necessary: My friend on the stretcher had suffered a fall; I needed to get him medical attention, and quick. But that need, clearly, was not going to arise. The man on the ground was staying there. The blood pool forming in the snow, the rock that appeared as the other lifted his head, assured it. Now, if the girl could just manage to join them in their little huddle—and she was giving it her best effort on her wobbly legs—my job would be simplified.

She couldn't, and her friend went back to her. I did the insurance on the one with the open skull as quietly as possible, but she saw the slicing motion of my hand from where the other man held her against his chest.

"*Mein Gott!*" she cried. "*O mein Gott!*"

I don't know why, but I simply stood up from the deed—scalpel visible in a hand drenched from the spurting artery—and bathed in it all.

"*O heilige Christ,*" let out the man as he dropped her and, very slowly, rose to stand facing me.

"*Ja*," I said. "I like that. I can see myself stretched on that frame behind me, promising redemption to my flock. Are you one of them, *Herr Mann*? Are you one of my sheep?"

We both cast glances at the stretcher as we faced off, but it was he who saw the movement first. By the time my eyes arrived, my college boy had begun to thrash against his restraints, issuing sounds out of his split mouth that clearly horrified the two mountain bikers. The actions, the reactions…they all happen so quickly when blood is involved. Are you looking, Captain? Are you watching with interest our stage play? Never fear, I'll be there soon enough to sign my autograph in your sweet throat. You taught me that, right? The dream of immortality?

The male biker, sportsman that he was, charged me. Before he knew what had happened, I'd shredded him.

In a complete, uncharacteristic, change of plans, I strode to where the college boy struggled and put him out of his misery. Leaving the loaded stretcher there for God and any of His children who happened to come along to gawk at, I took the girl to the designated spot, where I had my drink of her until I was full.

3.

Hua Hin, Thailand

It was the whiteness of epiphany, not the tropical heat, that seared me as I crouched behind the trunk of a mango tree, waiting for the monk in his unique, toga-white robe. The temple was ancient, made of stone—not one of the gilt, ludicrously ornate affairs that scourged the province of Prachuap Khiri Khan. How such a sublime faith could entertain, could *suffer* such monstrosities as those tourist beacons that had not even been built for the tourists, was beyond me. Thank the Lord Vampire God Albino for providing riches from the falsest of springs. Unto thee, I shall forever cast my lot. It is with thee I go and without thee I come to the final understanding. You are generous to have provided the monk, all in white, suffering from the long absence.

Previous reconnaissance had shown the holy man to be punctual to a fault, which was a Buddhism that I could not help but admire from so atypical a creature as he in his deviant dress. Indexing back through the weeks produced only orange robes, orange robes and gaudy temples. If he wasn't a disciple then neither was I. We'd both had our brushes with God, I was quite sure, but to stand in testament to it was something else entirely. Sure, *they* put your robes on you. They placed you in your temples. They called you by their names. But it's you who wear it all. You who come when you haven't verbally been called. You who fulfill your duty without question. You who sweep toward your brother even now, in your glorious whiteness. The palm fronds and the mangos and the monkeys swimming overhead. Unto thee, brother. This gift, this old trusty gift unto thee.

Strangely, and then not so strangely, it was the girl mountain biker who'd put it in my head. "You need faith, man. If you can't get it here then try Buddhism. They don't judge, you know? *You* are responsible for your own winds. I know. I spend three weeks there every year. I'm like you. I really am. I don't know which way to turn to accommodate myself. Thailand helped me. It gave me focus without the moral turmoil. I might have ended up *being you* if not for the direction that a few sticks of incense and a little prayer gave me. And the joy of it all is that it's *your* direction. It was never imposed. It was never a requirement."

"I find it hard to believe," I told her in utmost confidence, "that blood is not a requirement."

"Why?" she insisted. "It's all white in Buddhism. There are temples, cathedrals, personal audiences with God. If only you could understand…"

I'd wanted to. I'd wanted to so much that I'd let her live, at least in some part of myself, and maybe, just maybe, in reality as well, as I went pursuing this strange dream. The past was so unimportant anymore that I'd shut off the cell phone I'd never, in all my existence, had. This woman, throat so ripe for it, had made a modicum of sense…which was all I'd ever asked of my fellow human beings. I'd spared her. In some truth, I had, indeed, spared her.

But here he came now, my monk, looking at the clock on his wrist. His skin as unpigmented as his armor. His armor as ghostly as the universe itself, as luminescent as Heaven, as undying as Captain Ferrer's milky white countenance where she sat in her privileged seat, sharing in a laugh with the one who pretended to be God.

Would she know me in my bloodless uniform? Could she call me out on my deviations, my lapses in humility, without some representation on her own part? If this man, this being approaching me served whatever purpose it was I intended, then what was I to do with him by way of commitment? I'd failed so long, and so hard. What was anything anymore?

White. That had to mean something. And so, I extended my instrument to him.

He looked at it, both long and hard, and then back up at me, eyes so sympathetic I almost lost myself in them. But I didn't. I couldn't. I'd come too far to simply acquiesce to the elements. He must have seen this, for a mist seemed to come over his eyes. I detected a sacrifice, an offering, a coming to terms on the air as he looked skyward, prompting a similar motion of my own head. I'd but a moment to share in it before my answer, with the swiftest of movements, was delivered.

A fountain in which to bathe, mouth open, fangs retracting.

As I let the tool fall from my weary hand.

Cries from the Static

When purple precedes and shadows reach long
And white noise recedes and nothing seems wrong
Remember the glass, the encrypted glass
The faceted prism, the storms that amass
Where clarity finds
Itself in the blinds
And panes in the static reflect you in kind.

When purple refrains and shadows dissolve
And darkness holds reign and nothing resolves
Remember the song, the encoded song
The faceted chorus that never rings wrong
When clarity meets
Your own primal beats
And cries from the static reflect your conceits.

When purple implies and pigments infuse
A relishing sky, that fabulous bruise
Remember the bands, the enciphered bands
The faceted spectrum that fans from your hands
In clarity wrought
Of something long sought
And cracks in the static inflecting the thought.

When static refutes and nothing resolves
When purple dilutes and rainbows dissolve
Remember the voice, the encrusted voice
The faceted myst'ries that castrate the choice
Remember the call, the embedded call

The faceted madness that creates the pall
As clarity fails
Lucidity bails
And cries from the static now drawn out in wails.

Der Teufelobstgarten

It wasn't my style to stay at bed-and-breakfasts, being something of a loner and disliking all that intimacy among strangers, but you learn to live with your hang-ups when you have little or no other choice. *Gasthäuser* are as much a part of the German culture as hotels are in America. I suppose I should have simply been glad—as Laura reminded me all too often—that we had cheap rooms available to us in even the most remote places on our cycling tour of central Europe.

By the time we reached the source of the Saar River near Strasbourg, a long day's ride from the edge of the Black Forest, I had actually grown to enjoy immersing in the culture with our routinely polite and domestically gifted hostesses. Having ridden along rivers since we set out from Frankfurt—the Rhine, the Mosel, then the Saar—Laura and I had been averaging ninety kilometers a day with minimal effort. That figure changed significantly when we climbed into the mountains that fed the Saar River. The day we found the farmhouse at the foot of Donon, we had managed forty-five at best.

Laura had just pointed out to me that the map placed us below a Roman temple ruin, elevation 1009 meters, when I spotted a sign in the trunk of the tree beside us. We sat on a deteriorating bench, having stopped to take a breather before tackling the mountain looming in our path. The bright April sun lagged beyond the pasture that the bench overlooked, reflected among the roofs at the near cusp of the landscape. The sign, which depicted a bicycle and a fork and spoon, pointed rustily in that direction. I stood and, licking my fingers, rubbed some of the message back into the present. The price was in deutsche marks, not euros, which completed the mystique.

"You think?" Laura said, not needing to finish.

"I would seriously doubt they still rent rooms," I said. I looked at my watch. "It's nearing seven."

"Can't hurt to try. Worse case, we make the other side of the mountain as it's getting dark. I'm sure there'll be a *Zimmer frei* in the village where people access the Roman ruin."

Our tour went very much like that, Laura asking me my opinion and then settling on her own. Which is how it should have gone, as she had mapped out our route and knew a good deal about the language, geography and culture, having spent six cumulative years in Germany in a military household.

"Lead on," I said.

The cords of her legs were already in motion as she mounted her bike and started up the narrow road. As the view expanded, bringing the resplendent fire of a mountain sunset, thoughts of refuge from the coming night evaporated. The structures sharpened into their configurations, fences stabbing darkly at the sky, roofs sloping in deep humility, as if for their luxurious domain. We rode alongside a fence of electric wire, automobile batteries appearing intermittently, then *immediately* as we reached out, laughing, to touch the containment of animals unseen. The silhouettes in front of us comprised a farm, its current operators probably generations behind the makers of the decrepit sign in the tree.

"I love this place," Laura said, a sentiment with which I couldn't argue as we merged with the rest of the brush strokes in the pastoral scene.

A rock wall surrounded the main house and its grounds. The gate was fashioned from the front halves of two rusted old-fashioned bicycles. If that wasn't enough to make me mend my opinion about the place offering beds, then the laminated lodging info attached to the side of the wall was. Furthermore, the rear of the house, now visible, had a second-floor balcony complete with fresh flowers. The view from there, I imagined, would be fantastic, taking in both the sunset and the mountain. Impulsively my eyes found their way to the top of the steep, thinly wooded slope behind the farm, where I thought I could just make out an unnatural stone shape resembling a pavilion.

We parked our bikes in a rack inside the gate and walked the path's octagonal stones to the door. Before I released the brass knocker a woman's face appeared, her striking blue eyes tempered by expressive age lines. Her white hair was done up in some clever way that Laura would later comment on, and her hand on the doorjamb sported a blue gemstone to match her eyes. In spite of a thin, sad smile, there was a vitality about her that went beyond her welcome.

"*Guten Tag*," she said.

"*Tag*," said Laura. "*Sprechen Sie Englisch?*"

"Oh, a little."

"*Ja. Ich spreche ein bisschen Deutsch.*"

"*Dein Deutsch is sehr gut*," the woman smiled. "Do you wish a room for the night?"

"*Bitte.*"

"*Kommt herein.* We have two rooms with private baths and a view of the valley."

We stepped inside the house inspired—Laura because of the warm welcome, myself because of the unexpected turn of events. My muscles thanked our hostess as they finally relaxed for the day, knowing a bed was near; my senses did the same as they partook of the rustic interior of the farmhouse. A wooden chandelier reminiscent of something found in an upscale hunter's lodge formed the centerpiece of the entry area. The rough stucco walls were hung with woven or otherwise handcrafted pictures. The floor was a richly textured hardwood, as was the carved balustrade leading upstairs. In keeping with the wood theme, the scent of burning cedar seeped in from other parts of the house.

Laura's smile said it all as we ascended the stairs to the guest rooms. The two rooms were identical in nearly every way—traditionally spare but charming—except that the balcony of the second was that much closer to not only the mountain, but also a separate feature that lured the eye. Out in the field beyond the barn and the farm's lone grain silo stood an orchard of some thirty trees—apple trees, I knew at once, because of their twisted frames. In the midst of them grew one that was taller and more grotesque than the others, and bearing the glimmer of developed fruit on one of its distorted branches, though it was only April.

I found myself commenting on the loveliness of the view, not specifically naming the fruit trees. But she knew what had evoked my admiration.

"In the village they call it *Der Teufelobstgarten.* The Devil Orchard."

While my imagination bristled, my response was altogether unimaginative. "I can see why."

Maybe it was my taste for the dark but this time I didn't allow my virgin tourist status to be a factor, plainly accepting the room to our hostess without even a consultatory glance at Laura. When I did cast my eye her way, I saw that my assertiveness had earned me an almost desirous look.

Downstairs, we made introductions, filled out a card, and fielded what was a beautiful question from Helga.

"Do you wish dinner?"

I blinked at Laura. We had planned on eating chili out of a can.

*　*　*

Forty minutes later, with light failing outside, we were sitting down to a table of *Jägerschnitzel*, *Brötchen* (hard bread rolls), *Pommes* (fries), and beer. Helga declined to dine with us, but she proved more than happy to converse. We asked about her family and she told us her husband worked out in the fields till late and her son was away at Heidelberg learning surgery. We told her about our own families, in America and envying our dream of doing Europe our way. The talk went to this and to that, finally landing where I'd hoped it would as our hostess mentioned late spring blossoms.

"So why do the villagers call it Der Teufel Garden?" I asked. It was as pathetically close as I ever came to constructing a phrase in the native tongue.

"The villagers are afraid of *Der Teufelobstgarten*. The site has been a sacred one to some cultures. It has also been a…the word is *grim?*…yes, a grim one."

"What do you mean?" I said, chunk of pork suspended on the tines of my fork.

"The Romans built the temple on Donon because of the energy that is present here." She turned to Laura. "How do you say *Gelehrte* in English? Yes, *scholar*. A Roman scholar named Protus wrote of the Celts…condemning this place."

Laura translated the rest because of the obvious strain on Helga's ability. "Apparently," she conveyed, "Druid priests chose this valley as a ritual site because of the energy Helga mentions. But soon after they began performing their ceremonies, they died without apparent cause. Their bodies were found in the spot where the orchard now stands, which is also where their funeral pyres were erected. The Celts believed that the priests fell victim to the same force that had made them choose the site."

Helga went on to explain, with Laura doing an increasingly animated job of translating, about how Protus had witnessed a battle between the Celts and the Romans from atop the mountain where the temple would be built two hundred years later—a battle that resulted in the near total destruction of both the Celtic army and the Roman division with which Protus traveled. He wrote that during the Celts' customary pre-battle clamor of blowing trumpets and banging their swords and shields, they abruptly quit their intimidations, raising their arms to indicate something beyond the Romans. The Romans, believing it a ploy on the foe's part, charged. A fierce bloodbath ensued, with the Celts appearing to try to hack their way through the Roman soldiers without regard for their own defense. Protus later learned that the Celts believed they had seen their Druid priests beckoning to them from a terrace of higher ground. So profoundly were they affected that they never returned for their dead, which spoke volumes for a culture with such elaborate funeral rituals—particularly when it came to their fallen warriors.

A pause preceded Laura's unnecessary footnote that this farmstead occupied that terrace of higher ground. In the succeeding silence, I was about to ask a question that perturbed me when Helga began speaking again. Laura watched her intently before passing yet more history along.

"The farm was abandoned during the war after some sort of skirmish left a party of Nazi soldiers dead. After an SS probe that apparently revealed nothing of substance, no one wanted any part of the place. Helga and her husband picked the farm up for next to nothing after it sat empty for almost two decades. They started renting in sixty-five. Around that same time they planted the orchard that the villagers despise."

I seized the moment. "The tree in the middle of the orchard. The one that has fruit…"

Helga spouted off a stream of German that did not even attempt to recognize the language barrier. Laura interpreted: "Beneath that tree lies what has been dubbed the *Druid Stein*—or stone. That's where the valley's energy is strongest and what made the Druids choose the place."

I shook my head for lack of a more appropriate gesture. "This is fascinating stuff. Why doesn't she post a new sign on the bike path alluding to the layered history of the area?"

A minor discussion ensued. "They aren't interested in money," Laura finally related. "They much prefer someone perceptive enough to find and follow the sign already there."

"By *they*, you do mean Helga and her husband, right?" I smiled my smile and hoped I wasn't told on.

Laura cast a glance at our hostess, who winked and began gathering up our cleaned plates. She asked if we would like to take a bottle of wine up with us and we told her we would, gladly. As Helga retreated to her environs, Laura and I did the same, pleasantly nibbling at each other's ears as we locked ourselves in. The day and its expenditures dissolved and our intimacies took over. Somewhere between the hour of darkness and total darkness I wanted a cigarette—which Laura, as usual, invited me to enjoy outside.

I stood on the balcony in my boxers, looking out on a night as clear as the day had been. The stone configuration at the top of the mountain stood confirmed in the floodlights that were trained upon it, a tease to motorists and long since disinterested villagers. As I sucked on my Marlboro my eyes fell to the orchard. Its trees were sketched in black wax, darker than all their surrounds, silhouetted even against the ground itself. A half-moon hung off to the right splashing the land in its silvery light. One object captured its radiance more effectively than any other, that fruit so rare, so plump and rare on its jagged branch.

At the foot of the tree I could see the white surface of the *Druid Stein*. I imagined how delightful it would be to sit there smoking my cigarette, submerged in the mystery of the place, knowing the local culture in a way no bed-and-breakfast, of itself, could provide. To venture a taste of the forbidden apple…

Something moved out on the skirts of my vision. When I looked I couldn't find it, though I fancied its afterimage to be the right size for Helga's husband, lost abroad in his fields without supper. As soon as I returned my gaze to the tree, the flash occurred again. Even in a hallucinatory context, there was no mistaking it for some manner of passage. I glanced at the moon wondering if something had disturbed its surface, but my eyes were the only things disturbed, the fragment of motion a ghost on their lenses. The stub of my cigarette arced out into the night, spraying embers like fiery salt.

"Are you coming in?" Laura asked from the spheres of darkness behind me.

I poked my head in, not recognizing any of the outlines. "How would you like to go for a walk?"

"Are you crazy? I'm sticky, if you know what I mean."

"Who cares. It's beautiful out. Let's go exploring."

I couldn't tell, through the darkness, if she was afraid. I suspected not, knowing my Laura who conquered Europe with a pencil on paper. The pause allowed my eyes to adjust, the moonlight to seep in, the magic to re-invert. Laura's breasts came into view, sweetly rounded and milky white below her tan line. I thought of their resemblance to the fruit in the orchard, but of course I had only a glimmer by way of comparison. Which was why I must go there, with or without her, and cup it in my hand.

She opted to join me, with the stipulation that I take her bodily in the spring night.

I thought to deny her presumption, but the refreshed experience of her made me weak.

*   *   *

The night was magnificently unrestrained as we slipped out the guest door in back. The valley sprawled before us, the temple of Donon a celestial body to complement the moon. *Der Teufelobstgarten* seemed to crawl in place as we approached, its still somewhat stark limbs jabbing angrily at the owls of spring with their shining eyes upon the mice of the field. Among the expressive trees, one rose taller, meaner, more seductively than its fellows, dangling drops of honey for the taker. I asked Laura if she was the taker and she told me she could not be sure. Neither could I as we dared place our bodies on the broad, flat stone beneath. I started a cigarette and she extinguished it against the bark of the tree, drawing me down on top of her. Her gown, translucent in the moonlight, melted around us.

When my pace, or perhaps a quirk in my technique, didn't satisfy her, she positioned herself above me, riding her body against mine as if it were our last encounter. Over her shoulder the bloated apple seemed to dip on its branch, singing with moonlight, begging to be pierced to let its juices flow forth. I felt my tongue reaching upward as Laura won the rest of my body, refusing to release me until I had spent myself inside her. While I experienced the orgasm with her, I could not release everything because a part of me had been captured by the fruit above.

As Laura's eyes hid behind their lids, the apple alone regarded me, a lamp over our pleasures. Again I reached, but it was too high unless I stood. And if I stood I did so above the contented body of the only goddess I had known— until tonight. I closed my eyes and held her, no, clung to her, and the night was linen around us. It was she who withdrew, seeming to fail to see my distraction.

"Aren't you going to have a cigarette?" she said, placing her hands on her thighs.

"Really?"

"Don't you always?"

That's when I heard the distant music of a tractor, presumably Helga's husband working away in the realms below. As I looked that way I was sure I saw wisps of something slipping through fluid layers, but they vanished as soon my eyes found them. I turned back to see if Laura had fallen for optical tricks, instead found her gazing at me. "Cigarette," she reminded me, holding a lit one in her fingers. She must have brought it along with her—behind her ear, perhaps, though I had tasted a different type of retreat there.

I pulled on it, looking up at her.

"If that's not enough, how about this?" She reached above her and grasped the apple. Motion occurred spontaneously in every direction around me, strange light-like shapes emerging from nocturnal folds. Now Laura saw them too, a fact I gleaned as my gaze was torn between the flurried darkness and the apple in her hand. But then she froze, fixing on a point behind me, in the direction of the farm. Her lips parted slightly, her hand—*no don't do that, Laura*—released the fruit, the gleam of which seemed to intensify as it hung there unplucked.

The surrounding motion quit, darkness becoming only darkness again. "Look," was the word that came out of Laura's mouth, as insubstantial as the shapes still lurking out there, invisibly. I turned to follow her stare and saw at once what commanded it. A single window in the farmhouse was lit up. Silhouetted against it, out on the balcony of the room next to ours, was our hostess Helga. Watching us.

"Jesus, what's happening. How long has she been there?" Laura said.

"It can't have been too long," I said. "We would have seen her."

"It's the apple. When I touched it, it...was it my imagination?"

"No."

"Then something else. An effect of some kind caused by the moonlight— look, she's going in. Jesus Christ, my heart is pounding."

She spoke sense—or some semblance of it. I wanted to believe the apple was a disco ball activated by her touch. I wanted to believe it was all about mirrors and reflections. "You're right," I told her. "It had to be illusion."

"There's no other explanation," she said, slowly removing herself from on top of me. I hadn't realized until then how tightly she had been clutching me with her thighs.

We covered ourselves and started back across the field, hand in hand, looking around us, looking back at the tree with its luminous angry fruit. Nothing disturbed the night except shadows. That and the distant, barely audible grumble of a motor.

"Do you hear it?" I asked her.

"I can't hear anything but my heartbeat."

"Come on," I said, turning towards the sound.

"What? Where? I don't want to."

"Just far enough so that we can see what's below. I think I hear a tractor."

"So? Why do we care—"

"Come on." She didn't put up a fight as I pulled her with me, though she kept looking off to her right where the Devil Orchard flexed its twisted waxen limbs. As we reached the edge of what proved to be a deep slope of more grassland, we had a view that sprawled even in the night, with rolling hills stacked one on the other in progressive shades. Our eyes found the tractor idling in a field, headlights catching its driver digging with his hands in the turned earth in front of the machine. As we watched for a minute or so, he appeared to sift through the soil, finding a glint of something and stuffing it in a bag he wore like an apron.

"What do you suppose he's doing?" Laura said.

"Don't know."

"I want to go back to our room."

"Okay."

The house could not have looked less comforting as we walked along the wall to the gate, wondering which peephole Helga watched from. But as we stepped inside its sturdy framework and the silence of its interiors escorted us to our room, our fears seemed farther and farther away. Laura held me for a long time before I heard her breathe evenly. In that easing music I tried to pass out of time with her, but a persistent gremlin in my system kept me from doing so. I tapped two smokes out of the pack and went out onto the balcony to watch the moon bathe the devil fruit.

I found myself somewhat disappointed when I reached the filter and nothing of report had occurred. I was debating whether to have the second smoke or go to bed when I heard the tractor approaching. The flick of my lighter echoed across the night. Upon lighting the cigarette, I held the flame up to Donon and saw the goddess Diana there. Hadn't Helga said it was *her* temple? The cigarette tasted like a question mark as the sound of the engine drew nearer. When the machine appeared over the lip of the field, the universe had reached a tilted normalcy that flickered among my nerve endings. The tractor turned toward the orchard instead of the house, and I saw the ember in front of my face brighten to unfamiliar degrees.

Helga's husband dropped from the vehicle. As he began to pull the artifacts from his bag and place them on the stone that was probably still wet from his guests' encounter, I had the impression of bones.

* * *

In the morning, as is so often the case, things looked entirely different. Laura joined me on the balcony for my morning puff, and last night need not be visited again as the orchard was only what it was, with actual blossoms breaking out on its branches. We kissed there beneath Donon before donning our cycling clothes and heading down to a wonderfully traditional German breakfast of soft-boiled eggs and *Brötchen* and cheese. When our hostess asked if we had enjoyed visiting the orchard, we could only smile and wonder.

As she saw us off she apologized for the fact that we never got to meet her husband, who was already out in the fields tilling again. If we took the farm road, which was the easier route around the mountain, we might see him. While we had no practical interest in the drudges of a farmer, we did like the idea of an easier route around the mountain. We entertained only the briefest flutter of doubt when she told us we would save time by crossing the orchard field and picking up the road by the tree line at the base of the mountain.

As we pedaled across the grassy stretch, Laura watched the temple above us, I the orchard. I couldn't be sure without venturing closer, but it appeared as though the rock beneath the tree was vacant. The apple, too, had that look about it as it hung there in the sun, pulpy and bright, unplucked.

A Lonely Town in Alaska

"What's your name?" said the woman through the open passenger window of the weathered Jeep Cherokee.

"Hunter," said the man at the wheel.

"Hunter? That's a bit obvious, isn't it?"

"Not if you're from my generation."

"Your generation? How old could you be?" she said. "Thirty?"

"Actually, I'm forty-seven. Call it living well."

"Yeah? What do you do, bathe in the blood of infants or something?"

"Why? Are you an infant?"

She hesitated a moment, searching his face, and then, seeming to trust what she saw, said, "Not after the journey I'm returning from."

"Well, get in and tell me about it."

Again the hesitation. Again the look that said, *He's one of us...whoever the hell we are.* She had that air about her. That of the lonely spirit.

"Where are you headed?" she asked.

"Hooking up with the Alaska Highway eventually."

"You must have just gotten off the ferry."

"Do I have the look of the lower forty-eight states, is that it?"

"Where else would you be coming from? Road ends not three miles beyond the terminal." She smiled, and he thought, *She herself has a trustworthy face. Clear and open without being naïve.* He wondered if it was a universal Alaskan trait.

"Yes, I remember that now. When I look at a map I tend to look in the direction I want to go. Never backwards."

"Wise man," she said, idly fiddling with the strap of her backpack. "The Alaska Highway, huh? To get there, I suppose you know, you have to go through Chi Bay." Now the shadow lingered a little longer, bringing out lines in her face that had previously been invisible.

"And?"

"And nothing. I'm going there myself."

"Well hop in. I could use somebody to point me around. I plan to spend the night there before heading on in the morning."

"My backpack?" she said, pulling the strap forward with her thumb.

"Of course. Let's put it in back."

When that was done and she'd settled into the seat beside him, he put the Jeep in gear and glanced through the side view mirror before pulling onto the road.

"I tell you there's nothing back there, man," his passenger said. "The kids party at this camping spot at the end of the road, but that's on weekends. If you were the only vehicle off the ferry, you're the only one this side of Chi Bay. You might catch a cop out here pretending to be busy, but that's about it on a Monday afternoon. People in Chi Bay don't wander much. And the kids, well, they go in packs."

"So where are you coming from then? I didn't see you on the ferry."

She pointed over her shoulder with her thumb. "The trail."

"Judging by the size of your backpack, you've been at it a while."

"Since Tongass Cove."

"And how far's that?" He tried to remember another town on the map. Considering his way with maps, he wasn't surprised when he came up blank.

"Thirty some miles. A few nights under the stars. I'm used to it. Spent the last year and a half backpacking around Europe."

"Yeah? I've spent some time abroad myself. What is it the Germans call it? *Wanderlust*? But this is Alaska. A whole other animal."

"That it is. But you came at the right time of year. This is your best month in Southeast Alaska. It's why I decided to return home in May. It can still be a little cool at night, but at least you get a break, if you're lucky anyway, from the otherwise constant precipitation."

"Chi Bay's home then?" Hunter said.

"I guess you could call it that. I prefer Juneau where I went to college, but this is the area I grew up in. Honestly I don't really know why I've come back. I ran away at sixteen, haven't seen the place since."

He nodded, watching the road and wondering if she saw the empathy on his face. He said, "I've given you my name, but you haven't given me yours."

"Huntress," she said. And smiled that clear smile of hers.

"First name or last name?"

"Middle."

"Ah."

"Okay, enough with that. Call me Von. My parents called me Vera. My foster parents insisted on using my full name, Veronica. I like Von."

The road was narrow, cutting through fir woodlands when it wasn't hugging the rocky beach. He was driving through forest now, the path before him a shadowy tunnel through the trees. Where the sunlight filtering through the canopy drew designs, there was possibility, a sort of hope amid the muddle. There was no denying the beauty of it. As there was no denying that a story lay in Von words. A little vignette by Hemingway came to Hunter. An example from a college writing course of a short story of perfect brevity. *For sale: Baby shoes, never worn.* Nothing muddled in its spare words.

"Your parents..."

"They died. When I was fifteen. They hiked up Harrow Mountain to one of the Forest Service's remote cabins for the weekend. They never hiked back down."

"That was here in Chi Bay?"

Von looked at him oddly. "Funny you put it that way. *Here* in Chi Bay. There's not a hint of the town in sight."

"The sign at the terminal said Chi Bay Ferry Terminal. These are the outskirts, right?"

"Yes, but...it's the way you said it. Like the place already had you. Chi Bay—not the town itself but the area—has that kind of effect on strangers. I remember my father talking about it once. He did these backcountry tours and was always coming home with little stories for my mother. Odd remarks the tourists and out-of-towners had made. He said the strangers were more at home in Chi Bay than the residents. They were, quote, 'in touch' with the same loneliness that alienated the locals." She paused, then looking at the road ahead said, "He'd know about alienation. He was a master at it."

Unsure how to respond to that, Hunter pursued the less personal point. "Do you get a lot of strangers?" Though Von had set the precedent, the word "strangers" felt awkward off his tongue. Visitors would have seemed the better description.

"*I* don't get anything. Remember, I'm a stranger too."

He detected the suggestion of something in her voice, though he could not have named what. Maybe the clarity about her was an illusion. Maybe there was a muddled quality here after all.

The road in front of him curved to the left, and the sea was visible again. The slate beach strewn with boulders. A bald eagle perched on a lip of one of those boulders, watching the vehicle pass.

People in Chi Bay don't wander much.

He had the sudden compulsion to ask her how her parents had died. *What is it about your Chi Bay, Von, that inspires these expressions of yours? You seem disturbed in your homecoming. Haunted.* But he refrained. For maybe it was the tragedy itself that had seeped into the environment. Again he empathized with her. His own parents, who to his knowledge had yet to be covered in earth, were nonetheless as dead to him as if he'd committed the act with his own hand. And maybe he had. Maybe they were the infants that had kept him young. Certainly they had never grown up enough to raise two children. Ask his twin Hannah, who'd made sure no one could question whether or not the earth had come shoveling down on her. Leaving behind an example of brevity to rival Hemingway's own. Its very words: *You want a note? Fuck you.*

A house came into view. An impressive A-frame set in a crook along the shoreline. Its seaward-facing façade boasted windows from floor to rafter. A handsome hand-carved wooden bear stood on two legs in the yard, its maw open wide. To the left of the house a trailer on which rested an expensive-looking motorboat was parked. A Hummer sat inside a carport. The next house, nestled among the trees on the opposite side of the road, was much more modest. In its gravel drive was a battered Toyota pickup. Its bear was a porcupine, one of those knick-knacks for brushing off the shoes. It rested by a front door whose aged paint was flaking away in leprous patches. Hunter wondered which situation Von had come from. Had her people been affluent or had they struggled as his own parents had? Struggled without really struggling as they partied themselves to oblivion every night of every week into infinity. What did a backcountry tour guide earn for a living? Enough to estrange himself from his child, apparently. Always enough for that.

Von spoke, and in a faraway voice, and Hunter wasn't sure as she returned to the subject whether it was one he'd really wanted to tackle after all.

"Aren't you going to ask me about my parents? Aren't you interested in knowing how an expert on strangers could be a stranger to his own daughter? Easy. You see her as a nuisance, a thing to be swatted away for her familiarity, for the mistake she was."

Which said to Hunter that strangers were actually not the less personal point.

"My mother, though, she was acceptable to him," his passenger went on. "Because she helped him with his work. Once upon a time she'd been something of a local celebrity, a poet 'in touch'—yes, there's that expression again—with dark and mysterious Chi Bay. It's what drew him to her, I'm sure. He was already involved in his work when he met her. You see, he was what you might call an occultist. Eventually they both were. I don't doubt it's what delivered them to their end."

Hunter looked at her, wondering just why she was opening herself up to him like this. Was that the way it was with strangers and wanderers who'd mutually acknowledged the fact? Was there a brotherhood? Stranger yet that the conversation had taken this turn; that the word "occultist" had been thrown out there as though it was an everyday word. And yet somehow it was not so strange. Hadn't there been something peculiar about this whole encounter from the beginning? The way she'd turned and simply stared at him when she'd heard the Jeep round the bend? The way he'd almost automatically applied pressure to the brakes then pulled up beside her as though it was the most natural thing in the world to offer a ride to someone who was clearly not hitchhiking, judging by the nature of the bundle she carried, bedroll and tent attached. How strong she must be beneath her khakis, he'd thought at the time, to carry such weight. And now…to know she'd hauled her load across thirty some miles in "a few nights under the stars." Where'd she get the strength for the other? The demons surrounding her homecoming?

"No, Hunter, in case you're wondering," she said. "I do not spill my life to every stranger I meet. You just happen to be here when needed. Do you think that's the right word? 'Happen?'"

"Strangely, no," he said. Meaning it.

"Do you believe in fate?"

"Today I 'happen' to."

She smiled, and yes, it was the clearest thing in the world.

More houses appeared, a mixture of modest and not so modest as she went on, in a less faraway voice now, with her sharing. "I did my thesis at Southeast Alaska on the Chi-Ikuk, the native Alaskan tribe the town was named for. The instructor allowed me to change my subject matter before failing me for what she referred to as 'pure and inappropriate fantasy.' I knew it wasn't fantasy because I'd taken my material from my father's own notes, and my father, well, he was obsessed with accuracy when it came to this, his one passion in life. So in a way I suppose you could call him a historian, though that's not to replace the term occultist. Chi Bay has been a breeding ground for the sort of material he immersed himself in for as long as it's been Chi Bay." She paused, gesturing ahead. "And here the devil is now. Welcome, my stranger Hunter, to one lonely town in Alaska."

As the view opened up before them, the trees falling back to allow for the tableau of town and bay, Chi Bay was as one might have expected of a seaside

Alaska village. While more worn by the elements, it reminded Hunter vaguely of some of the towns he'd seen in Maine during his wanderings. Its dwellings were mainly scattered along the base of a mountain, with a few along the near waterfront, while most of the commercial and municipal buildings were clustered near a bridge that crossed to an island running generally parallel to the mainland. Between the two the wider bay funneled into a channel at whose mouth were harbored an array of boats, a newer-looking marina standing in the foreground. Rolling his window down, Hunter partook of the air of the place. As expected, it had its own charm, the brine a pleasant assault on the senses in spite of the underlying odor of fish.

"That delicious taste in your mouth is from the fishery," Von said, pointing to the left at a long aluminum structure. "The ancient building beside it, the one that's on stilts, is the cannery. Like the mine on the far side of town, it's just an attraction now. Fluffed up with the brown historic signs for the cruise ship tourism we got over a few summers before the locals decided they'd had enough of being overrun by gawkers. This back in the late nineties when I was still devising a way out of this place."

"You're telling your age," Hunter smiled.

"What's to hide? I'm twenty-nine, and aging as fast as you are de-aging. That's what you're doing, isn't it? You've reached a plateau and now you're aging backward and I'm the truth you missed on your way up the hill. The truth that age itself is an illusion. That there are still places on this earth like Chi Bay."

She looked at him as if expecting an answer. Since he had none, he went with the thought that failed at obscuring his own questions. "Are you sure you're not the poet in the family?"

"I don't have a dark enough soul for that task."

"You do paint a picture though."

"It's easy when you're a Chi-ite. But where was I? Oh yes, the tourism. The natives weren't as happy as the rest of the town about dropping the cruise ship traffic. They didn't like losing all that business. They didn't have much ground to stand on, though, considering that the death toll among our eager visitors had reached a half dozen over those summers. You can warn an outsider only so many times to stay on the trail, lose the perfume and loud deodorants in bear-populated areas—which is everywhere—and treat this particular Alaska town with a modicum of respect. Chi Bay is not Juneau or Ketchikan or Haines or any other place you can name. It's built on a fault, so to speak, and that fault tends to yawn open when it's hungry."

Hunter stopped at one of two visible traffic lights on this side of town, eyes drawn to the sparse afternoon foot traffic along the street while his mind tried to make sense of what was being generated by this special clarity of Von's.

"If the townsfolk seem zombies to you," she said, "it's because they are. Oh, there's no shortage of hospitality, or that pretense anyway, but you'll find a blankness in the eyes of Chi Bay residents that you'll not find elsewhere. It's the only substitute, in the end, for the terror."

"Terror?" he said, emphasizing each syllable.

"Sound extreme? I guess it would to an outsider." She smiled mirthlessly as she added, "An outsider coming home again."

As he looked around at this ageless town of hers he found himself feeling precisely that way. Like an outsider coming home again. He'd have thought a little conversation with the locals, some immersing in the culture would have been required to validate her father's observation. But no, just being here did the trick. And not necessarily as pertained to the town itself, but rather, as Von had suggested, the environment in which the town's props had been erected. There was a nostalgic flavor to being surrounded by the stage pieces, certainly. But there was a deeper something involved, an older, almost primal something. While many places he'd visited had inspired a certain bittersweetness, an indefinable yearning, a sense of filling up while emptying out, this was something different, something more. A strange wind blew in Chi Bay; there was no denying its delicate caress.

As they approached the next light, Von interrupted his philosophizing. "Turn left here."

"Where are we going?" he said, pleased with the fact that, wherever it was, it was on the waterfront side.

"The hotel. You okay money-wise? The Red Bear's a little on the expensive side, but it's the most charming of your choices. Another one of those historic sites if you go for that sort of thing."

"Sounds nice. But what about yourself? Do you have a place to stay?" Oddly, he didn't feel awkward asking.

"I'll be staying there as well. While I'm not hurting on the money end, I wouldn't mind sharing the expense of a room."

How natural, in fact, that what had started a quarter-mile from the ferry terminal should come to this. And without the sexual tension that might have accompanied such an encounter. Indeed, while she was attractive, and had the "natural" qualities he was attracted to in a woman, he hadn't thought of her in that way until now. Of course, offering to share the expense of a room with someone was not the same as inviting that someone into bed with you—whatever one preferred to read in that open, clear face of hers.

"Sure," he said, hoping it didn't sound too casual.

When the uncertainty in his voice didn't make it by her, he found it natural, also, to laugh along with her.

*　*　*

The room smelled of cedar from its rough-cut beams. Its furnishings were plush in a upscale hunting lodge sort of a way. The floor was carpeted in a rich maroon, and a fireplace stood between the two high-posted wooden beds. They hadn't had to ask for the room type, it had been the only one available, saving them any discomfort (which he doubted at this point) an option might have caused. When Hunter had asked Von where the hotel got its guests with no tourists around, she'd told him Chi Bay appealed to a certain breed of out-of-towners. Her words: "With Alaskans being the secretive lot they are, you won't find the town in any docudramas. But Chi Bay has its faithful."

"Occultists like your father?" he'd said.

"More like tornado chasers. Though they'd never admit, even to one another, what they're up to."

"And just what are they up to?"

She ignored the question. "I think brandy's the appropriate drink for this place, don't you? Or better yet, a good red wine. We'll get a couple bottles while we're out."

Evening had settled and they were preparing to go out now. She looked refreshed after a shower and a two-hour nap. Not in the least bit tired after sleeping much of the way on the ferry, Hunter had followed his shower with a stroll along the waterfront promenade, stopping in at one of the drinkeries for a couple beers while letting Von rest her joints and muscles from the day's hike. As she'd remarked, the locals were very hospitable, but equally detached. There had been no mixing among them, though the joint had been relatively busy. But Hunter hadn't been there to appraise them, only to relax with his Alaska Ambers and enjoy the view of the bay and snow-capped mountains beyond. It was everything he'd imagined it would be, his first sit-down view from Alaskan shores. Haines, beautiful in its own right, had just been a stop where everyone who'd driven or walked aboard in Bellingham, Washington had offloaded except himself. But the view from the Chi Bay waterfront, it was the kind of experience he'd subsisted on these past several years, first in Europe, then South America, then during this revisiting of the homeland. Lonely and beautiful and soul-satisfying. For at least those choice moments in time.

"You ready?" Von asked him as she stuck a pin in the knot she'd made of her long, honey-brown hair. She looked in the mirror, fussing with the knot a bit, then with a dissatisfied twist of her lips pulled the pin and let her hair down again.

"Hey, I rather liked it like that," Hunter said.

"Is that so."

"Yeah. It went well with the turtleneck. Gave you a certain sophisticated look."

"In spite of the lack of effort that went into it?"

"Less effort goes into leaving it down."

"Are you a woman?"

"No."

"Then shut up."

He smiled. The fact was, she didn't need to be a botherer when it came to her appearance. Nor, he suspected, did she ever put more time into it than he'd watched her do this evening. Deeply tanned, with a smooth, clear complexion, she'd put on very little make-up, and then only around the eyes, with a sparing tastefulness. The jade-colored turtleneck, the jade earrings, the fashionable if wrinkly jeans…granted, she was working out of a backpack, but she'd spent about as much time selecting these as it had taken him to wash the shaving cream off his face. Hell, *he* had been the one to run his outfit by the other.

She was really rather lovely, he'd decided. And appearance only a part of it.

"Are you ready? Or are you just going to stare at me?" she said with a girl's grin.

No use letting *her* know how he felt. "I've been ready, Von. I'm a man."

She stuck her tongue out at him. "I'll give you the benefit of the doubt and assume there's not a double meaning there."

He felt himself blush, a rarity for him. "So where are we going?"

"As I've told you, it's a surprise."

"Well, I hope they have food there. I'm starved."

"I should have thought that obvious. When a small-town Alaskan says she's going out in her small town, she means she's going out to eat and, if she's in the mood, have a few drinks. Where the hell else is there to go? The club? The symphony?"

"I get your point. So are we walking or driving?"

"Driving."

"After you," he said with a gentlemanly sweep of his arm.

*　　*　　*

Of all the places she might have taken him—okay, of all the *few* places she might have taken him—he'd never have guessed *here*. He'd known it would be outdoors after a trip to Wal-Mart ("You have a *Wal*-Mart?" he'd voiced in amazement as the store came into view) to pick up a tablecloth, a block of sharp cheddar cheese, a half dozen slices of semi-fresh deli ham, a loaf of semi-fresh bakery bread, and a basket of semi-edible-looking strawberries ("Fresh produce in Chi Bay?" she'd said. "Forget it."). At her insistence they'd split both that bill and the bill for the wine, which, along with a pair of red wine glasses and a corkscrew, they'd picked up at a legitimate dealer at a cost that had made him glad for her sharing spirit. But picnic materials evoke images of pretty parks and sandy beaches, not the sort of place to which she took him. Not in a million years would he have expected an abandoned turn-of-the-century gold mine, even with its brief mention earlier.

Thankfully, the only accessible part of the hundred-plus-year-old setup was *outside* the mountain, and it a skeleton of what it had once been. The mine was accessed by an offshoot of the road out of town. The main road, according to Von, continued on in a curve around the mountain, passing through a tunnel and a few residential areas before settling into its long, lonely pursuit of the fabled Alaska Highway. A foot trail led to the site from the spot at the end of the road where they parked, following the edge of a length of wetlands active with ducks and other waterfowl before entering a body of trees which Von identified for him as Western hemlocks. Ten minutes along, the path, by way of dilapidated wooden bridge, crossed a stream carrying the melt of winter snows to the sea. A short distance beyond, the trees opened up and the mine, in phantom shapes, presented itself.

The picnic spot was inside the larger and most intact of three concrete buildings standing in close proximity to each other. In the building's main room a concrete platform that must have been a work table of some sort provided a handy surface on which to place the tablecloth. As they laid out their gourmet spread, a light wind blew through the holes where the windows and doors had once been. The beach was easily visible from the room, the high tide line some forty or fifty yards from the building. The waves coming in now were far from that line, lapping softly at the lonely posts left behind by a collapsed pier; a bright half moon, visible through a gaping vacancy in the ruined roof, highlighting the gentle crests that occasionally formed. In the foreground rusty metal chutes extended from the next building, some broken and lying in the silt, others connecting to unidentifiable apparatus that stood silhouetted in the dusk. More of these chutes extended in the opposite direction toward the mountainside, where other, smaller structures lay in ruin. The generous moonlight contributed to the overall industrial phantasmagoria, and Hunter, taking it all in, found the surprise the location had brought along with it giving way to a sort of adolescent thrill.

He told Von she'd done well with her spooky site.

"Naturally," she said.

They sat on the platform, the food and wine between them. "You've been here before, I take it," he said as he picked up the Buck pocketknife she'd had the foresight to take from her backpack, and began cutting slices of cheese and bread.

"Once. With my parents," she said as she worked on uncorking one of the wine bottles. "They didn't like having their nuisance along when communing with the spirits. This is one of those sites, according to my father's notes, where the energy surrounding Chi Bay is concentrated. Not because of what happened here, but because of what caused what happened here. Meaning the energy is older than any tragedy."

He paused before asking the question. He'd known, hadn't he, that there was something? As opposed as Von was to her father's occultism, she herself was fascinated with that aspect of Chi Bay—if indeed there was such an aspect outside of the mind. But no, Hunter knew this to be rigid thinking. And a reversal at that, as he'd already allowed for the strange wind that blew around here. A man's skepticism had to yield sometimes to his subtler senses. And the subtler senses required no proof beyond the vibrations they picked up.

And yet, mustn't there also be some allowance for words? For expression? For the tenor and inflection of the voice? The nuances of the face and body? For the subtle power of suggestion? Von was certainly persuasive, and all the more so because of her innocence. That established, it seemed to him that the empirical should also be trusted. Not without reason did a person grow increasingly more skeptical, more reasonable in their thinking as they aged, the fancifulness of youth dissipating with hard experience. Von could talk all she wanted of his aging backwards, but the imagination does not revert after the plateau; it merely deteriorates. They were two different things. A person could dream, for example, of misspent youth, but a person could not dream the dreams of misspent youth; they were gone forever. Yet not without leaving a man susceptible to language, to the particular thrums of the vocal cords.

But Von, having poured them each a glass of wine to go with the food, was now answering his unspoken question, and he had to tune in lest he miss something that might make this debate with himself irrelevant.

"Tragedy is nothing new to Chi Bay. Examples of this force we're talking about were happening as far back as the days of the town's settlement. Maybe before that, who knows. It's not like there's a dependable record. Far from it. It's as though everything that had to do with the natives, the Chi-Ikuk specifically, was expunged. Why I link the tribe, which I presume you've gathered is extinct, with the tragedies of Chi Bay, I can't say exactly. Nor could my father, whose research was far more extensive than mine. For him it was life. For me, a thesis. A way of coming to terms with my parents' deaths. But that's a separate chapter. We're talking about what happened here at the mine, not up on Harrow Mountain."

She paused, taking a bite of the bread and cheese and washing it down with wine. Hunter added a piece of ham to his bread and looked through the doorway across the slate beach to a tidal pond where a swan floated contentedly.

"That's a trumpeter," Von said, noticing the direction of his gaze. "Not only big, but a mean rascal if it feels threatened. If young are around, stay clear." She took another swallow of wine before using the swan as a segue back to the subject. "The Ikuk believed any living thing, human, swan, what have you, was subject to the energy of this place, and that the result could appear in any number of manifestations, all of them bad. Madness. Murder. Suicide. Or in this particular case, disappearances. The mine employed dozens of people in its day, and had yet to reach its peak when it was unexpectedly shut down. It's output, already hefty, was growing every year, putting it on pace to give the Treadwell operation in Juneau a run for its money. Everybody was happy. As happy as a bunch of zombies can be anyway. The town was prospering as business flourished. It was almost enough to make folks forget that tragedy, to one degree or another, *always* strikes again in Chi Bay. And so it did. One fall morning the wives kissed their husbands goodbye for the day, and the husbands went to their various posts at work. When lunchtime came around and the wives who expected their men home for a bite found the food getting cold, they thought little of it. Their husbands had been late for lunch before. When mid-afternoon rolled around and still no sign of their husbands, a few of the wives, still not overly concerned, went to the mining offices to inquire."

She paused again, motioning for the wine, which had remained idle in his hand as he listened to her story, though he'd already guessed its end. Perhaps seeing this in his face, she decided to quit with the fluff and build-up and proceed straight there, drinking directly from the wine bottle as she did so.

"That's right, Hunter. The Devil's Triangle for the whole goddamn crew. Clerks, supervisors, miners, everyone. Poof. Gone. The only ones saved were those sick, or on their off-day, or on a later shift—security guards, evening bookkeepers, etcetera. At best, ten percent of the work force. The other ninety simply vanished without a trace. And I mean *no* trace. Multiple investigations turned up nada. Absolutely zero."

Thirsty suddenly, Hunter reached over for the bottle and followed her example by partaking directly from it. The wine felt good going down his throat. Cool, wet. His preference was white wine, chilled, but right now this seemed similar. Had his throat gone dry because of the story, or was it the flickers of movement he'd detected in the trees outside the windows while she spoke? As though the two could be separated.

"It's the breeze," Von said.

"What?"

"I remember the movement in the trees too. If I were the dramatic type, I'd tell you yes, the tales have it right, their ghosts linger."

"But?"

"But nothing. I'm not the dramatic type."

No, you spin your threads more delicately, he thought.

They were quiet for a while, letting their thoughts drift as they finished off the slices of bread and cheese he'd cut, waving off the rest in favor of the wine. As he emptied the first bottle, she opened the second. The glasses sat forgotten, lonely in their emptiness. The breeze off the water now had a perceptible nip to it. It felt good to Hunter. A sort of counterpoint to the warm embrace of the wine.

"So what about your parents?" he finally said. The words seeming as much an affront to the peaceful quiet as the voice that uttered them.

She sat near the corner of the platform, farthest from the door. The window across from her was the natural place for the eyes to stray, which hers did as she spoke, seeming to look through the trees into that not-so-distant place that is less a refuge than a reference point for the drifty soul. "It makes me lonely thinking about them. Because that's how it was living with them. Can you imagine existing as an outsider within your own family? Knowing their entire focus is elsewhere? On something that is not even tangible?"

"Actually I can," he said in a softer voice than he'd intended.

When she looked at him, lines of inquiry, of attempted comprehension, creasing her brow, he felt the urge to look away, or to explain himself, or to simply vanish as the miners had. But he owed her more than that, as fate had predicated when it brought their like souls together. "Go on," he said, in an even softer voice.

"My parents' is a short chapter really. Shorter than the miners'. There were no spouses to miss them, only a lonely child. And she left nothing for their ghosts to cling to, to find purchase in. Even the wind can't remember them. I hiked up that mountain three times after the first time looking for glimmers, but there simply are none. And yet my parents haunt me still. In my sleep. In my daydreams. Funny I never see the act. The act of their bodies being shredded. They are always whole, as whole as was possible for them. They're poring over books, notes, oblivious to the moth that has flittered into the room until its shadow disturbs one of the pages. Then they're fierce, especially him. This is when he's most whole. The fury brings him there. It ignites in his eyes, eyes grown almost totally black from the layers and layers of text imprinted on them. The fire itself is black, and the moth wonders if he, if both of them, aren't the very embodiment of the force that holds Chi Bay in its clutch. Not in the same way as the ones that went mad, the ones that turned on their loved ones, on themselves. Nor like the lost ones, the ones who retained only the most basic outline of their former selves. I'm talking about the very embodiment, the thing itself as they hurled their fury at this moth that would dare flitter its shadow across their work. And my mother, somehow it was even more terrible in her because it was less formed. Her flames fed off the central fire, which was his, only his, and came from the furnace of his heart and his bowels. He wanted to be in touch and oh was he, Hunter. Oh, was he…"

A fire of her own seemed to die in her eyes as she let her words taper away, shivering suddenly though the nip on the breeze remained slight, certainly no match for the wine's warmth. As Hunter removed his jacket, placing it over her shoulders, her gaze seemed to remain halfway in, halfway out of that place of reference, the ghosts among the trees reflected in them. But only momentarily as Hunter faced her, holding her shoulders and searching her face for answers that he had never been able to find. Then she was looking at him, focusing in on him. Her hand came up to touch his hand on her shoulder. Her trembling lips found his mouth. They were lost in the desperateness of it for a few moments before one of them managed to pull away from the other.

As they separated, Hunter saw that tears had formed in her eyes. She let them fall as he watched, saying, "They were ripped to shreds, Hunter. Beaten, *torn* to death. Though the authorities never found the weapon used, they thought it must have been a hooked instrument, an instrument that could be used with a pulling action as well as for bludgeoning. A fireplace poker—just like the family that died up there years before them. Only this time there was no evidence to show who had done the deed. No body in the lake outside the cabin. No father and husband to blame for killing his child and wife before walking out on the frozen surface of Harrow Lake and chopping open a hole in the ice with the murder weapon and then dropping the tool and himself into the crack for the police to find later. But what difference would the details make? My father killed his wife as surely as if he'd wielded the poker. He killed his child in much the same way, with swings and thrusts and yanks; he just took a little more time at it, stretching the deed out over the years of her shadowy little life. And you know what a year is to a child, Hunter. It's an eon. But fuck, where's the wine? Hunter, you drink, and then kiss me. Let me taste it on your lips. It's warm. It's life. I came back down the mountain that first time, but that's not life. I came back down, but even blood, that's not life—"

He kissed her, the wine spilling from his mouth and trickling down their chins. "I know," he said around their hunger, their need. "I had a sister...Hannah...I helped her. I loved her and I helped her do it. Our parents, they had forgotten her. They had forgotten both of us. Hannah was strong. I tried to be strong with her. We did it with Demerol. My mother's opiate of choice. Demerol and tequila. Three shots for Hannah, three shots for me, one pill for Hannah. Three shots for Hannah, three shots for me, *two* pills for Hannah. I lost myself for a while after. There was this piece of property in Florida. An expanding company wanted it and I sold it to them for a cool two million dollars. Thing is, it wasn't mine to sell. It was my father's. Hunter senior. A poor replacement for a fireplace poker, yeah, but it made things easier on me...the forgetting. The endless forgetting."

He was speaking in her ear now, and she was kissing his neck, clinging to him, digging her fingernails into his back. "I live for places now, Von. Landscapes. Scenery. Open spaces. Places that sing rather than suffocate, that broaden rather than constrict, that are apathetic in a pleasing rather than a crushing way. Sure, it's still props, but there's less poison in it. I admit I laugh at myself sometimes for this church I've found, but I attend anyway. While there are Alaska Highways out there, Alaskas and Canadas and places of sweeping, unpolluted beauty, I attend. Did I tell you I was on my way to Canada? Do you want to join me, Von? Where else is there to go really?"

"Nowhere," she said, releasing him finally. "Nowhere."

She drank more wine, passed the half-empty bottle to him, and then suddenly seized his arm. "Did you see me, Hunter? When I told you about it, did you see me coming—"

But her attention was drawn to something beyond him, through the doorway. He turned and saw what she saw, the swan making its slow, awkward way up the beach in their direction.

"It's only the swan," she said, eyes lingering there for a moment.

"Did I see what, Von?" Hunter had to know.

"Don't you know?" she said, letting the bird go. Looking into his eyes.

"What, Von? What should I have seen?"

"Me coming down the mountain that first time. Fireplace poker resting on my shoulder. I put it in my pack before I reached the trailhead, but it hung out so I wrapped the end in a rag. The rag I brought to clean myself with. No matter, our house was the third one you came to as you walked along the road from the trailhead. It was dark by then anyway, and no car passed. I remember thinking that meant something. Nothing to do with justice; it was more like I was being told I had a calling. A light, that's what it was. A warm light a little moth could fly to. But it didn't last. The light gradually flickered out as I sat naked by the fireplace and watched all traces of the thing disappear, knowing no one would remember the smoke, not in the late fall, not in the season for such things. Watching my clothes turn to ash and the caked blood on the poker burn away, I lost the connection with the force that has driven so many of us, us Chi-Ites. I don't know if I bored it or if maybe it understood that my pain would be worse if I were simply left alone. In any case I—"

Again her attention was diverted. This time her eyes catching fire.

Nothing to compare to the eyes of the swan though as it descended through the door, wings cast wide, throwing shadow over the whole room in spite of the moonlight from above. Eyes black as the pit of the soul as they devoured these homecomers then spat them back out again, blazed then disappeared in the madness of the beast's retreating wings. The shock of it leaving the picnickers breathless, holes of themselves, until Von, in a moth's whisper, uttered, "Can you see me now, Hunter? Can you see me fluttering down that mountain?"

Things That Tend to Disturb

The shadowy silhouette of a ship on the horizon. People died there, in one fashion or another, in that ghostly memory of a place.

The memory of your brother, then seven, waking up screaming in the night because he'd seen Jesus in the mirror. Let's hope it was only a dream. Epiphanies are not for kids.

The tadpoles with legs in the puddle in front of you on your hike. Evolution in frighteningly naked thereness.

The girl in Ibiza, high on ecstasy, watching you curiously as you try to make the Spanish taxi driver understand you don't want to fuck the girl, you just want to get a hit or two of what she's on.

The abandoned, decrepit, hollow house that regards you as you regard it on your way by. Bicycles were supposed to be for the breeze, the exercise, the time for thought. Not nightmares.

The recurring nightmare that you and your accomplices killed somebody and disposed of the body, which is about to be discovered by scary government people that are "on to you." Or was it a dream at all?

The missionaries at the door with the "Do you know the Lord Jesus Christ? Would you like to know more?" No. My sister dated one of you and spoke highly of the breakup.

The crabs in the tank clawing at each other for pastime, not knowing that a five-minute boil doesn't exalt. Crabs have gods too; they're just more confusing.

The moment in your aging years you realize *Star Wars* wasn't the bomb after all. Nor even the fuse. Acne and misbehaviour splattered out on their own. Good thing for your mind, which would have been repeating Darth Vader quotes forever if not.

The girl that got away suddenly appearing again after all the years. What was that last post to Facebook? That you landed an oil job in Saudi? "Fuck you," she says. "I'm a CEO at Apple." That you want her credentials is a testament to your vulnerability, not hers. A cow in a slaughterhouse disturbs your kind.

A cow in a slaughterhouse. They sleek it up for the animal people and slit the throats, stall by stall. Problem is, the next cow knows it's coming and moos like it's never mooed before. Thank you *Faces of Death*. We all like our burger that way.

Noises in a house that you built yourself. Contracted to build anyway. Settling boards, you tell your concerned mate, with no mention of the fact that there's no wood in sight and concrete blocks and stucco never have bad chemistry.

Darting lights in the night before your half-drunken eyes. Can it be a trick your friends are playing on you? No, not unless they have access to the best special effects artists in the universe that are willing to work outside the shop, the studio and in thin air. Still, they warned you about the hallucinations. You weren't supposed to keep using the peyote.

The motherless kitten with the bum leg and the propensity to bite and scratch. You took her in, you let her back out. Why did you take her in in the first place?

A look at yourself in the mirror after that ill-advised night in Ibiza. Had there even been a taxi driver? A rolling girl? Best you can remember you'd a half-pint of Sangria and walked away from any such nonsense. That Tiesto thumping in your head came from somewhere outside your own sphere.

The moon, clean like a sickle, and bright as the sun. Okay, what hell is going to rain down upon us now?

Words you said when you weren't in your right mind. Answers scarce in your inbox but always with something relating to subjects you were sure you hadn't touched on. Luck to them weeding your type out.

The snake hanging from the tree upside down, skinny lips seeming to relish the thought of you.

That time in Australia where they Jeeped you into the outback and wouldn't explain to you to what creatures the bones belonged.

The expired milk in the refrigerator which you could not possibly have refrained from, being the abstinent monk you are. Let alone the trace of whiskey left in the bottle after your friends stumbled out to be zeroed in on by the late-duty cops.

The Village People. (Who put that on?) Not because they're gay but because of the show itself. They can't even get away with that kind of shit in Vegas.

A frosty breeze in the house on a sweltering summer day. Thank God the children are playing outside. Time to get ice cream ready.

Jesus in the mirror. Forty-six times you've considered it, forty-six times he's still there in the mirror. Seven-year-olds do not wake up from such nightmares. Unless Uncle Lou got to them.

Uncle Lou. Do yourself a favor and just shoot him if you've a gun. He contributes nothing to the human condition. He wants to go south and work on a boat and cut fins off sharks and toss the finless creatures back into the water like they do in Asia. "The Orient," he's joked. "Let's see how oriented our friends are without their top fins!" Disturbing because he knows what brand of garbage he is.

Aunt Lisa. She never looks at Lou's face, chest, legs. She's always looking at his trap. Like the whole world of people do the shoes. Are Nikes better than Italian leather? Only Aunt Scarlet knows.

Swollen Betty Baker, poster girl for the local biscuit. Goddamned shame you married her before you knew about the yeast.

Anything that falls like angels from the sky. Or up from below like indegestion. *War of the Worlds*. Childhood's End. That rain you encountered last winter while you were thinking about something you can't remember.

The End. And then, The End.

Shall a Whisper Die Unheard?

He had followed his wife's brother to the Ban Pamai Kheiyw temple, where the cremated remains of two members of May's family were kept in ornate vessels, and was now sitting on his motorbike in the dusk watching his brother-in-law talk to a monk. Bhunma had also come by motorbike, but he'd parked his out of sight in a group of trees on the opposite side of the street. Randall had hung back until the other had gotten on with his shadowy business.

It was May who had alerted Randall to a conversation she'd overhead that afternoon, in which Bhunma had told a drinking buddy of his—hard types, the two, whisky guzzlers—that he was going to try a trick tonight that, if successful, would divine for him tomorrow's lottery numbers. May couldn't decipher all of it, as she'd been inside the shop assisting a customer while they were outside sitting at one of the tables, but she was fairly certain that when Tong, the drinking buddy, asked Bhunma if it involved drugs and dreams again, her brother had answered that no, he was going all the way now, danger be damned; he was going to lie with the dead and invoke their whispers.

That, of itself, wouldn't have concerned Randall. Whisky with a side of superstition wasn't a new diet in rural Southeast Asia (or anywhere else for that matter, including the backwoods he'd grown up in in America). Nor did he find it difficult to imagine Uncle Bhunma, as the family referred to him, dosing on a recipe of, say, psychoactive drugs and sedatives to such ends. What did stay with Randall was his wife's fear that Bhunma, rather than simply sleeping in the company of the dead to await the whispers—as was apparently the way this worked—might be capable of disturbing the resting spots of their sister Jang and her unborn daughter Yui who'd been removed from Jang's womb and given her own vessel after the crazed driver had killed them both on the very road that led from the village that May's family called home, to this temple.

And now he was being presented with mounting evidence of his brother-in-law's intentions as both Bhunma and the monk had climbed the short set of stairs between the columns of the open temple, the latter gesturing into the interiors, perhaps thinking his visitor a homeless wanderer and giving him permission to sleep there tonight. Bhunma wouldn't have had trouble convincing the monk in those soiled rags he wore. Indeed he pretty much *was* homeless when he wasn't sleeping in the spare room in Randall's and May's house, to which the shop and its groceries, including cheap whisky, was attached.

Yes, this was almost surely what was going on, Randall decided as the monk now left and Bhunma disappeared among the shadows inside the structure. Had Bhunma wanted to commune with just any dead, he would have done so at the smaller temple outside their village of Ban Hyok and saved himself the fifteen-kilometer drive. It was of course a leap from "sleeping in the company of" dead relatives to "disturbing" their resting places. But Randall didn't trust his brother-in-law. Even if you took May's feelings about her own brother out, Randall wouldn't have trusted the guy.

He didn't know Bhunma well, in fact stayed away from him as much as possible. You didn't want to know a man who could do what he did after Tommy died.

*   *   *

Randall had not entered into the discussion about where to rest the ashes of his and May's son, Tommy, until it had reached its rather heated conclusion. The majority among the dozen or so family members present, including a drunkenly outspoken Bhunma, wanted him with his grandparents in Ban Hyok. The other side, which should have had no opposition considering it was May's side, leaned toward building a platform outside the house to hold his vessel. When the thing culminated in May and her brother raising their voices at each other, with May periodically breaking away in frustration to translate for her husband the parts he didn't understand, Randall decided he'd had enough and told the lot of them in English to shut up. He knew exactly where his son's remains were going to be placed, he said, and that was at the back of their rather significant property of fifty rai, on the banks of the small lake where Tommy had so loved to fish and had in fact drowned when the old, rotting pier he was fond of casting from (despite his parents' continual warnings) had collapsed, and he'd struck his head on an exposed post as he plunged into the water.

Everyone had stared at him, some knowing a little English, others none, but May had been the only thing in his vision and she had slowly, then more decisively, more determinedly begun to nod. They were their son's parents, and rarely had they ever been in disagreement about him, not least because he had remained a beautiful, loving, tender, honorable boy through all of his eighteen years of life. Their already purchased birthday present for his nineteenth, which he had been only a week shy of on that fateful day on the lake, had been a new set of fishing gear and a weekend charter deep sea fishing experience on the Gulf. Without any further thought on the matter of Tommy's resting place, May had turned to her family and translated Randall's words, laying it down in such a way as to leave no room for additional discussion. Only her brother resisted the will of both of the boy's parents, storming out of the house spitting the words "fucking farang," which meant Westerner, foreigner of white skin or European descent.

But that wasn't what had done it. That wasn't what had sealed the deal for Randall with regards to his brother-in-law. It was later, on the day the ashes were placed inside the handsome, tastefully restrained ornate vessel on its platform by the lake, that Randall discovered a side of Bhunma he wouldn't have imagined even the most crude and pathetic and delusional of men could possess. He hadn't realized to what degree Bhunma thought himself connected to Tommy—which simply did not reflect reality as Tommy had routinely gone out of his way to avoid having to interact with his drunken uncle—until that evening when he went back down to the lake to be alone with his son for a while.

What he found waiting for him was absurd, demented, criminal, barbaric, pagan—he didn't know what, it was so perversely out of context with the tragedy. Bhunma was there, on the platform, seated but in a haphazard way as he sort of straddled the vessel, fully naked and tossing whisky from the bottle over it and humming a something that made no musical sense anywhere but in his own twisted mind. He might have been on acid at Jim Morrison's grave. Or worshipping a phallic symbol. Or summoning the ghost of his nephew for some sordid or dreadful purpose.

It had been all Randall could do not to pick up a rock on his way there and break his wife's brother's head wide fucking open.

"What did you do?" May would later ask him.

"I picked him up, dragged him away from our son, encouraged him to finish off the bottle, helped him a little at it, okay helped him a lot, went and got the ATV, drove it back and managed to get his half-limp body onto the back, then took his sorry piece of shit hell bound ass back to his room. What else could I do? He's your brother."

* * *

But even that wound, if such it could be called, had scarred over in the years since. No episode of its like had occurred since as far as Randall knew. Apparently this particular manic drunk had his spells of mania on the blue moons. There'd been discussion about committing him. There were certainly enough blood signatures to see that accomplished after May had let slip or intentionally warned others about that profane capacity in him, that inhuman potential for which even the Buddha, in his sacred reflections, could not have imagined a reincarnation fix. But after May, following a period of obviously violent internal debate, had nailed her brother against a wall and performed her awful surgery on him, his behavior had changed. On a tip from a cousin he'd begun supplementing that diet of his with marijuana, which seemed to reduce, to a degree, the alcohol intake because of the vomiting the two could cause in tandem when the whisky was overused—this no doubt the cousin's intent.

Where Bhunma was right now with his problems, Randall didn't know as he approached the temple on foot. Three years was a long time sharing scarcely a word with the stray that continued to suck on your teat like a ghost on lost air. For the teat never produced whisky—that was his to scrounge up—only food, which he couldn't stomach much beyond the soup at the bottom of a bowl of pork and noodles. He'd withered, was wisp-like—even compared to the monk who had let him into the temple to rest his head. Nothing like the bloated sack of flesh Randall had pushed up onto the rack of the ATV.

Wild dogs lay about the place, ears and tails starting to rise but then relaxing again, the beasts too lazy to worry about other possibilities after the meal of rice the monks had no doubt provided them in the trough outside. There were a couple restrained growls at the smell of a foreigner, but otherwise none of the dogs threatened to reveal him as he stole inside the temple, determined to see no harm done to May's family's memories. The right-hand wall provided cover from the lights outside, the dead lined up neatly along it in their vessels. The opposite wall, he knew—not here, but deeper in the sanctuary—preserved the memories of the family of May's sister's husband, of which Jang had become an inseparable part not just by marrying him—a good man, hers—but by conceiving a child. That Yui, a name on which they'd settled early, had never been born in no way diminished the value or meaning of the life in the cycle Jang had carried almost to term.

Bhunma was back there with those memories, those whispers that were not of the type he was looking for. He'd no doubt pulled his flask from among his ragged folds and was pulling on it now, pondering whether to rely on the sleeping with the dead method or to strip his rags from his body and crack open the vessels of Jang and Yui, take out their urns and pour the ashes all over himself in an ecstasy of numbers to which only he, in his mathematics, could hum the right notes. Could it really be lottery winnings he was after? Was there such ambition in him? Could the golden-amber translucence of Thai whisky let in enlightenment like that? How dazzling it must be for him imagining the vast implications of it? Alcoholic fountains in which to bathe into the lives after and beyond.

Having found the corner now, the place where he must turn, Randall crept through the semi-darkness, instinct as much guiding him as the memory of May introducing him to her beloved sister and unborn niece. That or the sense of suddenly unsettled ghosts. But as the outlines at last became discernible, he paused in his creeping tracks. For there was not one, but two shapes in the corner, a huddling Bhunma and a separate, standing figure. One that was not monk, unless the robe had been shed, but that of a lean, tall stranger who seemed to loom behind and over Bhunma, unbeknownst to him.

Randall eased closer.

*   *   *

"I am here if you wish to hear whispers," the figure said softly to Bhunma's back.

"Huh? Who's there?" Bhunma said, turning one way then the other, but not sufficiently enough to sight the figure behind him.

"My name is Game. I am here to advise you in the wording of your request."

"Game. It's a good name," Bhunma said, not trying to locate him now, perhaps instead finding the voice in a more comfortable place inside him.

All of this in English, which Randall knew Bhunma had in him, albeit mostly hidden, from his long years of military service doing exercises, cross-training, intelligence work with British forces. May faulted her brother for this—his refusal to acknowledge how extra-capable he was in areas.

"I detect a humming in your vocal cords," said the figure. "A thing you're not quite letting out. Is it a particular sound you are looking for?"

There was pause. One during which a normal human being might have been considering the question and an answer. "I think so, yes," he said at last. (Which proved nothing but a moment of clarity on the drunk's part, as far as Randall was concerned.) "But I can't remember the notes exactly."

"Could it have something to do with the pier?" said the figure.

The pier? thought Randall. What was this? Who was this creature?

"Yes, yes," said Bhunma, sounding excited. "Yes, how it moans, begs of you. Once, I listened to *it* for the lottery numbers."

"You did indeed, didn't you. Only it didn't answer, did it?"

"No. I was disappointed by that. I thought it had something in it. A message for me."

"Have you considered," said the figure, "that perhaps the set of numbers is its own entity and has no relationship whatsoever with potential beneficiaries?"

"But I know that," said Bhunma, trying to find the speaker again, but seeming to be limited by a failure in his understanding of physics or the notion of degrees and circles. "I know there is no relationship. I am trying to establish one."

"And yet you speak of an anticipated message."

"No, no, you're trying to confuse me. You are a demon, aren't you? You want the numbers for yourself."

"I don't need the numbers, and have them in any case. Shall I instruct you as to the wording of your request of the dead?"

Bhunma lifted his arm, elbow out, which meant whisky was going down the chute. "If you are not a liar and trying to trick me."

"You must start like this: 'Tommy, I know I—'"

"But Tommy is not here." Looking over his shoulder.

"That is so."

"I'm sleeping with a real accident. Everybody knows it has to be a real accident. That the deceased must be vulnerable like that. Blameless. And a baby too?"

"You are not sleeping."

"Am I not?"

"You are not. Therefore I must ask you, was Tommy not a real accident?"

In his shadows, Randall felt cold skittery things all over his flesh. He wanted to leap upon them, bash their heads against the nearest available surface. But he couldn't and mustn't do. Not when there was potentially more to learn.

His brother-in-law was speaking again, and it was awful, sickening, savaging, un-fucking-bearable enduring such drawling corruption, streams of slime from a creature so undeserving of pity or mercy, the creature ought to have been torched, doused, torched, doused, torched again long before it ever reached these huddled corners. "I never touched Tommy! Sometimes I wanted to—I'm human. But I never did it! He was so sweet. So remarkably gifted. Such an artist. The gentle way he removed the hook from the fish's mouth, looked at it in the eyes before tossing it back in the lake. And that long hair May and that smug farang bastard let him grow.

130

That skin…the color of it. Who would not want to caress, to intimately know such a thing? But I never did. I never touched him. Am I really not sleeping?"

"You are not sleeping. Your brother-in-law perhaps is, but that is of no concern to you. Tommy is your concern. It is he who has your numbers. I will meet you there with the instruction you need. And again, lest we lose our way, my name is Game. Think of me by my name, not my presence."

With that, the figure turned, seeming to stare directly at Randall out of its dark face for a moment before striding out of the place. Leaving the huddled perversion that was Randall's wife's brother finding his hum now, and the father, the sire, the protector of the victim of the creature's fantasies on the precipice of vomiting as he tried to creep away, every movement causing his insides to lurch anew.

Wife's brother or not, Bhunma would be dead but for the fact Randall had to know.

*   *   *

Yes, wife's brother or not, Bhunma would be dead but for that Randall had to know. He waited on his motorbike for some little while before Bhunma emerged from the temple, then was on his way, wanting to be in place before his brother-in-law arrived. There was a back way into the property, the lake entrance as he and May called it, and he would go in that way as he knew Bhunma would do, even if the latter's fugue had exalted him into the ethers by now. For the risk of alerting his sister to mischief transcended sobriety tests. The awareness of her was ingrained. At least in the night, of which she was ever alert with creatures such as him around.

The fifteen kilometers did not go by quickly, though he drove at higher speeds than normal to stay comfortably ahead of the game. Game. The stranger that had introduced itself by that one simple word was the real reason for haste, not the perverted slug that was Randall's brother-in-law. The kind of thing Bhunma represented in his corruption, while reprehensible to a catastrophic, nearly unimaginable degree, could still be accounted for, explained, broken down. Game was another matter. Where had it come from? What was it? What did it want? Was it a manifestation? Was Randall, in fact, dreaming?

Bugs dancing in his headlight and battering his face and arms and hands as he went, he knew that if he was dreaming he was dreaming for the most important reason of all—truth. Memory, history, yes—but above all, ever above all, truth. Truth not for the world, not for the family, but for him. For him and, if he decided it worthy of his wife's grace and sublimity, May as well. That he would get to the truth tonight, he'd no doubt. For if it didn't come of the progression, the sequence, the waves, he would beat and cut it out of the monster that was Bhunma.

Should he relish the idea? Probably not. Did he? He wasn't yet sure. Bhunma was sick, there was no question about that. And more than in the drink way, even with the dementia that set in with abuse over time. He wouldn't go as far as to reference evil—it never worked blaming evil, which was far more amorphous than insanity. But insanity, too, was abstract, couldn't be considered directly without a license and then only if brain imaging or some other kind of physical evidence proved it to be true. Certainly a person's behavioral patterns couldn't. Which ironically led back to evil, didn't it? An independent pre-existing agent. That or cosmic humor. Merry-go-round. That's what Randall was on as he drove back home through the insect-ridden darkness.

At last he arrived, parked in the trees, a recurrent theme tonight, and went to a spot he knew near his son's resting place, the jabbing posts of the pier, the ghosts of the arcing casts of the fishing rod, Tommy's hair sweeping across his face in the breeze that regularly blew through the coconut palms, to await what was to occur.

*　*　*

Thinking he heard the sound of an approaching motorbike, Randall looked in that direction, but no light came through the entrance of the gate in the old fence that surrounded the property. He gave it several seconds before admitting his imagination was playing with him, and turned back to the only thing that mattered, the resting place of his son—

Where now stood the lean, tall figure from the temple, seemingly but not certainly looking back in his direction. Indeed, a moment later it had turned back to the vessel, the ghost that must be stirring in there, being the object of so much interest tonight. Rest, Tommy, his father bade him. Soon I will have rid you and those who love you of your tormentors or will be there with you instead. Either way will do—if must be—so long as you and I have the ability to comfort your mother, to assure her we are waiting for her on your side of the veil. If reincarnation's in the mix, then I know it will be a journey together because we have done no wrong as individuals or a unit that hasn't already been righted by your joyous presence in the world.

The sound again, this time for real as the shaft of light pierced the trees.

Randall, watching from between the low, divergent branches of the mango tree Tommy had loved to climb when a younger boy, anticipated something in what was coming that would not only absolve him of having developed such inexplicable, irrational expectations during his time waiting, but would also free him and May from endlessly pondering questions that had never quite been answered. Questions like: How could Tommy, who was a light and smart foot and agile as a cat, quick as one too, allow himself to take any wrong step on that pier? And further, not avoid making any kind of contact with the pier's bones when the merest creak from its decrepit frame would have alerted him to what was about to happen?

Bhunma didn't stumble as much as Randall might have imagined as he made his way down to where Game waited. This brought some sense of peace and justice to Randall. Killing a man, or what tried to pass as a man, on his two legs, no matter how rotten he was, was much preferable to feeding his powerless body, what was left of it, to the fish. Should such in fact prove necessary. Randall continued to vacillate. Revenge was not in his nature. Neither was poetic justice. It sounded fine, and tasted in future memory real fine. But where did it really get one? Or worse, land one? What happened after you'd returned to your safe shores? Would they be safe anymore?

Maybe Game had the answer as he welcomed Bhunma up onto the pedestal of Randall's dead son. Not once did Bhunma look at Game, though he had never actually seen him. He seemed to have simply accepted the other's voice as authority, leaving him free to focus on other matters.

"So," said Game. "You want your lottery numbers."

"I do," Bhunma said, staring at the vessel that contained Tommy's remains.

"Then this is how it must be worded—and listen close here. 'Tommy, I know I was not a real uncle to you and that I disturbed you with my behavior. But I wish to make amends now.' Okay, Bhunma? Let's start there."

"Now?" said Bhunma, continuing to stare at the house of his nephew's ashes.

"Now."

Without a breath first, Bhunma said, "Tommy, I know I was not a real uncle to you and that I disturbed you with my behavior. That I was unhealthy in my thoughts and desired things that—"

"I did not say to say that," interrupted Game.

"I'm to come clean, right?" Bhunma said, finally looking at the other but perhaps without really seeing him.

Had Randall even seen him? Always the shady side of a face.

"No," said that face. "You are bargaining, not atoning. You give him what happened, he gives you the numbers. I'd as soon mediate for your wife's husband back there in the trees. Are you loving the dead or getting rich off them?"

Though Randall was ready for him, Bhunma did not follow Game's gesture. He was struggling somehow. Seemed...pained. "I...I don't know that I ever wanted to get rich. I think I just wanted to...I'm not sure what."

Game nodded. "That's right. You're coming into it. Now tell him, tell the boy, lottery numbers aside, what you were going to trade. Tell him what you did."

"Must I?"

"After you retrieve the sledge hammer from where you hid it, yes. Present it to him. That is the only way. Not only is Tommy watching, his father is as well."

Bhunma broke down then. In a way Randall had not seen before. Into sobs. Violent, temporarily uncontrollable sobs. Now feeling pity for him, like when he'd first encountered the tales of him, from May and other family members, early in his marriage, Randall was becoming increasingly uncomfortable, shuffling, hands trying to find restful places among the tree branches, like here with this smooth long branch, no, not a branch but a handle, the handle of a heavy, very heavy tool that someone had stashed up here.

"I did it," Bhunma wept. "I came down here with the sledge hammer and I went into the water and I beat the posts till the whole structure began to moan in the wind. It was one of those days, little rain, lot of breeze, perfect fishing with the bugs all over the place. I knew Tommy would come. It had to happen, he was too beautiful. I watched him, the way he carefully placed his feet where he knew the pier was strongest, but I'd taken away that strength. I'd crippled it like he had crippled me. I'd never again have to watch him cringe when in my vicinity, shrink from me in fear. I did it. I killed him as surely as if—"

He never finished the thought because an emerged Randall, with a single merciful yet decisive stroke of the hammer, had bashed his skull in. Game, littered with the splatter, bowed his head slightly at Randall, turned and strode away into the darkness.

Waiting, came a whisper in Randall's ears. Though it could have been the night breeze just pretending to be a young man's familiar voice.

Darren Speegle

Lathered Spit in the Calloused Palms of the Demiurge

Was then, in that reality, I encountered my whole-life
Rotten, wracked, reeking, wrecked
Wretched
Like something from a film

A frighteningly vibrant, astonishingly pristine dream
A pulse of clarity
Shattered
As suddenly shattered

By knowledge that best kept its own fierce company, indeed
Horrid, alien, alive
Human
Like the loss of it, that

Familiarly human something, what was it in the whole-life?
Whisper, flutter, flitter
Of wings
Mine and mine only, yes

As the whole affair coalesced into this silverish ball
Sparklingly maddening
And true
Strangely fascinating

If alternatingly, alternatively, savagely rough
Like raw uncut diamonds
Spittle

Oil in the fractured skin

Was then, in that reality, I encountered my whole-life
A measure anyway
A taste
And relished it I did

When the song I'd previously known ended without the fare
And I saw a certain flush, flash
The blush,
Joy of having known it

That one moment, that glimmer, wherever it's disappeared to
I saw it there, saw true
Had wings
The whole-life figured out

There for a second, staking mine, imbedding mine deeply in it
My whole-life, my life-grip
My thing
A glimpse of it, a touch…

The Moon, a Roman Token

I

Heike was the most difficult case I've ever had, which is probably why I fell in love with her, though she would have claimed even *that* had been orchestrated by Kanz.

My mother called me Constantine.

Kanz…bringing the waters of destiny swirling around Heike and me in the pool of strangers that is humankind.

Destiny. I had spoken of it in my book, *Illusions, Perceptions, and Gods*, and not in a favorable light.

Light: what Heike had brought out of the obscurity of existence. It was easy to leave the *Klinik* in Wolf's charge and accompany her when she returned to Trier.

* * *

We arrived on a windy fall midday jammed with tourists. Our hotel overlooked the two-thousand-year-old Roman bridge, which we admired from our balcony as we stuffed ourselves on *Bratwurst* and *Pommes*. When we were finished Heike wanted to walk around the old city. I knew from the endless hours of interviewing my patient, then listening to the idle talk of the lover she had become, that she had lived near the Hauptmarkt, in an upper floor, looking down on cobblestones and tourists. During the two-hour drive from Heidelberg, she had shown a giddiness that I had not previously observed in her. She missed her home. It had been two years since she had known anything but walls, grass, and my face, which eventually she came to trust.

Face.

As we approached the *Porta Nigra*, mighty weather-blackened gate of the ancient walled city, a face looked down on us from one of the windows of the sentry paths. It might have belonged to a tourist but for the young man's toga, and the suggestion of a crimson band caught brightly in the September sun. We joined a few gatherers in wondering over him, but he did nothing of interest except suck on grapes, spitting the seeds out on the court below. As Heike and I passed under the gate's arches, his eyes followed.

I looked at her but she had shifted her attention to the shop windows along the cobblestone way. I realized the footsteps behind me were the echoes of my own. A glance back revealed only the massive scarred gate, which somehow did not stand in contradiction to the bustling modernization surrounding it. In the shop windows the togas were silk and velvet and all the fall fashion. A strangely cooperative melting of elegance, power and decadence occurred in this city, its product a voluptuous bouquet.

A trio of Chinese men passed by on hurried feet, one name emerging out of their native chatter: Karl Marx. Heike had told me one could visit the eighteenth-century town house where the philosopher had been born. No doubt these men were on their way there now. The name hovered for a moment in their wake, then was gone on the breeze, replaced by the hint of fish. Early for that, but people were moving about in gradually increasing numbers, gravitating towards the square and even more particular aromas. We went to the booth that emitted the sweetest odor, where Heike left me while she wrestled her way through the crowd to the mobile *Toilette*.

When the man serving realized I wasn't a native, he invited me to try a mug of *Glühwein*. "Glow wine," he said in his wielded English. Off the rich Mosel slopes and into your cup, heated to perfection. As I put my hand around the plastic mug, choosing not to tell him I'd had many a cup of *Glühwein* during the eight years I'd lived in Germany, a toga bumped into me, causing me to spill some of the blood-hot fluid.

"*Entschuldigen*," laughed the one standing there, crimson band on his cuff.

I looked at the deeply colored saturation in my own shirt sleeve, then at the curls pristinely arranged on his head. "No harm done."

"Cheers!" he said.

I raised my mug and its diminished contents in a half salute.

"That building over there..." Heavy accent bleeding in. "The Red House, yes. The inscription, do you know what it says?"

The words were visible enough: ANTE ROMAM TREVIRIS STETIT ANNIS MILLE TRECENTIS PERSTET ET AETERNA PACE FRUATUR.

"No," I said, fresh off my Latin.

"It says, 'Trier existed 1300 years before Rome. May it continue to exist and to enjoy an eternal peace.' Do you realize that makes this city more than two thousand years older than *me*?"

I drank the rest of my *Glühwein* by way of answer. What could I say to such logic?

It didn't occur to me until after he had dissolved into the crowd, to be replaced by a British couple ordering two cups of the mulled red wine, that we had been speaking in English.

"I tell you that boy *is* the statue of the young Constantine."

I stared at the woman, who was looking in the direction the toga had gone. Her husband shook his head at me. "Don't mind my Marge. She has her fantasies."

*   *   *

Heike had often spoken to me in English during her *possession*, as Wolf and I referred to it. Schizophrenia. Split personality. These were archaic terms when it came to Heike. Her invader was a consciousness of its own. The only even remotely similar case I had encountered had involved a reincarnation delusion.

As Kanz she spoke routinely in my tongue…

When I was a boy living in Trier, my father worked in a shoe factory. I remember, one time he brought a pair home. I was about nine at the time. I nearly cried for joy when I saw the shoes, I was so happy. But my father said they weren't my size. He had brought them home for Hexenmeister, our shepherd pup. He placed a piece of bloodliver in each shoe and whistled for the dog, then went off to smoke cigarettes and read the Trier Morgen. *My mother was dead by then…I think. As I've said, during the time I knew her she was always in bed.*

Hexenmeister licked up his meal, had some fun burying his snout as far as he could inside the shoes, then went off somewhere to have happy dreams. I found myself alone with the shoes. They weren't all that stylish really, plain with a square toe, but I hadn't had a new pair since I could remember. I peeked into the living room to make sure my father's cigarette had mutated into a bottle of pear schnapps, then I stuck my feet into those new specimens. They fit as if God Himself had fashioned them for me. I gave it lots of thought but as usual refrained from killing my father. Hexenmeister wasn't so lucky.

I hung him out on the line with the laundry, tongue sticking out of his mouth, still dark from the bloodliver. He looked like that dog from the big billboard over on the viaduct by the Southside.

The viaduct? Southside?

I lived not far from there as a boy, in Birmingham, Alabama. Little Pittsburg. There was this big advertisement for pet food. It kind of scared me as a youngster, lording over the traffic, tail wagging endlessly. It spoke more about the future than all the religious trap I had been fed since the moment I reared my head out of the baptismal font.

Baptism wasn't for me.

Yes, Kanz routinely spoke in English, and on occasion he spoke through the filter of my own memories, which he had presumably gleaned from one of the interviews following the success of my book ten years before.

Tell me, doctor, how significant was your father's hand in shaping your perceptions? Did you ever probe your father for answers to the existential questions?

"We all do, I suppose."

Only you weren't asking for philosophy, were you? You simply wanted to know where people came from. It should have been a biological question. And what did he tell you? What did he tell you about the origin of people?

"That they came from God."

And your young impressionable mind took this as meaning that people materialized on this Earth in the exact form that your eyes saw around you. God made them little and big, young and old right off his wand. You still have dreams about it, don't you? About a giant people factory. I know you, doctor. I know your illusions, I know your perceptions, and I know your gods.

"Tell me about Kanz's gods."

Do you know why my mother called me Constantine? Not because it was a natural elongation of my name. Nor even because Constantine the Great built an imperial palace here in Trier, which was to be Rome's northern capital. It was more ironic than that. Constantine, she said, had brought the light of Christianity to Rome. I had brought a light of my own into her house.

"Ironic?"

Ironic because of what I am.

"Do you think you are God, Kanz?"

I am as close to it as your perception allows.

"I don't know what that means."

If you don't know what that means, then who? It was God perhaps Who invented reality, but you invented perception. It was only a matter of time before I came to you, the one person on Earth who enjoys the same plane of thought as I do.

II

We found ourselves at the hotel before the sun had properly hidden from view. As we watched the river transport its ghosts towards a faraway rendezvous with the Rhine, I asked Heike if she was okay. I'm more than okay, she said, taking my hand and leading me inside. As we made love on the stiff bed, the effortless communion of our bodies reaffirmed that she had indeed been exorcised.

We ate in, sharing our plates, talking about the cathedral and the basilica and all the other places we had seen today. When we came around to the Roman baths and the service tunnels underneath them, where we had teased each other behind every corner, we grew aroused again. We took a shower together in the little cubicle before abandoning the room to our wafting secrets.

As we walked out into the slightly crisp September night, all I could see was the lit-up bridge beneath the stark Roman token that was the moon. I asked Heike if she wanted to walk across and she told me without hesitation that she did, though I suspected she had done so a hundred times. We bought a bottle of wine from a merchant capitalizing on the weekend class, and opened it with the complimentary corkscrew before we reached the bridge. As we stepped onto the pedestrian walk, a man appeared out of nowhere, peering at me with shining eyes, grinning as Germans simply are not wont to do. He was gone before I could react, the perfume of him lingering, like a misplaced warning.

"Do you smell that?" Heike said, looking behind us.

"Yes."

"It smells like blood."

I scanned the street, but he had disappeared among the shadows, the tourists.

"I'm sure it's nothing, Heike. The guy probably works at the *Imbiss* we passed. I noticed they were selling that disgusting bloodliver."

"I happen to like bloodliver."

I looked at her and she responded by handing me the wine. She seemed as light as air as we proceeded, even strange evening encounters failing to perturb the relief she had found since the illness had departed. I consumed at least three healthy swallows before she repossessed the bottle. By then we were nearing the center of the span, the surface of the river shimmering under the clear night sky. As we stood under the tall stone crucifix looking upriver, Heike seemed to have forgotten entirely about the man. We kissed and drank our wine and let the troubles of the world melt away.

"Divers still find Roman coins down there," she told me, pointing at the water below.

"Do they," I said, expressing too much interest in the disinterested night.

She failed to stifle her laugh. It felt good to be laughed at in that way, by her.

Not like the man who had passed us, smelling of blood and purpose.

*   *   *

I thought I heard her sometime during the night, but it was too close to my dreams.

Featureless buildings, silos, smokestacks in the night. A factory silhouetted severely within the blossoming mushroom of its silvery exhaust. Metallic sounds, motor sounds, the regular chugs of generators, conveyer belts, the irregular screeches and clangs associated with heavy industrial production. An emerging shape, life-sized cardboard cutout; then a second, and a third, Ingmar Bergman characters skipping hand in hand along a medieval hillside...

Stone temple, marble columns shining, bodies writhing in a Caligulan ecstasy. Fingers on strings producing music, breasts swelling beneath dark wine spilling from mouths and tongues and the fruit of the vine...

A youthful body rising to stature. Hands extending as if to offer oblivion, but instead unfurling a papyrus manuscript...

Sound: as of some dry, crackling passage. Leaves swirling in the dead words inscribed upon them.

I reach, but the funnel escapes my grasp, it's echo sandpaper on my fingertips as my hand falls to the vacancy in the bed beside me.

I call hers or some other name; rise to chase the words, the ghosts. I think I hear a response, but it is only the Roman sheet in which she is so elegantly, so lightly wrapped.

Light: as the air.

Air: in whose caress the garment stirs, wine murmuring on her breast. Goddess that she is, draped over the balcony railing against the backdrop of the bridge and the river and the Roman moon laughing down on all.

I am awake but I can't remember what is illusion. Perception. Who are the gods.

If Heike could answer, she would. But this was never her story.

Hexerei

As I sit here partaking of this strangely calming, strangely exhilarating thing I hold in one hand and contemplating the pen poised in the other, I realize I am no closer to finding a starting point than I was two and a half hours ago when I first opened my empty notebook to the waning afternoon. I've started my tale no less than three times now, from three different angles, three different points in time, and still Reiss's talk of sorcery and *Hexerei*, spoken only the day before yesterday, overlaps with Wagner's even more ominous words, uttered more than two decades ago to an eleven-year-old boy.

There is that sound again, fading in, a rhythmical central gear in a system of memories. As it increases I pull from the object in my left hand, pour from the instrument in my right…and it occurs to me that, instead of trying to work the prism's facets into some kind of linear sense, I should leave them just as they are. For essentially each is a beginning in its own right…

I

I wasn't sure what I had expected as I stood there, having just emerged from the trees, looking down on the forbidding structure that was Old Man Wagner's drying house. The vision was precisely as I remembered it, the planks of the tall barn stained dark against the painted afternoon sky and the lush fields of tobacco rippling in the early September breeze. A door at one end of the deep building stood partially open, revealing the nose of a rusty green tractor parked within. I imagined the rows of drying tobacco leaves hanging from beams above it. I imagined that and more, much more.

Scanning the valley and finding no disturbance beyond the ebb and flow whisper of the tobacco blossoms, I moved to the spot affording the best view of this place out of my boyhood and nightmares (if the one could be distinguished from the other). A pile of electric wire lay beside a deteriorated gate post, a former boundary of the pasture extending between me and the tobacco fields. Stepping across it, I dropped my bag, retrieved the beach towel I had packed and spread it on the grass. Next I dug out my notebook and pen, then the slab of *Käse* and the bottle of richly dark Neckar Valley *Wein* my new landlord had given me as a move-in gift. Lastly, the cigarette. A lone, filterless, machine-rolled cigarette that, when held up to the light, was touted to have none of the white specks of impurity an American cigarette had.

I wouldn't have known. I had never brought myself to smoke after playing as a boy among the aroma of Wagner's fields, an aroma I could smell now, more bitter than the cheese I unwrapped, more sweet than the wine I uncorked. The cigarette felt duly odd between my fingers. Odd as the face, the smile of Herr Müller as he'd produced it out of a metal container.

The lighter in my hand felt appropriate, the flame like prayer, incantation, its kiss in the blunt end of the packed tube a sort of saturating magic that could not be undone. Taboo like the orange-purple sunset melting in streams towards nightfall. Mojo like the fields inviting the old friendly trespasser back into their midst. Voodoo like the wrenching singing of swings and beams; the tickling of little girls' feet with pinkish blossoms; their last breaths, in a tall deep *Tabak* house with a green rusted tractor parked under a bestirred yield.

A cigarette under a flame. Smoke into my lungs, almost smoothly, as if I had been indulging all my life, of my own devices.

Then a murder of crows off to my left lifted as if spooked—in the process, spooking me. I watched the cigarette begin to shake in my hand. I had no idea why I had lit the thing to begin with. It was too early, too fucking early for symbolism. Three days it had been since I'd arrived back in Germany after the years, three days to find my way across the fields and forest to this place again. Three days to face my terrors. The cigarette could wait as I pinched it out unceremoniously, setting it aside in favor of the vine-purple wine, steadying agent, organizer of thoughts.

As I let the wine play its less than obscure part, the sun gradually fled from Wagner's property. Alcohol, nicotine, the being there brought the taboo into focus under the horizon—the voodoo, the juju, the mojo as the dark castle of hanging tobacco became a silhouette against the swelling dusk. The September sky became speckled with stars. I watched the structure with calm, restrained wonder. With every swallow I further suppressed the basic fear. But the expectancy, the watchfulness remained as the evening, in strange new effects, took hold.

The warmth of the wine seemed at odds with the startling sharpness of the crows that came and went at their fancy and with the fresh bent of the wind, seeming to warn of the coming hour. The warmth of the wine could not combat the threat and suggestion of the cold September night—its wrenching sounds, its laughter—and yet I found myself longing for that dark house where I had once been caught trespassing. I found myself…picking up the cigarette again, looking at it…

The light like incantation. And not a soul down there in the valley to disprove it, though I did begin to detect, fading in and out, a regular and cyclical sound. Like a wheel…

II

Somehow I always knew I'd return to take over for my father when he retired from the *Heidelberg American*, the newspaper he'd started in '71, year of my birth. I'm not sure whether duty or nostalgia played a part in it or whether I was simply haunted. As my childhood had continued to linger through college and then a teaching job that barely paid for life, much less living, it could easily have been the latter.

My parents and their golf cart were already part of the Floridian landscape when I landed on European soil again to stay. Herr Reiss, who'd leased and then optioned to us the house I had spent the first twelve years of my life in, was gracious enough to put me in touch with an elderly neighbor of his who had an available apartment in the same lovely farming region southeast of Heidelberg.

The three of us met on the evening I drove my rental down from the Frankfurt airport, a round of schnaps sitting on the rickety table of the room I'd be spending the night in whether I thought the place worthy of my money or not. Other than the table, two rusty scissors-legged chairs, a small refrigerator, a few dishes, and a horrid orange-patterned sofa—my bed—the first-floor apartment was empty. The upper level of the functional two-story house constituted a separate apartment, as is common in Germany, but it remained empty most of the year, reserved for Herr Müller's relatives when they came to visit from Würzburg.

It surprised both men when I accepted the price without viewing the place by daylight. That it stood on the northern skirts of the village, accessed by its own small road—albeit a rough one—was enough for me. The stooped and venerable Müller actually clapped his withered hands at the news, while Herr Reiss, frowning at this sort of rash decision making, offered to show me around in the morning.

"No need," I told him. "I remember the area like yesterday."

*   *   *

Reiss was there nonetheless when I rose from the deep and dreamless sleep that follows a transatlantic flight and opened the door to the new day. Framed by a clear September sky, he held a coffee in each fist, last night's frown replaced by the cheerful face from my youth—a face that seemed to have aged none at all since the last time I saw it.

"*Was hat denn das Leben so für dich getan?*"

I wiped the traces of oblivion from my eyes, accepting the mug presumably brought from his own cupboard. "Can't complain too much. I'm here, as they say."

"So you are, Reed." He put his hand on my shoulder, doubtless glad to have around some remnant of my father, with whom he had developed a friendship through the years.

As I started to invite him in he gestured with his coffee hand to his right. "Have you been around to the patio?"

"No, actually. You're the first thing I've seen this morning, Herr Reiss."

"*Albert*, Reed. Albert."

I felt a strange thrill at this luxury. The twelve-year-old boy had known him only by the respectful title due elders and landlords. "Then no, Albert," I said. "I've not visited the patio."

We walked along a footpath of octagonal stones, textured and substantial under my naked feet, to a tiled semi-circular patio with a view that managed to take my memories and transform them into verdant lace. As we looked down over the rolling fields of tobacco capped with pink-white blossoms, I sensed both his pride and his unease.

"Old Man Wagner?" I said. "Is he still around?"

"Yes," he exhaled, seeming relieved to have it out in the open. "I hope you will forgive that this house borders his property. It was the only available apartment in Zuzenhausen in your price range."

"No problem," I said, choosing to withhold, perhaps even from myself, that this very distinction had been a selling point. Meanwhile the rational part of me was somewhat disarmed by not only his frankness about the matter, but also his considering it deserving of the sober look on his face. A far cry from my father's opinions on Wagner.

His next statement found a cold place retained from my boyhood. "The village has grown rapidly in recent years. North is the natural direction for expansion, but no one will live near him."

"Because of the murders?"

"Because of *him*. Has your father said nothing to you about this? Wagner has become a blight on the land. In terms of impact on the community, he is worse than the rumors describe."

I looked to my left where the edge of the village was just visible beyond the fields. "Wagner's still a sore subject with my father and me, Albert. From all the way back to…the girls, the hangings. He feels I wasn't truthful with him at the time and that I've never admitted to it."

He peered at me over the rim of his mug. "Benjamin never said anything like that to me."

"No, I'm sure he wouldn't. After all, who would want their friends to know about their deluded boy?"

"Deluded? Is my English serving me?"

"You know exactly what I mean, Albert. Don't pretend to miss the point in defense of my father. That's the kind of thing…never mind."

He gestured inside the house. "May I get the chairs?"

"By all means." Along with the table, they'd probably been patio furniture to begin with.

We sat looking out on the waves of leafy abundance, the rich odor of untainted tobacco riding in on a sporadic morning breeze. Albert seemed to savor the scene even as his words cast a shadow over it:

"The villagers speak of strange sightings on his property at night. They avoid any dealings with him. He has his regular buyers for the harvested *Tabak*; otherwise he is a social…what is the word for an outcast of this type?"

"Pariah?"

"That is the exact word."

"But what are the villagers' reasons? When I was a boy there were two sides: those who accepted the findings of the police and those who accepted the findings of the police with the stipulation that Wagner was nevertheless involved in some way." I swallowed. "Never mind what came after—his wife found practically torn to pieces in the fields while he was away at market."

Albert studied me a moment, having detected the lump in my throat. "Yes," he said, "the stigma on the Wagner name." He sipped his coffee, letting his gaze drift out across the fields, adopting a look that could best be described as one of remembrance as he proceeded to elaborate on the subject.

I had probably been too young to understand, he told me, but the attitude towards the Wagner family had gone back to medieval times, when they'd farmed rye, the food of the poor—quite the opposite of tobacco, which only the rich could afford when the 'medicine' of the New World natives became fashionable. During the fifteen and sixteen hundreds the Wagners were rumored to have been actively involved in *Hexerei*—witchcraft, sorcery, black magic. One story, at least partly based in reality, told of two of Gerhard—Old Man—Wagner's ancestors, a mother and daughter, being put to death as witches. In retaliation the husband/father, along with his son, the village baker, intentionally ground ergot-infested rye with regular grain and poisoned the entire village.

Ergot, Albert explained, was the fungus from which the drug LSD was derived. It had been known at the time, even used by alchemists for various potions, but it hadn't yet been identified as the cause of outbreaks such as St. Anthony's Fire— attributed to the mass consumption of ergot-poisoned bread—whose symptoms ranged from hallucinations and madness to gangrene so severe in the body's extremities that people were described as having blackened stumps for arms.

Legend had it that the Wagners had known what they had, that they'd experimented with it, made serums with it, used it to practice sorcery. "While many of the locals," he said, "will claim they don't believe such nonsense, you won't find them taking a shortcut across his property. Not then, not now." He regarded me from under the shadow of his brow lest I mistake his meaning. "But tell me, Reed, what did you share with your father that he would not believe?"

There it was, on the table between us, rigid and naked as the coffee mugs. In the silence I heard what I thought was the duet of hooves and wood on pavement. His nod invited but did not encourage.

"I told him about seeing Old Man Wagner with the girls at the *Waldspielplatz* prior to their deaths, about watching him tickle their feet with flowers—tobacco blossoms—as they swung on the swing set. I knew Wagner hadn't killed them, that the MO of the accused and later convicted drifter was hanging young girls. But the removal of the eyes post-mortem was another matter. I told my father what Wagner said to me when he caught me trespassing in his drying house after the girls were found. I was an eleven-year-old, you understand, and terribly curious..."

III

If my mom had owned her own church bell she would have been ringing it by now. I could feel her worry, palpable as the odor of the fields, as I finally watched the lights go out in Old Man Wagner's barn, the tall skewed doors of the structure screech shut, locking in the bunches of dried leaves that looked (through the windows of the tilted slats) like so many cocoons for God knew what.

I had stolen over hill and dell to be here, chased by my mother's words:

"You're not to go past the stream, son. I know they caught the man, but the thought of how vulnerable a kid is out there…"

"I'll be all right, mom."

"…it simply kills me."

It simply kills me.

Driving words, though she hadn't realized it.

Simply.

As if it were so.

Kills me.

As though her own daughters had been found hanging there, with black and empty eye sockets. But only I had any such connections, having often played with the children, a kind of older brother to them.

As I walked down the lazy slope toward the barn, I willed myself to shed all the extraneous matter and focus on the object, which was to look within the building upon the site of the crime. Whatever deeper compulsions might have been at work, they too became extraneous, dissolving in the night like Herr Wagner as he wobbled away on his bicycle. I was a slave to my fear, and my fear was a slave to me. The drying shed was the terrible medium where the two realities clashed.

The house of planks and beams rose above me in dark mystery, reaching for the moon but settling for its syrup dripping over the suspended leaves of the product. A house of magic and terror, a young man's dream to be explored, its contents known. I squeezed my skinny body through the rectangular hole where one of the planks was missing, finding myself engulfed in a silver-tinged blackness. I heard my mother's voice, but it was a long long way from Wagner's barn.

The stench of oil managed to seep through the sweetly pungent fragrance of tobacco, with the further elements of hay and chemical fertilizer and my own sweat. The mid-September air was cool, but my flesh didn't know chill from heat. Children I had played tag with had died here, carcasses among cocoons. I gingerly felt my way around the wall, the hulk of the tractor and the pods above my head the only shapes visible in the dusk. My hand found a wooden shaft; I let my fingers crawl up it until they found metal prongs. I removed the pitchfork from the wall, a warrior now against the place.

A noise from the other side of the tractor, a creaking like the wind forcing two tree trunks together, made me clutch my weapon more tightly. I made my way along the wall so that I always retained my bearings, touching the beams and planks with my right hand while the other held my pronged lance extended by my waist. My searching fingers found a ladder, the possibility of actually climbing up above the beams where the girls had been hanged, and I was compelled to take it. I was halfway to the first of the drying levels when the door to the barn scraped open. I let the pitchfork fall and scampered behind the cocoons, one foot planting on a wall brace, the other resting on a main horizontal beam. Tobacco bunches from the next level hung in my face, a reeking camouflage.

A flashlight searched the spaces as the visitor walked through the barn. I could tell my hiding spot was at least somewhat secure by the densities the beam had to penetrate. If I remained utterly still, perhaps I would not be discovered. Then the light froze beneath me. For several seconds there was no motion within the building except that of my heart against my feeble shield of a shirt. Then, the beam shot upward, swimming among the tobacco, wanting me. I watched it pass across the crotch of my jeans, burn in the tobacco leaves I straddled, then die as the main bulb of the barn came on, the light filtering through the bundles indiscriminately.

A hesitation ensued, a period of foreboding, and then the game took its inevitable turn as rusty tines stabbed up through the murmur-glow below. I heard the word but did not utter it. Instead I remained stretched across the spider's corner I had chosen, feeling the silky webs over my mouth like gauze. The tines appeared once more then slipped out of sight. I hung there like a bat as Old Man Wagner's thrusts now took the form of speech.

My two years attending a German school and learning the native tongue paid off now as it never had before.

"*Hallo, Reed. Ich weis das du in meiner Scheune bist. Ich weis wo du dich versteckst.*"

—I know you're in my barn. I know where you're hiding.

"*Dort habe ich mich auch versteckt und habe zugeguckt wie er die Mädchen von ihren Hälsen an den Balken wo du gerade draufstehst aufhing.*"

—I hid there myself and watched him hang the girls by their necks from the beam you are standing on.

"*Willst du wie sie werden? Wilst du deine Augen weggeben und für immer mein Geschöpf sein, um mich zu dienen, wie sie mich dienen?*"

—Do you want to become like them? Do you want to give up your eyes and be my creature, to serve me as they now serve me?

My legs were shaking so wildly I could barely stand up, much less maintain my position on the beams. If there had been any question as to my exact location, it was gone now as the clusters of leaves around me shivered with my own fear. Even as I squeezed my eyes shut, knowing the next thrust of the pitchfork would not miss, I wanted to act, to obey the instinct that seemed to find connections through my paralyzed body.

He spoke again, the German adding a certain coarseness to his otherwise unaggressive timbre. *The eyes, they are your liaisons in every transaction, physical and otherwise. They are your last link to the world. They are strange vessels…strange orbs to hold in the hand.*

It was too much to bear. I let go my perch and launched forward into the cocoons, praying that if the tines were waiting on me as I dropped, they find my exposed stomach, my chest, my neck, anything but my eyes…

The last thing I expected was to land on a vacant floor, with a terrifying though unimpeded path through the brightly illuminated barn to the open doors at the opposite end. I scanned the surrounding area for him, but nothing disturbed the fields except the tocsin of my mother's voice from the other side of the hill and forest.

IV

And maybe Old Man Wagner has been waiting on me all these years as I keep hearing that revolving wooden noise, inevitably bringing to mind the fate of Frau Wagner, who liked to go out for a horse-drawn buggy ride at around dusk, to enjoy the land, the sweet scent of the fields, the materializing stars. Like tonight. I wonder, as I take another puff, if she, herself, smoked of the product. If she looked over her demesne exhaling silver clouds and never imagining to die a brutal death among the crops.

The noise increases by the second, echoing in the valley, the wrenching sound of wood on pavement, rope on wood, hooves in oblivion. I don't want to be here. I have only been back in Germany three days and I don't want to be here…as I place the last bit of cheese in my mouth. Chase it with a swallow of wine. Draw from the cigarette yet again…

I see the buggy appear below, from the direction of the village. Frau Wagner might as well be driving it, the twilight hour remaining hers in death. But the lamp hanging above the carriage exposes that theory, showing Old Man Wagner in the driver's seat, a whip in hand, like a tendril of ribbon in the light of an invisible moon. At the barn he stops, waits. I watch, drawing from the cigarette again, alert—peering and alert in the undeveloped night. I smell something more bitter than tobacco, or even my half drunkenness. I smell Herr Wagner. I smell necromancy.

The doors of the drying house open and out come three small figures, shadows at first as they approach the buggy, then golden haired angels as they enter the glow of the lamp. I cannot move. My petrifaction is such that I can't bring my hand down to grip the bottle of wine. Even from this distance I can see the infinitely black holes that are their eyes, dense spaces that the lamplight fails to penetrate. The wind touches at their hair, lifting gold flames around their oval faces as they stand looking at their master, hands by their sides.

I watch the whip sing in the air and manage a gasp as the first lash meets flesh with an eloquent *schpack*! The next lick comes immediately behind the first, the ripping sound of its all too successful landing filling the whole valley. The girls react to the vicious spurs by dancing, but not in the way the recipients of such abuse might normally do. The leather in Wagner's hand acts like an instrument, an instrument of sorcery, long licking wand that lifts them in a rotating funnel from the ground—hair sailing on the night, sleeves of dresses clinging to flesh as the girls raise their arms over their heads in a ballet beyond reason. The whip/wand keeps spitting, snapping, cracking as the three, in their elegant, slowly spinning dance, rise beyond its reach, and then begin to move…

In my direction.

I hear the word but, again, can't speak it. The muscles of my mouth make the attempt. I feel the No form, but by now they are halfway up the slope, black figures contrasted against the early night, but still dancing, still posing in the slow-motion whirlwind of Herr Wagner's *Zauberei*. *Hexerei*. Before I can address the sudden alienness of my own body, the hole that reaches up out of my insides to eat me alive, they are descending. Black sockets finding me with every turn, mouths now opening perhaps in memory, perhaps in appetite. All I know is nothing. No thing can be known in this world as the funnel slows, and they touch down on my towel, the three of them staring at me out of blackest oblivion.

"Ines. Selma. Karin," I am somehow able to produce. "It's me. *Reed.*"

But I have gone to hell; words are meaningless. There is only the searing agony in every nerve ending as these creatures surround me with their fathomless sockets. Suddenly—or so it seems to me—one of them, the oldest, Selma, reaches toward me. My blood freezes as I can think only of what they did to Old Man Wagner's wife, indeed why he must have made them his slaves to begin with. But she merely extracts the nearly burnt out cigarette from my paralyzed hand, long snake of ash falling on the towel. She puts it to her mouth and sucks. The inhaled smoke collects in her empty eyes. For a second I see pictures form, house, swing set, tractor, then the memories become a word on her lips.

"Reed?"

"It's me, Selma. Reed."

Her head snaps sideways, toward the barn below, where the lamplit buggy still sits, its owner anticipating the satisfaction the night's deeds should bring him. Perceiving my stare, he pops the wand in my direction, playfully, a little kiss of goodbye…

I look at Selma. She regards me a moment, if such a thing is possible, then turns to the other girls. "Reed," I hear in the strange wind.

And as one they rise up off the towel, briefly levitating there, looking down on me…then they are spinning over the slope, three black dancers on the night. I look in the direction they are moving and find Herr Wagner's whip now upon the flank of his horse as he flees across his fields of tobacco, fragrant as blood in the beautiful, flowering night.

The Horticulturist's Daughter

1.

How do you console an unreachable child? How do you tell her that the one thing that has inspired any emotion in her, the one thing that has penetrated the moroseness that has surrounded her all of her eight years of life, is gone and will not be coming back?

I will never forget the expression on my wife Haley's face when she came out of Jonna's playroom that September morning, her weekend routine of drawing curtains and opening windows having been bluntly interrupted. I will never lose the image of her grasping the door frame for support, tears welling in her eyes as she looked at me, trying to get the words out. I was standing by the hall table, had just gotten off the phone with, coincidentally, the most recent therapist, the one who had suggested getting Jonna the parakeet in the first place. It had been a month, you see, since our last visit, and Jonna had been improving remarkably. Because of the bird.

The bird that—as Haley finally managed to get out the words—was lying on its back in its cage, dead.

*   *   *

"We have to make a decision, and quick," Haley said when her crying subsided.

We were in the kitchen now and could see Jonna idly wandering the pebbled path through the flower garden. If there had ever been a place of comfort for her, then it was in the backyard among the flowers and fruit trees, a paradise my wife and I had built around the darkness and pain. Haley liked to think our daughter was attracted to the garden's cheerfulness. I knew it was the gloom, seeping between the petals, the leaves of the bowing branches.

"Haley, I'm not sure what decision there is to make."

She turned from the window, anger amplified in her moist eyes: "We've got to do something with the bird, Ray. This will just kill Jonna." She glanced outside again and suddenly grew taut. "Oh no, she's coming. Go and occupy her while I figure something out."

I didn't argue. There was no point. Besides, I hoped to god she did.

I called my daughter's name as I stepped outside to meet her at the mouth of the maze she walked. Once, I had come around the side of the house and caught her in a pile of potting soil I had dumped by the pansies a couple days before. She was eating a worm she had dug out of the black mound. I liked to think that I had embarrassed her. That the reason she paused was because she knew what she was doing was not normal.

The therapist, when told of the incident, had disagreed. "Do you have a lot of birds in your garden?"

"We have quite a few, yes," I said.

"And does Jonna seem to take to them?"

Haley and I looked at each other as though the realization was just dawning.

"Then you must keep her out of the garden," the therapist said.

"Keep her *out*?" Haley echoed, clutching my arm. "After all the work."

"Clearly, she is imitating behavior she has witnessed. It is not wise…"

But this had been the previous therapist. Cheltenham, the nearest population center of any size, had only three that fit our needs, and we were on the third.

I held my hands out to Jonna as we met between the trim edges of grass. She looked up at me with the saddest expression you have ever seen—her regular one. I let my fingers trickle like water and she placed her hands, more by wont than desire, in mine. She was frail as well as morose. A September flower of her own. I spoke to her quietly as I always did, so as not to damage her.

"Hey little golden one."

Her vocabulary—what she was willing to use, anyway—consisted of perhaps a hundred words. I had inadvertently invoked one of them.

"Goldie," she said.

Yes, Goldie, her poor dead parakeet.

"Are you having fun playing outside this morning? Look at the sky, how blue it is."

But she was finished talking now, letting her finger communicate instead. Following it, I was surprised to find Haley emerging from the back door, having already settled on a solution.

"Honeydrop," she announced. "Honeydrop, I have something to tell you. It's about Goldie. She's flown away."

*   *   *

It might have worked had Jonna not paused on the way to her playroom to look in the drawer of the hall table, where Haley had stored the bird until she had more time to figure out what to do. Jonna did random things like that, though I could not rule out the suggestion of the eyes, a la that memorable scene in Steinbeck's *The Pearl*. How many times have I read to her from my favorite author? In any case Haley was so stunned by Jonna's action that she could only gasp as the drawer came open.

As always, our beloved daughter did not offer much in the way of expression. She lifted the limp bird in her hands and, stroking its feathers, looked at Haley quizzically but without expectation. I saw that Goldie's head lolled as with a broken neck, its wing lay at a tangential angle, which said so much more than "Goldie's dead."

Haley knelt before Jonna in remorse and contriteness and supplication and reverence. "When I said Goldie had flown away, I meant her soul, Jonna. Goldie is a ghost now. She has left her body and flown away to heaven. Do you understand?"

If Jonna did, she didn't indicate so, the melancholy as entrenched in her face as I had ever seen it. Without a word she turned and stepped into her playroom, where the cage door as well as the room's window lay open to that heaven suggested. Goldie cradled in her hands, she went to the window and looked out on the garden and orchard, suddenly grotesquely plastic against the equally artificial September blue. My wife and I, having agreed long before to let Jonna fulfill her moments, however unidentifiable for us, could do nothing but watch—Haley's hand over her mouth, mine clutching the neck of my tee shirt in a habit that never dies.

This situation of course fell well within the identifiable, but there was nothing we could do but our classic stances as Jonna raised Goldie in her hands as if in offering. Haley and I saw in advance what was to come, and yet had no choice but to let matters follow their course, for Jonna's sake.

"Bye," said our daughter as she let Goldie go. There is no language for the way the bird fell out of her hands, striking the windowsill before dropping into the yard below.

"Oh, Jonna," said Haley, rushing to her.

In the face of it all, I somehow maintained the presence of mind to suggest to my wife that we formally bury Goldie. "There is no closure otherwise," I said.

She nodded in affirmation as she clutched our daughter to her breast, bleeding, "Honeydrop."

Hands lax by her sides, Honeydrop watched me.

*   *   *

Honeydrop. Haley had begun calling her that when Jonna was three and the blue of her baby eyes had surrendered to the melanin that gifted her irises with their unique long-term hue. Haley rightly equated that hue with the color of a drop of honey pierced by light, and indeed it was a central feature complemented perfectly by our daughter's whimsical blonde hair and slightly dark complexion. We were still in New York then, and the people on the street would stop to look at our undersized Jonna in the carrier on my back and comment. "How lovely she is. And those eyes, how *unusual.*"

Like her mother and maternal grandmother, Jonna was born in the United States and answered England's call later. Haley's American mother had met her British father while on vacation in London and they'd later wedded and settled in the States. Haley had been born in Virginia and in the course of time met an ex-Airman turned commercial airline pilot in New York City. They had soon left their lives behind, subsisting on his retirement as a fighter squadron commander (veteran of both the first Gulf War and Kosovo) and both their savings—his from his five-year stint with the airline, hers as a standout artist from a rebirthed psychedelic art movement in NYC. Disenchantment with their respective careers had brought them together in some random bar at JFK, where she had confessed that she had always wanted to go back to England and her heritage.

And so they had, settling in the Cotswolds in a little stone house on the outskirts of a hamlet called Abury-on-the-Wold, a peaceful place to continue to raise a five-year-old child with golden eyes and hair and a love of birds that extended beyond pigeons and seagulls and the mocking parrot on the arm of the indigent on the corner.

*   *   *

I woke in the night and discovered Jonna outside exhuming Goldie.

I had been trapped in one of my recurrent F-16 dreams, in which I fired upon and fired upon, pounded and pounded, the same stretch of long since defaced foreign soil. I woke, as always, before the scream rising within me found escape. I woke hating what I was, even afraid of myself and of what I was capable. Beside me, Haley stirred in her sleep, but she was used to my disturbances and rolled over without waking.

It was an impulse, possibly the same force that had driven Jonna to open the drawer, that made me pull back the curtains and look outside. The night sky was as clear as the day's had been, casting the rolling wold in that wonderful unreal twilight knitted by moon and stars. The movement revealed itself almost immediately, but my eyes had to adjust before I could make the determination that it wasn't an animal out in the garden. As the nature of the figure took shape, I found myself conscious of the scent of my shirt collar in my fist. Sickly sweet, fruity. Like the pears that wouldn't make the cut when we harvested our nine trees next week, tossed into their pile at the back of the garden to rot.

Then the creature in the yard became Jonna. My Jonna digging at the grave of her own creature, Goldie.

I stopped in the kitchen to fetch the schnapps from the cupboard. As always I cringed at the sugary buildup around the mouth of the bottle. We make our own schnapps, Haley and me. Or rather, I do. The flower garden is technically hers, the orchard mine, but they are one and the same, really. I smell the flowers on the both of us sometimes, like perfume. The fruit, too, though sometimes I smell it on my own person when we haven't even been working in the garden. Lifting the bottle and taking three deep swallows, I recalled a note I had seen on a bulletin board once at Aviano Air Base, Italy: *Life is a grape. Those brown spots are just a sign of sugar oxidation, resulting in a sweeter, more mature fruit.* I took another swig of the gin and stepped outside into the night.

What is her name again? You know her name, my Jonna, with the fleet little hands and the words that come and go as of their own wings. Funny that when I called to her, I called Haley's name. But maybe the word didn't actually come out; maybe it was a fancy of mine. When she wasn't crying, Haley liked to say that my fancies reminded her of her abandoned art. (*Will you leave me, too?* I asked her once. We didn't speak for days after.)

Jonna held the exhumed body in her hands and was kissing it, whispering to it, now letting it go. And so it did, engaging its green and yellow wings (the pet store had commented on the unusual amount of yellow in the wings; hence, the name Goldie) and flittering away into the starry night.

As she closed the cigar box, carefully putting it back in the hole, another impulse overcame me and I looked to my bedroom window and saw Haley's face there, stricken with wonder, dark and ripe.

2.

How do you console an unreachable child? How do you tell her that the one thing that has inspired any emotion in her, the one thing that has penetrated the moroseness that has surrounded her all of her eight years of life, is gone and will not be coming back?

If you know, please tell me. For I have no expertise in things of emotion and instinct, except as they trail back to me like the worms in Ray's pears. I did not breast feed my daughter for fear that I would poison her. Nor can I do this. Ray will take care of it. My husband will know what to do with this broken bird in its cage. It might as well be Jonna, for all we have given her out of our wretched lives. No, that's not fair to Ray. He at least served something besides his selfish ends. What did I serve, in my LSD-induced flare of a career? I served a scene. I served Haley's art. I served Haley.

Leaving the parakeet where it lies, I gather up the horror of the thing into the package of my mobile soul. But as must be expected in our world, I find Ray on the phone with the child therapist. The hot tears fall, and I rejoice that I can feel anything, an increasing occurrence as the distance between the mother I am and the artist I once was widens with every month, week, day that passes. He puts the phone down and I tell him, in gasps so much as words, that our daughter's only meaningful reference in the world is lying on its back in its cage, dead.

*   *   *

"We have to make a decision, and quick," I tell him when my crying subsides.

We are in the kitchen now and can see Jonna idly wandering the pebbled path through the flower garden. If there has ever been a place of comfort for her, then it is in the backyard among the flowers and fruit trees, a paradise my husband and I have built around the darkness and pain. Ray likes to think our daughter is attracted to the garden's cheerfulness. I know it's the moroseness lurking beneath the vivid, psychedelic splashes of color. I have seen what she sees. (My agent used to wear a dark purple tee shirt on which was written in lavender: *I was there to hear the tortoise sing.* I never asked him what it meant; all that really mattered was that he had been there.)

Though Ray knows that I'm right about the urgency of the decision, he stalls. I hate him when he is like this. He watches Jonna in the garden with more of the horticulturist's eye than the father's, and seconds, precious seconds pass, unattended. At last the response: "Haley, I'm not sure what decision there is to make."

I turn from the window, anger blooming as starkly as the afterimages of the roses on my retinas. "We've got to do something with the bird, Ray. This will just kill Jonna." But my eyes, my vagrant eyes have returned to the garden. "Oh no, she's coming. Go and occupy her while I figure something out."

He does. Thank god he's finally acknowledged how critical these moments. He calls her name as he steps outside, a warning, a tocsin: but it isn't she eating the worm; the worm this time is eating her. She is one of Ray's pears.

Now what do *I* do? I am the one who found Goldie. The strange mechanics of fate say that I must also unfind her. But how? I cannot just wish her to go away as I did my own (infinitely less real) reference to existence, my excuse of a profession. Or can I? Parakeets have the actual power of flight, whereas professions have only that illusion. I will not see Jonna peel back the garden's layers so far that she looks upon death. Goldie will fly away first.

I open the cage. I open the playroom window. I hold the bird in my hands and realize its neck and one of its wings are broken. *Oh god, Jonna, I know, I know. Please forgive us for all of your suffering.* Hiding Goldie in the first place I find on my way back to the kitchen, I open the back door and the words come as if I'd rehearsed them a thousand times. As if I'd always been the liar:

"Honeydrop. Honeydrop, I have something to tell you. It's about Goldie. She's flown away."

*   *   *

I hear her voice inside my skull as she walks in front of us. Rather, a voice of my own that I attribute to her; a fine line there, as I used to also hear it from the womb.

Why have you put her in the drawer, mother? You know that I know she is there. Why put yourself through this?

Her wing is broken…her neck, Jonna. She was so fragile.

Putting her in a drawer will not mend her. Only flight will mend her.

But she cannot fly, my honeydrop. She will never fly again.

I flew.

So she had. Ray never knew how close to dying she was during that first week. He was aware that there were problems, but I begged the maternity ward staff not to reveal how severe. As far as he knows, she was kept for ten days after delivery because of her size—five pounds and change.

Will you open the drawer for me or will I have to do it?

I warned you then, in the womb, about this world, Jonna. But you wouldn't listen.

She stops at the hall table, looks down at the gilt handle of the drawer. Though I have seen it coming, I can only gasp as she reaches out and pulls the drawer open.

I don't know what to say as she lifts the broken bird in her hands. So I kneel before her in remorse and contriteness and supplication and reverence. "When I said Goldie had flown away, I meant her soul, Jonna. Goldie is a ghost now. She has left her body and flown away to heaven. Do you understand?"

If she does, she doesn't indicate so, the melancholy as entrenched in her face as I have ever seen it. Without a word, verbal or otherwise, she steps into her playroom. I can only watch as she crosses to the open window, raising Goldie in her small hands as if in offering. I see clearly what is to come, yet have no choice but to let matters follow their course, for Jonna's sake.

"Bye," says my daughter as she lets Goldie go. There is no language for the way the bird falls out of her hands, striking the windowsill before dropping into the yard below.

"Oh, Jonna," I say, rushing to her.

Behind me, my husband, the voice of reason, suggests that we formally bury Goldie. "There is no closure otherwise," says he.

One wonders if even a funeral is closure as I clutch my honeydrop to my breast, nodding back at him for lack of anything more.

* * *

Honeydrop. I remember Ray's face the first time I, quite innocently, used the expression. Like most babies, Jonna had blue eyes until age three when they started developing that unique color and quality for which I had no other description. It might have been the way the word resonated along the bustling New York streets that struck a chord with my husband, but I rather liked the thought that we were going someplace more appropriate to honey and sunshine, more rural.

When I met him you would have thought he was going nowhere. Just like me. He showed up in his pilot's charade and bloodshot eyes from hours on hours of East Coast flights (he did not specify just how many). He preferred European flights, he said; at least you got to rest at the other end. In the bar, with his white shirt and its un-exalting shoulder emblems, he seemed a dead thing. That's what called me, I think. And maybe that's what called him, too. Because I was in my own inglorious outfit and bound for the farthest reaches of nowhere.

He saved me, it is certain. I like to think I saved him, but that is not so certain.

*   *   *

Ray dreams in the night. In his former vocation he has killed and killed, not face to face, but worse—from a great distance. I can hear the horror in his voice as he talks his squadron through the mission before them, the individual pilots through their trepidation as the targets begin to appear on the radar. I hear it all in the night, with my own radar. Ray there, upon his back and clutching the collar of his tee shirt. The smell about him is different in the night, in the closed bedroom; it is as though he is made of candy.

I am made of candy, dissolved in the saliva of dreams and nightmares. I refer to him because he is all that is left of the active part of me. He *feels* as I will never do again. He pretends that I channel through him, as I in turn pretend our daughter does me, but there is nothing vicarious about any of it. Life is about tides, and reality and perception certainly, but mainly tides. We were swept by them into the most beautiful land on the earth, and though still we dream, and hide, and mourn, Abury-on-the-Wold keeps our souls and is the only thing that matters to us besides our beloved child.

What was her name again? Jonna. Yes, sometimes I forget that she is not just a drop of honey there in the light. There in the light of the moon, with the unburied body of her bird in her hands. Kissing it. Whispering to it. Now letting it go. Now watching it fly on its green and yellow wings away into the night.

3.

We found in the local newspaper that the Forestry Commission was doing a bird banding down in Tetbury at the Westonbirt Arboretum. It was Haley, actually, who brought the article to my attention, pointing out that it might be something Jonna would enjoy. When I told her that I had happened upon a bird banding in the Tongass National Forest during an Alaskan cruise I had taken after retiring from the Air Force, she cited that old friend of man's, fate.

"We have to go then, don't we?"

It was well over an hour's drive down to Tetbury, but yeah, we had to go. A bird banding was about more than being close to the birds. It was about interacting with them—on both a personal and biological level—and then letting them go. A prospect that seemed to have been easier for my daughter than my wife during the days since Goldie's funeral.

The information appeared in both the *Gloucestershire Echo* and *The Forester* on the weekend after the loss of Goldie. The event was to happen the following weekend when I'd planned on storing and canning pears, but that could certainly wait as the formula for harvesting pears was imperfect to begin with. Nonetheless, we went ahead with the picking of those fruits that fell from the stem with the slightest twist and pull, and laid them out in the cool barn on shelves lined with the very newspapers that had diverted attention from our orchard of nine trees and its modest yield. Walking back through our farmer's market of gleaned fruit, Haley commented on the lovely smell. Of course it was an association. We weren't back in Sicily on our honeymoon, with the smell of lemons on the breeze. I checked my collar, in case.

* * *

Meanwhile Jonna had stolen an elongated look from beneath the hood of her metaphorical shell. It happened so naturally, so seamlessly, that her whole case might all along have been a question of moods as opposed to anything medical. Not only was she less reticent than usual, her vocabulary increased by uncounted words that week. A simple overview of what a bird banding was all about—compliments of the *Echo* by way of my wife's mouth—set her tongue and honeydrop eyes adance.

"*Will I see Goldie?*"

Haley looked at me, master of words and situations that I am (in some reality that I have not quite come to terms with). "You will see all kinds of birds," I told Jonna, "and be able to touch them." *And whisper them goodbye.*

"It's okay," my daughter said. "Goldie is home again. She is safe."

I looked at Haley and she at me, and there were no words. Just as there had been no discussion about what we both knew we had witnessed.

*   *   *

We arrived early at the National Arboretum, the parking area near the designated spot vacant except for the Forest Commission vehicle. Seeing it, I was reminded of shuttling from the cruise ship at sunrise to the Mendenhall Glacier in Juneau, Alaska, where I had stumbled upon the uniformed lady unloading her equipment from her wagon. There hadn't been anyone else around then, either—at least not for the bird banding. I'd slipped away from the group snapping pictures of the glacier and waiting for the Visitor's Center to open, curious as to what the uniform was up to. Little did I know that fifteen years later I'd be taking my daughter to see what the morning mist had given up in the Cotswolds of England.

The *Echo's* in-depth article had detailed that visitors arriving before 7:00 a.m. would stand a better chance of seeing a variety of birds, but that they would have to find the biological technician—named Melissa Henry—on their own. A series of colored markers would lead to the first of the vertically erected nets, then it should be easy to the follow the path from one net to the next. As it turned out, that first net hidden among the beautiful autumn maples wasn't so easy to find, the markers having obviously been placed in a hurry. We didn't care. The September air was slightly crisp, but refreshing. Condensation clung to the foliage and the sky was a patient blue waiting for ribbons of platinum-white to burn off.

When the first net appeared from behind golden leaves, Jonna cried out. "Look! A birdie."

Sure enough, there was a wren caught in the net and looking around in alarm or bewilderment, though not struggling. As we drew close enough to touch it, Haley invited our daughter to do just that. I knew from my own experience that this would not sit well with the tech, but before I could utter my wisdom, Melissa

Henry herself appeared—suddenly, and in a high state of excitement.

"No, no. Please," she said, exhaling as from a sprint. "Wait till I'm able to do the round with you. We don't want to cause the birds any more stress than we have to."

The first thing I noticed about Melissa Henry—aside from her being wound a bit tight—was her fingers. They were exactly the fingers of the bird bander in Alaska: rough, with dirty nails clipped to the quick, knuckles swollen as with arthritis or tendonitis. Otherwise she was perfectly presentable, even good-natured behind her aura of urgency. I suspected she would prove gentle as the morning dew when handling the birds.

Jonna seemed to take to her at once (it was as Melissa was extending a hand to our daughter that I observed the knobby tools of her trade). Actually, *seemed* to drastically understates it. Melissa made more progress with Jonna in her introduction than the hired experts had in all their sessions combined.

"Would you like to see where I do my work?" Melissa asked, smiling down at Jonna.

"Where you let the birds go?" said Jonna.

"Well, yes," the tech said, looking up at Haley and me. "Where we let the birds go. But we don't keep the birds too long after they're caught in the nets. We make some notes then band them and let them fly away again."

"I wish I was a bird," said Jonna.

Melissa's smile grew ever wider as she touched Jonna's face with her hand, "Me too, honeydrop."

Jonna was hers upon those words. That word.

"Follow me, troops. My workstation is back this way."

*　　*　　*

We passed three other nets but only one other caught bird before arriving there.

"Looks like a second or third-winter goldfinch," said Melissa, turning to toss Jonna's hair as if to accentuate the *gold*. Jonna, wholly against her nature, was outwardly *delighted* to be a part of it all. Haley's hand found mine, warmer than it had been in days, since that night out of dreams, when what was real escaped both of us in favor of a bird's flight.

To Jonna's evident fascination, the tech had already bagged three birds during a previous round and now pulled one of them out of a canvas tote she had been carrying inside her coat. This one was a song thrush, she told Jonna, as she held the bird delicately in one hand while recording her observations in a notebook with the other. These observations consisted of blowing the feathers below the bird's breast to determine gender, then fanning the wings in her bulbous though expert fingers to locate the stripes that determined age. Even though I had been through the same lessons in another lifetime, I was as fascinated as my daughter. Haley merely watched Jonna for those reactions that must be savored now, on the moment, lest the world collapse tomorrow.

When she finished with the third bird, fixing the band on the colorful blue tit's leg, Melissa let Jonna hold it. "Like this, with the neck between the fingers, but very gently...that's right."

"Can I let it go?" Jonna asked.

"You may stroke its feathers first if you like."

Jonna looked at Haley, then me. She held my gaze as she said, "I just want to let it go."

"Of course," Melissa said.

Jonna whispered to it before releasing it. She did not let go of my eyes until the blue tit had disappeared into the foliage.

"Okay," said Melissa. "Shall we do the next round then?"

Haley felt the need to interpret. "Would you like to go see if there are any more birds in the nets, Jonna?"

"Does Daddy want to?" said Jonna.

Caught in my own net, with my collar in my fist: "Sure, honeydrop. But you three go ahead. I need to...relieve myself."

*　　*　　*

There is literally no description for what it is to live with such moroseness, with such distance, with such failure. It consumes you until all that is left is the memory of what you'd hoped for, the dull realization that what your fanciful optimism has gained you is not salvation, but penance for what you have been and done. And then even those vestigial wisps of thought and feeling begin to succumb to the general numbness. A winter-white calm descends, covering the graveyards of fruits and flowers, stilling the vivid expressions and impressions of life.

But not fully, not ever *fully*. There are moments, beautiful, terrible, majestic moments when emotion finds you again and you lash back against the mocking futility of it all. When you *feel* and you *acknowledge* in one magnificent rush what it is to be abandoned by your god, your dreams, your illusions, your soul, your child. For that instant you are closer to freedom than you have ever been before, but you know it cannot be attained, the instant cannot be *fulfilled* without action, that your chance is already slipping away. So you reach again for the bottle of schnapps, the great prolonger of moments…

*   *   *

Their sounds as they moved up the trail were unreal to me as I took the flask out of my inside coat pocket and drank so deeply that I nearly heaved the gin back up. As I removed the container from my mouth, liquid dribbled down my chin onto my collar. I started to cap the flask but thought better, drinking another long swallow. Smelling sugar, pears, rot in the air.

I stood for a long time with my penis in my hand, nothing delivering itself from me.

Somewhere among the trees, now devoid of mist, now vivid and vivacious in the clear morning, I heard Jonna squeal in happiness. I knew what had come. I knew what had found its way here by migration patterns that could not be measured by summers and winters. I knew what had inspired the moment, that moment which exists separately from waking and sleep even as it calls its servant out of those very wastelands.

I had come when it called then. I did so now. They were one and the same moment as I picked my way along the corridor, brushing aside shadows, pausing a time or two to partake of the bottle again, remembering the spring, when Haley was fresh and beautiful and round with child. Remembering when salvation emerged in the form of a bloody squirming babe.

I came and I saw that the cage incorporated the same basic principles it always did, only was of a different material and configuration and scale. There she was, my Jonna, caught in the mesh and trying to free herself, her arms batting against the fabric, her eyes where they had always been. On me. Always me, as I extended a hand through the open door, seizing the creature in my fist. Hating it for what I could not accomplish. Hating it for what it had. Hating it as I had hated every target that had appeared in front of me, every action of my finger on the joystick, every emotionless look my daughter had given me. Hating it as I did her, with her frail wings and monopoly on expression.

Then withdrawing my hand, green and gold feathers peeping through my gnarled fingers. And her voice, Jonna's, growing more confident with every breath, singing, "Can I let her go?"

4.

Jonna fell asleep in Haley's arms on the way back to Abury-on-the-Wold. Her mother had elected to ride with her in the backseat, maybe feeding off Jonna's strange complacence. Maybe afraid of it. A smell accosted me as I drove. I looked back at them through the rearview but they were ignorant about the subtler things. They were victims as I was. The road stretched before and I thought about pears, and canning, and by turns Steinbeck. I wondered what he would have thought of Kosovo…

We arrived home before eleven a.m., but for some reason it seemed more like eleven p.m., perhaps owing in part to the fog that surrounded the vicinity of Abury. I joined Haley in pulling Jonna's curtains and putting our daughter to bed. As seemed appropriate, we were silent as we performed these duties. The suggestion of a smile on Jonna's face spoke all that needed to be spoken.

Haley retired soon after, cuddling up with the pillows on the living room couch.

At two I went in to wake Jonna for lunch. She was not in her room. Her window was wide open, the breath of the wold lapping in. Out beyond the roses and the pear trees, I thought I saw a wind in the mist. But I knew it was only a bird, going wherever birds do.

Dear Whom

Thy labored sigh
    Thine errant eye
And never ought
    Thy will comply
To tortured dreams
    Thine own extremes
        Nor ever heed the wild dogs' screams

Relax thy mind
    Maintain thy will
And never mind
    This wretched swill
Of howling hound
    And snarling bitch
        Raw dog screaming its own pitch

Thy logic lose
    Thy fear to choose
That thou wilt not
    Such wretched rot
A moment more
    One stinking spore
        Suffer one last beast implore

And still the howls
    The hungry growls
Of devils 'bout
    Thine exit out
Its seamwork tight

Its promise bright
    Raw dogs sav'ring one more bite

Of ceaseless wails
    From canines nailed
Upon such frames
    As ne'er will tame
The ceaseless cries
    The insane eyes
        The raw dogs screaming last refrains

Yea, raw dogs screaming
Lost laments
Howling verses
Long since spent
Yea, howling verses
    Lost laments
        On dev'lish verses long since spent

Was this what Whom
    Our parent meant
Between two sons
    Let one relent
Dear Whom, dear you
    Thy laughter spent
        Devil, angel, what e'er thou meant

Yea, devil, angel
    Thyself repent
Thy children, pray
    Thyself relent
Still the dogs
    The howls, the scents
        Of long dazed kids and mir'cles spent

Darren Speegle

Kiss of Chromium, Caress of Isolation

For Ingmar Bergman, a master artist

I

Through the lens of Hadrian Dellenbrant's archaic 35mm camera, the approaching island of Spöke looked as forsaken as its name implied, a phantom in a forgotten sea. The breaking crests of the otherwise gentle waves washing in over its rugged beach ignited in the effulgence of the silver-coin moon, already risen thanks to trouble with the rigging, rendering rock and sand as monochrome as the sea. Dwarf trees, the only sign of life along the rugged shore, cowered in long crooked fingers from a wind that danced in the sails of the two-masted vessel which bore Hadrian to his reunion with his long-lost mother.

As he clicked the button, releasing the shutter and capturing the image in time, he doubted future eyes would be able to draw a history, to tell it was a late April evening off the North Sea coast of Sweden and that two inherently connected but inconsequential lives were about to come together again for the first time in two decades. Even he couldn't know the latter with absolute certainty, though a quiet prescience had found purchase in him the moment the words had passed from the source's lips to his ear. He could only hope that the information he'd been given was accurate, that his mother was truly here, and still alive in her self-imposed exile.

The captain announced they were dropping anchor and instructed his lone passenger to be ready to help him with the skiff. Hadrian was ready to help with whatever needed doing; this was the end of eternity for him, where all the tangled roads that had sprouted from the seed of puberty delivered him. Putting away his camera, he stepped across the deck to stand patiently by as the captain operated the windlass. As he had the entire voyage, the captain remained intent on his work, displaying not the slightest hint of interest in his passenger or why Hadrian had commissioned transport to this desolate place. On those few occasions when they'd made eye contact, Hadrian had sensed a loneliness as great as his own. Indeed, both he and the captain might have been fixtures in the same bleak memories.

The splintered oars groaned in the skiff's rusty locks as the captain rowed them ashore. In spite of the scrutiny of the vast moon, Hadrian couldn't help but think of the coming landing as a secret trespass, an invasion. A violation.

* * *

Line in hand, rubber boots clearly reluctant to abandon the surf, the captain asked Hadrian if he should wait. The grizzled fellow hadn't blinked an eye back in Nirvall when Hadrian had requested one-way passage. The hour doubtless played a part in this sudden swell of conscience or duty, for when Hadrian had placed the money in the captain's hand, neither of them, he was quite sure, had imagined they'd be arriving at their destination after twilight.

"No need to wait, captain. But a question if I might. How long have you been in the charter business in Nirvall?"

"Twenty-five years and more."

"Do you remember ever bringing a woman out to this island? It would have been a long time ago. At least a—"

The captain's expression, a conspiracy of the lines on his weathered features, relieved Hadrian of specificity.

"When, sir?" Hadrian said.

"Twenty years ago. Such a lovely woman to be traveling to a ghost island, thought I. But she looked the phantom herself, with her pale skin and her hollow eyes. When I tried to engage her in conversation…her words, they seemed…lost. It is a silent voyage to this place."

"Yes," agreed Hadrian. "*Adjö*, captain."

"*Lycka till.*"

Hadrian watched him row away toward the schooner rocking beneath the light of its lanterns, themselves astir in the wind which he suddenly felt acutely against his exposed cheek and ear. He pulled his hood around his face and turned to the island. Spöke seemed to know him in its drear welcome, its chill caress, born less of the weather than the place itself, at the end of eternity. Rock formations along the Frisian shore created a medium between element and essence, carved to the line of his own set jaw as he followed the rough natural path that wound gradually up from the sea. Though the hour had settled, and the gibbous moon established reign, the going was easy, as if each step brought a luminosity to the shingled underfoot. The wind howled among the bodies of rock, shaping them, sculpting long, watchful, expectant faces.

He moved among them as through memory etched in stone. *You are different than the boy who went into the shower. The shower has...transformed you. Was it the heat? Did your thoughts drift? Do not be ashamed.*

"I am not ashamed, mother."

Come here to me.

Such easy memories, in this place in the drift. He'd thought them forgotten—which effectively rendered them perpetually remembered, if only in reaction.

Come here to me.

And then, through the countenances, he spotted the subdued, half-timbered, thatch-roofed cottage defying its environment even as it sang with the erosive wind. He knew it was the end of his journey because in such a place the journey had begun. There had been a father to go along with a mother, a father now dead, drowned, forgotten.

A noise distracted him, drawing his eyes to the right and behind him where a pebble tumbled over tiers of ancient rock. He looked up searching for the author. For a moment there was nothing there but the crag against the sky, silver edged, bright. Then a raven lifted from the bust of stone, black against the lustrous silk of the dome. When he turned back to the house again, it and its immediate setting had changed. A great clock, mechanism worn down by the weathers, had ceased working, leaving the image frozen in the moment, as if stolen by his own camera.

II

On the stoop, what little there was of one, stood a woman as ancient as the expressive rock garden among which she'd made her dwelling. She leaned forward on the crook of a sturdy cane, a sunhat upon her gray head in spite of the hour, a crooked smile on her wrinkled face. Like the lost world of which she was a part, she was brilliant in monochrome, a queen in molten time. Her hair blazed, her flesh throbbed, her eyes consumed. Her mouth writhed as she shifted on her staff, the only thing in her environment that moved at all.

For the wind had stalled in the smoke that rose from her chimney, such that the vapor smeared against the backdrop of night, trapped in some terrible retreat. Likewise the weeds in front of the cottage lay bent at an angle that mocked gravity; the picture of the dwarf trees along the beach, only trebled. And not the faintest hint now, neither sound nor sensation, of the actual concrete wind, though the case of its indulgence seemed to permeate every corner of the picture. Including the lady's dress, which clung to her otherwise naked legs, and her hat, on which she placed a protective yet unnecessary hand as she spoke:

"You are looking for someone."

Hadrian nodded. "My mother. Petra." He thought to ask, *Are you she?* But Petra could not have been as old as this woman, even in despair.

"If it is milk you are looking for, I am not yet dried up." She smiled in the direction of the frozen wind, and pulled a breast from below the neck of her dress, offering it to him.

Hadrian looked at the sagging gland and for a moment became part of the surrounding scene, caught in perpetuity, in flight. The word wanted to remain behind, untouched by wind and weather, but before he could will it so she uttered it for him:

"No. I see you look for more than physical nourishment. Come then. You can't stay out here all night. The animals…"

He glanced around him and the only animals he could imagine possessed flesh of stone and fangs and talons of silver. It was enough to prompt him indoors, where she took his coat and hung it in space.

*   *   *

The fire was not so cursed as its vapor, lapping freely at the prospect of air somewhere up there beyond the flue. The hearth was a great circular thing, as staunch as the cottage's foundation buried in the natural cement of the island.

"I can read your thoughts," said the old woman, taking him by the hand and guiding him to the low stone platform, directing him with her cane to be seated beside her.

Obeying, he replied uncertainly, "If you can read my thoughts, then you know I am here to be reunited with my mother."

"Where is your father?" she said, encouraging with her cane.

He stared at her. "He is in his grave."

"Why?"

"Because that's where I put him. I failed to help him."

"When he was drowning, you mean?"

"Yes."

She nodded and the fire in her hair streamed. "Drowning is not so bad a death. We all drown in our way." She squinted, perhaps with a deeper secret.

"We do," Hadrian said. And removed her cane from his thigh.

She returned it, this time placing it on his crotch.

He clenched the shaft in his fist as he said, "This is a small island. Surely you know my mother."

"Tall or short, small or large? There are many animals on this island."

He swung the cane aside, observing her silently.

"She cannot help you, Hadrian Dellenbrant," she said. "You know this, surely."

"It is not I who needs help."

"Isn't it?" she said. Her body, as if switched on by the wink she offered him, glimmered. They maintained sensory contact for a protracted minute... then she was gone by way of the chimney, leaving him alone in the cottage, surrounded by the motionless wind.

Hadrian sat on the hearth for some time, remembering another wink, less ironic, delivered long ago across a table set with food. Hadrian remembered a father tossing a napkin in his plate, pushing back his chair and rising noisily from the table, uttering words that had lived far beyond him:

"The both of you disgust me."

Across a table set with food. To a boy, a mere boy in his mother's caress.

* * *

Time passes slowly. With or without expectations, time passes slowly, and deliberately so. And yet wasn't it only yesterday, indeed just then, that he'd felt her hand upon his thigh. *Such strong legs for one so young.* Her fingers grazing the soft blond hair as they traveled their fateful course. *Such maturity.*

Do you remember when I used to feed you from my breast? she had said, stroking him, causing feelings that he'd previously felt only in private, and then ashamedly, burying his face in his pillow, suffocating his tears even as he resumed his explorations, which seemed to lead to nowhere, a carnival ride that skirted but never found the truly ecstatic. *Your suckling sometimes aroused me. Made me touch myself. Like this.*

175

Wasn't it only just then in time that she led him into the room that she shared with his father, pushing him back on the mattress, gently at first but then aggressively, hungrily. Her breath, her tongue hot on his flesh, and no pillow to turn to, no fabric to bite, nowhere to hide his eyes, not even behind their lids as he watched her welcome him to manhood. Hadrian but a boy, there on the stuck second hand of a watch, the tears spilling from him and into her.

Spöke. A fitting name for the place of her retirement. She, a ghost herself, superimposed on reality. He never knew her so much as the image of her. And yet, what she gave him was not abstract. What she gave him was not elusive. What she gave him was not poetry. What she gave him was a moving picture. And the subtitle: *How real a mother's love, how real a father's pain.*

From the language of perversion to the North Germanic. To the Swedish, ahowl with symbols.

III

There was a knock. The rap of a phantom at the cottage door, and maybe it was that wasted American, Edgar Allan Poe, looking for the pebble that had fallen into the gutter to be washed away by the wind. Or maybe Tamino tapping with his Magic Flute. Was it indeed Pamina whom the Three Ladies had had in mind at all? Perhaps it was that vagabond Zarathustra about no good.

He rose from the hearth, the flames still dancing warmly about his face. He passed a window and, though the pane was opaque, could see animals, tall and short, small and large, dancing to a music of wind where there was no wind. The tap came again, and he could hear the breath from the flute. If it was Mozart himself, Hadrian would kiss the phantom and then go, wherever the wind led him in its utter stillness. He placed his ear against the surface of the door:

"Mother?"

"It's your father," came the long-lost voice. "They found him near the pier…dead, Hadrian. Drowned."

I know, thought Hadrian. *I know. I was there.*

He heard the music of the flute as he opened the door, though it might have been the exhalations of the fire playing games in the chimney. She stood there, lips as full as he remembered them, body as curved, breasts as round and self-supportive. She had not aged a day, except in her eyes. In her eyes he saw the weathers of her domain.

"Come in, mother," he said, pulling out of his pocket a bottle of lotion, brought with him from civilization. "I wasn't sure what you were able to get out here so I bought this for you. I know you used to be fond of it."

"I did," she confessed. "It's been awhile, Hadrian."

"So it has, mother."

She squirted some of the lotion on her fingers, rubbed it into her cheeks before stopping suddenly, looking bewildered. "Then you know about your father…"

Yes, I know.

"He was a good man," she said. Still not seeming to know herself.

I watched him die.

She walked into the kitchen, stroking the doorframe as she let her eyes roam. "It is a good place, yes? Much like home?" She drew a wooden chair from beneath an equally rustic table, sat down with a sigh of what might have been satisfaction, what might have been concern. "I wanted it to be just like home."

Hadrian closed his eyes as he went to her, kneeling at her feet and hugging her legs. "Are you real, mother?"

She looked toward the window, impenetrable there in the wall. "Sometimes I wonder what is and what is not real. Do you have a camera? Is it one of those immediate violations ? You know what I mean."

"No, it's not an instant camera."

"Take my picture anyway. Pretend I am an actress and you are the director."

"The director does not take the picture."

"No? It doesn't matter. Look at me, Hadrian. I have missed you." She let the strap of her gown fall over her shoulder, her fingers gather the hem around her milky thigh. "Do you remember when we used to play the seeking game? You would play shy and I would come seeking. Even your father used to participate in that game. Have I mentioned that they say he is dead, Hadrian? I don't believe it, you know. Do you?"

*   *   *

The sound of the water on the rocks. Like a movie, a testament to the reality of our existence. A clock. A beat of surf on stone, and the tap, perhaps, of a toe on the rock. A man fishing, away from the worries of the world. The wind tossing his blond hair, turning his lips to dry, glorious flakes. A beer there, by the tackle box. A sky without a sun. It is strange that it has taken this long to be found out. Are the fish biting? Are the fish biting?

You know it is only the way the clock ticks, the way the hand lands, but still he asks, *Are the fish biting?* Dare he ask such a mundane question after he has been between her legs, where you, her own husband, have not ventured for so long? Were you invited? You cannot remember. You know it is only the way the clock ticks, the way the hand lands, but still he asks, *Are the fish biting?*

For he is what he has always been, steadfast, there, concrete. And you… you have been elsewhere. So you turn your fullest attention on him, like a man, and the stench of fish about you, and you say to him, "I would die here, father."

And he returns, "I would let you. I would let you, son."

The wind is enamored of the place, gathering over the rocky outcrop, swooning among the crevices. The sea contributes its refrain, the silver wash hissing at feet and line, salt spraying like magic dust. What did he do anyway, your father, casting his line out on the water? The chromium world receding from him even as it engulfed him. There were factories, stores, boats, houses, all manner of discussion, but where indeed did he do whatever he did? Just a moment of your time…are they biting?

Come. Come see. Come see what I have caught here on my line.

The wind and the sea, and the churning reunion that never ceased, no matter the distractions. You reach out your hand, but it is an afterthought. An afterthought of nature, an afterthought of you. And yet…

* * *

A disturbance beneath the elements. There she stands, on a higher shelf of rock, cane in hand, scowl on her face. A face that always scowls, even when it smiles. How you love it. How you despise it.

"Are they?" says she.

"Are they what?" say you. Disdainfully. Adoringly.

"Are they biting?"

"No, mother." And yet there it is, the pull, as if of your own flesh. The water whirls as your catch materializes. You know that youthful, beautiful face, though you must not speak its name. You must not say what you have done. Done to your own son.

"No," you repeat, watching his visage fade beneath the waves. "They are not biting."

"Good," she says, touching your naked ankle with her cane. "Good."

Yet there can be no ridding of it, that name. *Hadrian*, cries the water. *Hadrian*, cries the night.

"Come," says your mother, turning on her cane. "Come back to the house. Petra prepares a good bed."

You gather up your materials and as you start that way, a noise distracts you, drawing your eyes behind you to the right where a pebble tumbles over tiers of ancient rock. You look up searching for the author. For a moment there is nothing there but the crag against the sky, silver edged, bright. Then a raven lifts from the bust of stone, black against the lustrous silk of the dome. You take a step backward and your fingers, of their own compass, find the pebble. Its heft isn't right, but then what *is*?

What *is*?

IV

You wake in a wooden bed with a sagging mattress, and you hear singing. It seems the world to you, the very wind. Life where there has been none, milk in the desert. You find on the table by your bed a timepiece, a clever thing with the ticking seconds set in a small nondescript stone. You shake it, but that isn't the way it operates. It is light as the lost days in your hand, reminding you of your dreams. The singing is Petra's. She is about the work of a new season, you recall; hanging summer clothes, finding joy. You call her name, but it is snatched away by the breeze. You marvel that there can actually be such a thing as breeze.

You are naked. Your penis is partially full, in keeping with the fullness of everything else. You do not bother clothing yourself as you step out into the morning. The flowers scratch at your feet. The sound of Petra's singing ushers you through the squat trees, leaves vibrant in the sun. She is about, somewhere, though you can't quite place her location. You remember games of long ago, seeking games, but you shut the memories out. Those were other times, other histories, other aeons. Suddenly, you want to find her and pull her to you out of the sparse camouflage of the foliage, tell her she is magnificent, a castle against the North Sea.

Naked, peeking behind the wind-carved faces, becoming the phantom that she aspired to be, and finding...finding out on the sea...

The ship from Nirvall, the unmistakable figure of its captain standing on the bow, clutching a taut line from the foremast in his fist. His eyes, seeking and finding. His loneliness echoing across all the Frisian Islands, wherever they were. Gazing from behind the arthritic shapes that are the island's trees, you mourn and you do not know why. Somewhere behind you is Petra's song. Somewhere in the random blow of sand. You call out to him, the captain. He waves.

You wait until he nears and you shout, "I told you I did not need passage back."

"It is not you I am here for," he returns.

Petra's song following along, her face suddenly appearing there beside you, at the cusp of the beach. How long has it been since you have seen her? An hour? A month?

It isn't known among the waves or the actions of the ferryman as you prepare to venture to the mainland again, your Sweden out there, to be kissed upon arrival, to be died upon.

"You've no cargo, then?" asks the captain, sporting the same disinterest as remembered, indeed his very own claim to the bleak memories among which all any of you can hope is to be props.

"Only this," says your wife, materializing, bundle in her hands.

The captain looks upon it with ever knowing eyes. He glances up at you as she turns to offer the infant to its father. You cannot be sure but the baby's eyes seem to devour the sunlight.

"Let us call him Hadrian," says Petra.

"The world," you tell her, "needs not another living thing."

Indeed, the bundle seems to have no weight in the universe. See how it hangs there, over the bulwark, as though the wind has never blown. Nor the disease of motherhood ever taken course. You watch it drop from your hands into the embrace of the sea. You consult your timepiece, and perhaps the instrument is what it is after all, a twitch of a raven's claw, a kiss of chromium, caress of isolation, a random pebble of memory, a goodbye to love.

The captain meets your eye. There is a moment…how long is a moment? Long enough to realize that it was inevitable, his company and yours. Inevitable as the seasons trudging toward winter. Inevitable as that.

American Kisses

1: Affairs of the Id

Jason Sully woke up that evening, showered, did up the front of his hair with gel like his favorite European football players, and went out on the town. Prague was a city he could relate to, having visited several times during his tours in Germany and Italy. The girls were still as sexy, still as forthcoming, still as wet when he stroked them the right way with his fifty-five-year-old parts, as they'd been when he did his stints as an enlisted man with the army. There was so much satisfaction here, in fact, that he was considering making Prague a base of operations now that he'd the money to do whatever he wanted to in the world.

But it wasn't his lottery winnings he was thinking about as he entered the Jazzy Digg, a spot that had been recommended to him by one of the aforementioned girls before he'd gently kissed her goodnight. He'd other things on his tripartite mind, other things on his id and ego and that third part that Freud had falsely identified as super-ego. Had the grandfather of the Great Psychic Dance but once considered his own thoughts and feelings and urges, he'd have recognized that super-*id* better characterized the third element of the psyche for the majority. Sure, there were managing angels on the shoulders of some, but they did little more than polish their wings in their role as conscience. The rational part, the simple ego—not some sadly moralistic archetype (cheers, Jung)—balanced things out in the favor of order. Shame on all of psychiatry for its craven penetrations into the true human condition. Had the forefathers participated in their experiments a little more subjectively, their legacies and follies wouldn't have to endure such exposure.

Fortunately, Jason wished them in his dismissive way, *my attention is turned to more interesting people now. People who are vibrant and able and full of Czech beer. Take, for instance, that girl there at the bar. Is she a tourist with her uniquely black hair or a dyed local about her business? I'll take either if I'm game enough, though the former might put a strain on my ability to use up the days my American passport allows me to be in the country.*

He touched his hair to make sure it was still upright and then, waiting until the busy bartender was in the area, stepped up beside her, calling for an Urquell. The bartender nodded without pausing from the magic tricks he was doing for his customers, an activity which didn't appear to be a labor of love. Flipping a glass this way, a bottle that, he moved from one end of the bar to the other with the practiced grace and attitude of a secretly lit fuse. The tart beside Jason was no more oblivious to this than he was, saving him the tiresome deed of making first contact.

"Will you look at how fast, how mechanically precise, he works," she said in English. "It's like he's harboring an urge to——"

"Murder all his customers?"

She looked at him, and he knew immediately she wasn't Czech. She was simply too exotic. Gypsy maybe? Mediterranean?

"Why are you looking at me so strangely?"

"Visa stamp," he said. "I'll have issues with you."

"Issues?" The odd look suddenly changed to one of understanding. "Aha. It's a come-on, right? Hook up with me and you'll overstay your visa and the whole world will stop revolving on its axis for our heavenly, sweaty partnership? Is that about it?"

"'Sweaty' was your adjective, not mine. I hope you remember that. Can I get you another drink?"

"I'm tempted, but…"

"Yes?"

"Sure, my American friend. I'll have what you're having, with a splash of honesty on the side."

"That obvious, huh?"

"That you're American or that you're not being forthright?"

"Take your pick."

"Name's Via," she said, offering her hand.

"I'm Jason," he said, raising it to his lips.

She watched him kiss it. "You're kidding me, right?"

He wasn't, and the trick, as always, warmed her in spite of herself.

"You want me to be honest?" he said. "I mean completely so?"

"Dazzle me."

"I'd like to take you out of here and open you up like you've never been opened before."

"That's hardly original," she said, licking her lips and seeming to take him in through her nostrils. "Considering where we are."

"Right. Ivana mentioned it was like that here. That one could find a partner to share in his fantasies without all the moralistic ado."

She laughed. "Invoke your Ivanas all you want, but you still have to perform."

"Might be able to do. The chance is yours to take."

"Confident in ourselves, are we?"

"You asked for forthrightness. I've given it to you. Would you like to be opened up to another world or not?"

"You have drugs, Mr. Jason?"

"Some coke, some pot. Some special side dishes."

"Including Viagra, I hope. You've kept yourself fit, it's obvious. But no amount of gym time or gel or flashy dress can hide the years."

Jason faced her squarely. "The day I stop performing, lady, is the day I die."

"Sign me on then…assuming of course your blade is big enough?"

"Oh it's plenty big, baby. It's plenty big. And just for your knowledge, the visa reference was to do with how fast I have to get out of the country after."

Wordplay of the damned, Jason thought as he paid their bills and led her out. They both knew the metaphors, the suggestions behind the teases. He'd forgive Via her victim fantasies if she'd forgive him his murderous ones.

After, that was, all urges had been fulfilled.

* * *

"Still tempted to say no?" he said as he traced the arc on her throat.

"Tempted, yes, but I never said the word 'no.'" She was moaning, pleasuring herself as she said it. And so was he, though in a different way.

"Let me know when you're about to come," he said.

"Getting there," she panted. "Press the knife closer. "That's it. Yeah. I'm almost there…about to…yes! I'm coming, goddamnit, I'm coming!"

"Let it out then," he said quietly. And having released himself by his own special means at the moment of her climax, ran the blade's bloody sides, one then the other, across her naked hip.

Fuck her for the foreknowledge, he thought. Pretend though it was, he'd have to find better slaves in the future. The lack of uncertainty on their part, however misled, was simply unacceptable (he might as well go back to finding his zest through the cream he was supposed to be lathering his nuts with before shaving them). It made the complicated process of disposing of the corpse all the more unpleasant. Normally the reducing of the body through available machinery would be an activity during which he'd smoke his cigarettes, drink his beer. But cases like hers, they weren't like cooking omelets. Being rid of her was a chore. An inconvenience of a major sort. Wasn't he supposed to have spilled his juice, too, while performing the deed? Goddamn her, her smugness. The hole in her decapitated head wouldn't even be worth the effort.

2: An Unlikely Threesome

Harry Hinterlove, forty-eight-year-old widower and retired army officer, moved from his last station in Europe to Tennessee in 2010, when things at home looked their bleakest. Making frequent forty-mile trips between his rental home in Chattanooga and the small town of Culter Brook, where his parents lived until their passing that same year, he waited until the foreclosures littered nearly every street before making his bid. What he got for his patience was a home that had previously been valued at over $250,000 for roughly half that price. And resting at the privacy end of a cul-de-sac at that, on the edge of a golf course that had sat idle and on the market for nearly three years. His only neighbor in the circle turnaround was a reclusive single mother of one with whom he didn't carry on a full-blown conversation until the fall of 2014, when circumstances insisted.

Those circumstances, unfortunately, preluded a succession of events he'd never have imagined to find himself involved in.

* * *

As usual, her twelve-year-old son Lyle returned home from school several hours before she finished her shift at the factory the boy had told Harry she worked at. Harry happened to be looking out his kitchen window—wondering as he watched the lad mow the grass when Lyle ever had time for homework—when the accident occurred. It was a freak thing. As the boy tilted the older-model mower to work around a young crab apple tree on the side of the house, one of the long laces of his untied basketball shoes was sucked into the rotation of the blades, bringing his foot behind it. Even if Harry hadn't been watching, the scream would have brought him running. The fact that he had been, though, might well have saved the boy his foot. Because when he got there moments later, the lawnmower was on its side, motor still running, and the boy still hadn't disentangled himself.

"Get your shoe off, Lyle!" Harry ordered him before arriving and shutting off the machine. As the rotor responded by winding down, the boy's shoe, finally off his foot, clunked repetitively against the dying blades.

Ordering the boy to shut up and quit his squirming, Harry took his foot in his hand, seeing at once the abnormality at the end of the blood-soaked sock. "Christ, Lyle. How many times have we been through this? You have to be careful with machinery."

Indeed, this was not the first or even the second time Harry had caught him being careless. Last summer, when Lyle was trimming Harry's trees for some spending money, the kid had cut first his jeans and then nearly his throat in a completely avoidable backlash of the small chainsaw. And those were just the occasions Harry had witnessed.

Removing the opposite foot's sock and wrapping it tightly around the foot whose big toe was clearly severely damaged as it hung at an angle to the bone, Harry helped him up, putting his arm around the boy's shoulder and leading him, hopping on one foot, to his SUV.

As they drove to the hospital, the boy said, "Will you call my mom?"

"Does she have a number? Three years we've been neighbors, and the impression I've always gotten from you is, she can't be bothered."

"This is different."

"What's the number?"

"Here…it's on my mobile. I'll call it for you."

"You have a phone? Why can't you talk to her yourself?"

He avoided Harry's look. "It's only for life-or-death, she told me."

"Wait," Harry said, having been jarred by similarly odd clues in the past. "And you carry this lifeline with you while you're mowing grass? What's with that, Lyle?"

Lyle held up a finger. "It's ringing."

"Give me the damn phone, kid. Jesus, you're—Hello? Yes, hi, Ms. Sullivan. This is Harry Hinterlove. I live across the street from you? I'm afraid there's been an accident involving Lyle. Don't be alarmed. He got his foot caught in the lawnmower blades, but everything's still attached, don't worry. His big toe's hanging pretty badly. The bone could be broken, or maybe it's only a matter of stitches, I'm not sure. I've dressed it up and we're now on the way to the hospital. I don't know if you want to meet us there…?"

"She'll come," Lyle said. "She won't believe it's from the lawnmower until she sees it for herself."

"Yes? Okay, good, Ms. Sullivan. Yes, yes, you're welcome. Don't worry, he'll be okay. We'll see you there." He clicked off and looked at his passenger. "What do you mean by that, Lyle?"

Lyle looked at the blood-soaked package of his foot, which Harry had had him rest on the dashboard to stem the bleeding. "Nothing."

"Don't nothing me. Don't even think about retreating into those secrets of yours, kid. This is a serious matter, and I don't have the patience."

It was the first time he had pressed the boy about comments that had seized his curiosity, so he wasn't sure how the other would respond.

"It's Dad," Lyle said, still looking at his foot.

"Dad? I thought you said your father was dead?"

"To us, he is. I mean it's like that. But really we just don't know where he is."

"Go on."

"Mom can't quit thinking he'll come back and it'll all start over again."

"All of what?"

He was quiet.

"Never mind that for now, Lyle. I think I understand. But when did your father leave? It must have been years ago. Yet you're still afraid of him coming back?"

"Mom thinks he might. I don't know. I was kinda young."

"You've no idea what became of him?"

"He won the lottery. One of those big cross-state ones. I remember him holding up the ticket and laughing at us. A few weeks later, after he had the money for sure in his account, he was gone. Mom didn't even try to get part of the money, she was so relieved he was gone."

Harry nodded. He'd learned more about his neighbors in the last couple of minutes than he had in the three years since he'd bought his house. No wonder they were so withdrawn and secretive. Assuming he was on track in inferring abuse, who wouldn't be under such circumstances? He was grateful he'd at least come to be acquainted with Lyle along the way. While their family business was theirs and no one else's, maybe Harry could provide some subtle positive influence on the boy.

It was the strangest of times to begin such a relationship, but why not while trying to keep the kid's mind off of his foot? "I saw you playing in the street with a remote-controlled tank after Christmas a couple of years ago. Do you know I was a lieutenant colonel in the army?"

"Really?" Lyle said, displaying genuine interest.

"Yup. And might have made colonel too, if not for a mistake late in my career."

"What kind of mistake?"

"I disobeyed a superior's order while in Iraq. There was a family suspected of supplying arms to the bad guys. We got the father and I thought that was the end of it. But they wanted his wife and young son as well. I said no. My superior said yes. I refused to arrest them and was temporarily detained myself, if you can believe that. A lieutenant colonel? They just don't do that unless the situation is very, very bad."

"Was it?" Lyle asked, wide-eyed.

"Yes and no. It was a major operation, don't get me wrong. But I had intelligence suggesting it wasn't a family affair, but rather a partnership among certain men in the village. Wives and children were off-limits as far as I was concerned."

"But they must have had a reason or they wouldn't have been bothering the guy's family."

"That's smart of you, Lyle. And you're partially right. On the one hand, war doesn't necessarily need a reason. But on the other, the guns and ammunition and missiles were in fact going through this guy's house."

"So why did you try to stop them from taking the mother and son?"

Harry looked at him, making sure the boy met his eyes. "Because, Lyle, they were *victims*. Victims of the actions of another. Do you understand me?"

Lyle knitted his brows as he thought about it. Finally, he said, "You're trying to say something about me and my mother, but I'm not getting it. Why would anyone want to blame us for anything?"

Had Harry realized Lyle was such a thoughtful, reasoning boy—his experience with him had never been that deep—he would not have made the analogy. "I'm just saying, Lyle, that victims are victims. Whatever went on in your house, it was about your dad and his problems, nothing else."

Lyle clearly wasn't liking this, as evidenced by the way he'd begun to squirm uncomfortably in his seat. It should have been left there; Harry recognized his own intrusiveness and would have said no more on the matter. Lyle, however, wasn't that dismissive.

"Who ever said anything else? What do you know about it anyway?"

"I apologize, Lyle. I shouldn't have spoken out of turn. But it's true you and your mother live in a secret world and that's no good for—"

"Just leave it alone, okay!"

Harry looked at the road ahead. For there was nothing else to do.

"And don't talk to my mother about any of this."

"I wouldn't do that, Lyle. This is between you and me."

"There's no you and me, all right? I'm sorry I ever mentioned my dad."

"Okay, Lyle. We never spoke."

Harry replayed the conversation as he approached the hospital. By the time he'd pulled into the emergency area, he'd come to the conclusion that, regardless of his experience as a leader and mentor in the service, he would never have made a good dad. You simply didn't brandish invented analogies in order to get close to your pubescent boy. Especially ones that made no sense. What had he been thinking comparing victims of abuse to *suspects* in a military operation? If his purpose had been to confuse the boy to the point of clarity, he'd succeeded admirably.

*   *   *

Ms. Sullivan was a pretty woman, Harry thought as he rose from his seat, watching her hurry down the corridor in her soiled factory clothes. Pretty, but not particularly attractive due to the facial creases that made her look older than her years—whatever her true age was. Subtracting for wear, he guessed she was somewhere in her early to mid thirties. Though who knew with these cases. He wasn't about to pretend to be a specialist on the matter. Not again. He'd made a fool of himself once this afternoon; that was quite enough.

"Why aren't you in there with him?" she said without a hello as she arrived. She was panting, probably having run from the car in her rush to be with her son.

"They're doing surgery on his toe," Harry said, nodding at the door across the hall. "They told me to wait outside. Maybe you can get in, being his mother."

"How bad is it? Did they say?"

"Please sit and catch your breath, Ms. Sullivan. Your face is beet-red. You're even shaking. Sit and I'll fill you in."

She started to protest but then put a hand out as if to calm herself and did as suggested. "Tell me."

Seating himself beside her, Harry said, "The right big toe was nearly completely severed, so they have to repair the bone, the nerves, the whole bit. They assured me he'll keep the toe because we got here so fast. But I've got to tell you, Ms. Sullivan, that boy of yours can be clumsy, and one of these days there's not going to be anyone around."

As soon as he said it, he regretted it. That's how self-conscious he'd become after speaking with Lyle about his father. Lyle's mother, of course, was nowhere near that arena; her focus was only on her son.

"Poor child. He's like that, I know." Then, seeming to guard her words more carefully: "How is it you came to be there anyway?"

"Ms. Sullivan," he said, trying not to sound like he was sighing. "I live across the street. My kitchen window faces your front yard. Thankfully, I happened to be at the right spot at the right time."

She looked at him, quirking her lips a certain way. "Yes. Yes, of course. And thank goodness, as you say. I'm sorry. As you know, I'm not the most outgoing neighbor. Listen, you can call me Billie, okay? This Ms. Sullivan, it's like the bill collectors and that." She almost put her hand over her mouth as she turned away, clearly experiencing her own share of the self-conscious.

Harry placed a hand, hesitantly, upon her knee. When she didn't perceptibly flinch, he said, "Billie it is. I'm Harry, as I think I told you back when I first moved in. Let's just relax, shall we? I'm sure we both feel uncomfortable, but let's get past that for Lyle. Agreed?" He lifted his hand from her knee in a casual handshake offering. It felt weird—it was something he mightn't have done in another circumstance—but she accepted the gesture, if tentatively.

"We think he'll be all right then?" she said.

"He'll be fine, Billie. I can assure you of that. I'm a former military man. I've seen worse out of a day's drills."

He smiled as he said it, and to his mild surprise, she smiled back. "Thank you for taking care of him. And for knowing how to take the worry off a girl."

It was only then that he realized she was still holding his hand. He thought to remove it but decided to leave her that choice lest any false signals were sent. Besides, its warm, slightly damp clutch happened to feel good.

*   *   *

When the doctor finally came out, it was with the best of news.

"Can't say how, Mr. and Mrs. Sullivan, but the cut was clean enough that we were able to put everything back together without a hitch. There's always the possibility of infection, but I think there will be no nerve or other long-term damage and he'll be able to pursue his career as a superstar professional soccer player with no problems."

Her face went slightly pale at the last of it, but she recovered quickly, pretending she'd known it had merely been a playful, doctorly remark. But Harry was watching her. Every sign was a telling one now that she'd let him in a little. Why he should care other than in a neighborly way, he wasn't sure exactly. He'd shared wounds and both warm and damp hands with others. God knew he had in combat. But this wasn't combat. This was small-town Tennessee, where the bonds were made not in blood, but in other, less immediate ways.

"We thank you so much, Doctor," he said. "And for the record, we're just pretending to be married."

"Oh? Oh, sorry, you two. My mistake. We doctors sometimes fail to get the details when we're dealing with urgent cases."

"Harry's joking," Billie said.

Both Harry and the doctor looked at her.

"We were married two years before Lyle was born." She winked at Harry.

The doctor, who by definition didn't care for the flippant stuff unless he himself delivered it, bid them good day and went about his duties.

They peeked in on Lyle, whose wound was being neatly dressed up by a blueshirt. He looked at the two of them, their faces side by side, as if he was looking at two strangers.

And that's where it began, their tenuous and unlikely threesome.

3: Songs of the Pipe

Jason Sully left Prague on a Monday. By Tuesday night he was on the streets again, now in Berlin, where everything operated pretty much as he remembered. Who would know from whom among the heroin addicts on the city's mostly ignored skid row? Drift among them as a fellow member of society's dredges and when the time came, produce your Pied Pipe and seduce your chosen rats out of their misery.

Such was the fantasy he built for himself as he strolled among their lolling ranks like a god, picking *her* because she was the most reduced and vulnerable among them, picking *this one* because she wouldn't put up with the other in a closed room. It was getting easier with each visa stamp, and he'd no plan to relent as long as his subjects kept bowing to his money and licking the street off the soles of his feet. He'd wondered, after wandering around Mexico and South America for a few years, how his game would fare in his old stomping grounds of western Europe. Paris, his cosmopolitan starting point on the continent, had not disappointed. When, without a hitch, Paris had turned to Rome had turned to Barcelona had turned to Vienna had turned to Prague, he felt almost guaranteed the immunity that came with anonymity and mobility. Berlin wasn't special. He might have conquered all the friendly cities of Europe on a single Schengen visa. But that wouldn't have been his style even if he hadn't had the luxury of his American passport and its 30-day per country flexibility. Even at the risk of leaving a stamp trail, he preferred entering each and every country by its airport so that he knew exactly how much time he had to work with before he had to move on. When and if he caught wind of authorities closing in on him, he'd think about more subtle border crossings.

He took his limp bodies back to his hotel in a cab, promising the driver immortality for his silent efforts. At the back door, through which one could only gain entry by a room key, he met another guest coming out. When the guest could only marvel at his obvious prowess with the fairer sex, he left the young man to die another day, proceeding by elevator to his fifth-story suite in the otherwise ordinary house of permitted sin.

Placing his friends in comfortable spots among the suite's various sofas, he conjured up the scent of crack to remind them of their full range of devotions. He'd gotten the pipe and rock from a gentleman in an absurd white suit with matching shoes who might have been a pimp of one of the girls, might have been her overseeing angel. Jason had taken a moment to contemplate which description better applied before piercing the creature through the throat with an awl a corner hardware store had been gracious enough to provide. Indeed, he'd almost mourned his servant as he'd gently let him down in a pool of liquefied heart that no one would miss until it was found, and likely not even then. Rarely did he experience such spontaneous impulses, but the cat had been so repulsively *obvious* in his living contradiction, he'd had no choice.

He sucked on the crack pipe, holding the vapor in for a moment before blowing it out over the general company. The nose of the nearest girl twitched before she came awake to this dirty little trigger, mumbling, "*Was ist los? Hat mir jemand vergessen?*"

"We haven't forgotten you, sweetheart," Harry said, stepping around the end of a glass coffee table to stand over her. "Just letting you dream, that's all."

"English?" Her pupils adapted to the room's light, their instruments focusing in on the pipe. "I speak a little English…"

"Good for you!" Jason cried happily. "We like when we get effort like that. Would you like a taste?"

"*Gott, ja.*"

"I thought we were speaking English," he said—not as pleasantly.

"Yes…yes of course. Where are you from, friend?"

"America, naturally. I've brought some kisses from home for you if you'd like. Are you game?"

"*Ja.*" As she reached for the pipe.

"No, no," he said, pulling it away. "After, I mean."

"Sure. I mean *natürlich*."

"Just what do you mean?"

"I'm a little foggy."

"What's your name, child?"

"Rox."

"No way," he said, tartly puckering his lips.

"Really! It's not a street name. If you don't believe me, just ask Ing—Is that you, Inga?"

She was looking beyond Jason's shoulder—and not far beyond, Jason realized. Without turning, he immediately dropped to a crouch, swinging a leg around to intercept the object of her gaze. The other girl, having apparently awoken to his games before sneaking up on him, crashed through the glass-top coffee table, the weapon she'd picked up falling harmlessly aside. Deliberately lighting and sucking again from the instrument he'd never let go of, Harry regarded the one, then the other, then the translucent glass lamp that the one had intended to use against him.

To the fallen girl, he said. "You're bleeding. It didn't have to be like that, you know. But since it is, why don't you pick up your weapon, or better yet, one of the shards surrounding you, and hold it up to the light."

"What are you going to do?" she half-whimpered, half-challenged.

"It's not what *I* am going to do. It's what you are going to do."

"Fuck you," she spat.

"I've enough smack to keep you going for a month. Do you really want to play super-ego?"

"What the fuck are you talking about?"

"Break the lamp."

"*Was?*"

"Just break it. There on the floor."

"*Wofür? Warum?*"

"Here, let me make it more clear." He pulled a bag out of his pocket, dangling it in the air. "Do what I command—"

"What you *command?*"

"Very well, do what I ask and it shall be given unto you."

"What do you ask?"

"Kill this bitch. She spoils the high." Jason glanced at the sofa.

The bitch in question immediately propped up. "Are you talking about *me?* Inga, no. You can't be listening to him."

"Inga?" said the other. "You're out of you mind, bitch."

"Which is what I'm trying to get at," Jason said.

The bleeding girl broke the lamp against the floor. "Is this what you want?" she hissed, holding the broken vessel up for inspection.

"Exactly that," Jason said, winking at her.

"Give me a taste first."

"A taste?" he said, teetering between expressions.

"A fucking taste. Isn't that fair?"

"If it's a taste you want, then it's a taste you shall have." As he stepped over the debris of glass and kicked her full in the face before producing the awl and driving it through her presumptuous eye.

The other girl, lost between past and future highs, offered herself to him in reverence, but it was already too late. She could be of no use to him now. "Go," he told her, realizing but not caring what he was doing. "Go and tell your Ingas and your pimps and your street police and all of your sort all around: I'm here. I'm staged. The whole complex is going to come down, cinder block by shattering cinder block if need be. Go. Get thee hence, Satan."

Though she didn't comprehend his words, she did know the sound of escape when it came to her.

He watched her go out the door, then at the last minute thought twice about it, chasing her down and dragging her back into the apartment. Mornings were not to be sold off like this after the effort brought to them. If nothing else, she could help in disposing of the other body. How much flesh could she consume, he wondered, in a day's time?

4: At the Risk of Damnation

The morning after Lyle's admission and release from the hospital, Harry Hinterlove found himself actually sitting in Billie Sullivan's kitchen drinking coffee with her. He'd been somewhat stunned by her invitation when he brought the two of them home yesterday evening, and he was equally surprised now, with the cloudless October day spilling its light over the table through the amazingly *open* blinds. Had he woken her from her nightmares? Dare he let his imagination run like that, knowing that her weekly day off only happened to coincide with the morning after the event?

"You're not wearing a ring, Harry. Is that because…"

Strange detour. But he wouldn't shy from it—not since she'd begun to show him similar courtesy, if in small bites. "She's gone now," he said. "We were quite the item once. I took her to all the balls, I fed her to all my superiors and anyone else who might care or matter. But like the users we both were, she used herself right out of my life."

"What do you mean?" Billie said over her coffee.

He thought about it a moment. "I think she wanted to climb to the highest rung and I wasn't quite getting her there. Don't get me wrong. I didn't necessarily mind her ambition. She certainly wasn't hurting my cause, as beautiful and charismatic as she was. But I think, in the end, her will was stronger."

"I'm not sure I'm getting you. You were also trying to climb the ladder?"

"Only as much as anybody in that position would. What I mean is that I wanted to keep up the appearance of a parallel path. To that end I worked pretty hard, though at some point I found myself supporting *her* at all the functions, rather than the other way around. In the end I couldn't keep up. I wasn't as devoted to it as she was. There's a lot of politics in climbing that particular ladder. You might get there by your military record, but more often you got there by networking, politicking, kissing a lot of ass, if you'll forgive the expression. I just didn't have it in me after several tours in the field, a few of them brutal. I remember sitting with a drink at one of these events watching her work, and it dawning on me that this was not what my mother and father, may they rest in peace, would have expected of me."

She'd started nodding somewhere in the middle of it, and now did so emphatically. "Yes. You have it right. If you can't take any kind of earthy pride in it…if it can't face the scrutiny of your deceased parents, then it can't be right."

Harry stared at her, marveling. Where had this bit come from? In its way, it was poetry. Which he'd never have imagined of her, limited though his experience of Billie Sullivan was.

"If they're the best kind of parents, of course," he smiled, not bothering to explain that his hadn't been deceased at the time. "I get that yours, too, were special?"

"Mine were just…perfect. They knew the outcome of every mistake I ever made. Especially the…" She hesitated, clinging to her cup.

"It's okay. I understand the—"

"The last one."

"I beg your pardon?"

"The last mistake I made. They pleaded with me not to do it. My father even offered me money, if you can believe that, to get away from him while I had the chance."

"Him?"

"Jay-Jay. Lyle's father. I wanted the money, don't get me wrong. Thirty thousand dollars can go a long way toward raising a child. But I was hopelessly in love. I'd known him as far back as girlhood when I'd been a cheerleader for the youth soccer squad he starred on."

"So you were pregnant at the time of the offer."

Suddenly teary, she excused herself to get a tissue. Returning a few moments later, she seemed better equipped to meet the task that she had remarkably placed on herself. Still, she hovered over her chair, grasping the back of it, rather than sitting. "I don't know why I'm talking to you, Harry. I know this can't be what you expected out of a coffee—"

"Tell me," Harry said.

"Yes," she said, blowing her nose in the tissue she'd brought with her. "Yes, I'm going to do that. But Harry…I'm not looking for sympathy or anything."

"Tell me."

She took a deep breath, seemed to teeter between breaking down and sucking it all up like the strong woman that had gotten her this far. With another, more deliberate inhalation, she regained control of herself. "Jay-Jay turned out to be not just a deadbeat, but a literal monster."

"How so, Billie? Sit down and talk to me, okay? It's all right. There's no need to feel uncomfortable with me."

"It's not that," she said as she did as invited. "It's the subject matter." She looked at Harry through blood-stained, virtually wrecked eyes. "I won't tell you all, okay?"

"Yes, of course. I understand. Tell me what you can."

She nodded, still trying to keep herself composed. When she'd summoned up the strength, she said, "If ever there's been a freak in this world, Harry, it's him."

"Go on," Harry said gently.

"It's not just what went on inside the house. It's what he was doing outside. I remember watching the news when the rash of slayings in Chattanooga and surrounding areas was the main topic. They named the killer the Psycho Disciple for the notes he was leaving on his victims. Comments relating to Freud and... who's the other one? Jung? One paper called him the Super-Id for this pseudo-philosophy he was trying to espouse. I knew then, when they were talking about the primal instincts overtaking all other urges, that it was my husband they were looking for. It was his hobby, you see. Abnormal psychology, as he often liked to brag to our friends when we were all drunk, was the only meaningful class he ever took in his three semesters of college. He'd quit Vanderbilt, he said, because they spun you this way and that without spinning you where they should have been spinning you all along—toward the naked truth. According to him, there were some classes that were worthwhile, but until you were able to freely pursue things that curricula like philosophy and psychology and even criminology were hinting at, what point wasting your money attending lectures. Experimenting on your own, he told me, was the only reasonable way.

"I accepted his line of crap, I suppose, because I'd been attending similar classes at his encouragement. Together, we were going to shake the foundations of something, but I was never quite sure what. We'd get high at night and he'd babble about the importance of putting ideas into practice and eventually I became so lost, I just let him ramble. I turned my full focus on our baby while he did whatever he did. Which in the end, as I've said, turned out to be terrible things."

Harry observed her. "And did you go to the police?"

"With what? Speculation? Gut feelings? At first it seemed to me I would only be making a fool of myself, trying to describe something that I didn't even comprehend. Later though, when things got closer to home, I did go to them. They heard me, they wrote down their notes, but I don't think they ever *listened* to me as I tried to resolve into words a husband's incoherent fantasies. During the next week I waited for a return phone call, anything, but do you know what I eventually got for my efforts? This after the story of yet another slaying broke? What I got was a restraining order issued at the request of a husband who claimed, rightly so, to have been struck in the head by his overwrought, if not mad wife. I was guilty, there was no hiding from it. I'd been baited into it by him and was now at the mercy of the same system that continued to allow him to prey. I know it sounds fantastic, but that's exactly the way it was. Jay-Jay is a genius in a way. And he'll have it his way or bust. What's scariest about him is not that he'd use his own family to polish up his identity, but that he treats the whole world as his personal mirror and relishes what he finds looking back. He'd call it Nietzsche or some such garbage. I know it's a god complex. Okay, I won't pretend to know the full meaning of the term, but that's what I'm certain it is. This is why we're Sullivan and he's Sully. We had to change our name to rid ourselves of him."

There was so much to think about in her words, and yet Harry couldn't help returning to the core—to the people he was beginning to know. "You're omitting what happened at home," he said. "Is that by intention?"

She frowned. "That's not as easily explainable."

"Try me…I mean if you want to."

She sighed. "It's just that it's not the kind of abuse you might expect."

"It was psychological, you mean?"

"Yes, there was always that. The elevating himself by diminishing us. Or at least me. With Lyle, though, it went much, much deeper. Unknown to me until not long before he was gone, he'd have him act out scenarios and situations with him that mirrored the scenarios and situations I now realize he put his victims through. It was a game, he told Lyle. They were playing out a mystery, a crime, like on TV. Later, the game became serious business as they were doing Dad's secret work for the government, which was to understand the behavior of people who followed rather than resisted their urges. He'd have Lyle…"

She paused, eyes tearing up again. "I need a glass of water."

"If you don't want to tell me, don't," Harry said as she rose and fetched a glass. "I'm getting the picture."

"Are you?" she said as she filled the glass from the tap. "I doubt it."

Harry didn't know what to say so remained silent. He wanted to know, but then he really, really didn't, for everyone's sake.

"Can you handle it, Harry?" she said, startling him with the question as she leaned back against the counter by the sink, looking at him through her bloody eyes.

"I can handle anything, but—"

"When he made Lyle play out his part, he sometimes simulated, sometimes performed the sex acts involved. Thank god he never completely committed his son to the dying part, though I'm now quite sure he routinely performed the act of drawing the knife across the throat or whatever other method he used."

Harry was now, it was safe to say, pretty close to shock. There was a reason, former military man or not, you stayed away from the neighbors that stayed away from you. While he'd so wanted to know what troubled their family, so wanted to contribute in some way to their healing, whatever the wound was, he'd never have imagined a history like this. As caring a man as he liked to think himself, the knowledge of what went on in this house made him want to run, and as far away as possible. Indeed this victim, herself, frightened him. What had made her disclose such things to him, curious as he'd been to know? As he continued to stare speechlessly at her, he couldn't ignore her bloody eyes. Weren't they more than what they should be? Wasn't her suffering too psychosomatic for her own good? Christ, she might have been the Man Himself upon the cross.

Maybe realizing her error, maybe reveling in it, she said, "I've had no one to talk to, Harry."

He clung to himself lest he get away, "No," he swallowed. "No, I suspect you haven't."

"You're afraid of me now, aren't you?" she said quietly.

"No. *No*, Billie. Of course not."

She flung her glass at him. It barely missed his head, shattering against some surface behind him. "Get out!" she screamed. "Get the fuck out of my house, you liar!"

He did, and in a hurry. If they were damned, he wanted away from it. If not, he'd regroup and deal with the situation later.

At the risk of his own damnation.

*   *   *

When the knock came at the door of his hotel room in Amsterdam, Jason Sully knew they'd caught up with him. If he'd been sloppy in Berlin, he'd been downright stupid in the City of Freedom. He'd of course not called it that way. Berlin had at least taught him not to leave a witness who'd seen a man of his exact description entering the hotel they shared carrying two incapacitated women.

If anything, Jason would have thought Amsterdam more lax. Sure, he'd gotten bolder with his kills after the angel in the white suit he'd left in a pool of blood on a decrepit Berlin street. But this was the City of Freedom after all. You slipped the deserving their due and dropped them into the canal and that was that. Or should have been anyway.

"Who is it?"

"Room service, sir."

"I didn't ask for room service," he replied as he measured in his mind how far a fall it was to the street.

"Open the door now, Mr. Krank. We have a search warrant."

Yup, he knew these people. They were the sort of people who fell for the false identity one Europhile had dug up at the last, requesting the name of that character from the French steampunk film, *City of Lost Children*. We don't make up names, the Russian had told him. We use previous identities. Or do you want to be caught?

"Well, find me another Krank. There must be some."

They hadn't, and maybe he wasn't actually hearing the name, but projecting it. Hard to say, high as he was. He tried to remember when the chemicals had quit being the servant to him in favor of assuming this stronger role, but he couldn't come up with the exact hour or date.

"Open up, Mr. X."

Mr. X. Now it was all feeling better. How far, again, to the street? He checked one window, found it unappetizing. Checked the other, and to his surprise, discovered that the building's wall on that side served as the canal's bank. Without hesitation he opened it and leapt out, feet first, hoping he found a friendly place among the gondolas.

When he realized he had, he immediately refocused his attention on home. He'd get back to Europe one day when things had settled. Home didn't really have that bad a taste when he thought about it in context. Sure, he'd failed to realize all their goals. But he'd achieved enough for now, he thought, to satisfy his family.

5: Like a Cat, Offering Its Offering

Harry happened to be standing at his window again that afternoon when the change in the flow occurred. He was washing dishes and not paying much attention to what went on outside when the taxi pulled up in the circle, its loud color drawing attention to the fact as it deposited its passenger on the scene. While he'd never seen the man who stepped out, Harry knew immediately this was the source of the trouble that now plagued them all, the people at the end of the street.

He wanted to approach the beast, to take his father's old Ithaca shotgun, or better yet, the assault rifle, and confront the trespasser. But something prevented him from doing so. Amends had not been made between him and his neighbors. Starting now might cause the ground itself to shake as the devil came up to swallow them all. So he elected instead to watch the stranger, who held a limp something in his hand as he approached the front door. Don't answer, Harry sent to Lyle. Not while your mother's at work. Don't do it—

But the boy was opening the door now and running freely, with all the abandon of a soul that had never encountered discouragement, into his father's arms. Together—father and son holding each other like life itself—they disappeared into the spaces of the Sullivan home.

"We're Sullivan. He's Sully!" he remembered Billie screaming at him through the window she'd flung open as he rushed across the street to the safety of his own residence.

God, that it were only like that, he thought.

Harry weighed his options for only a moment, and then, exiting the house by the open garage door, crossed the street in a hurried crouch, which must have looked the parody to any onlooker, considering the day had not yet begun to die. Approaching at a wide arc, he made the side of his neighbor's house his immediate aim, planting himself momentarily against the brick wall before easing his way, in a more credible crouch, back to the front where he could peek through the kitchen window. As he did, he just caught the back of the homecomer, that limp, still unidentifiable something held hidden behind him as he followed his son through a doorway into what Harry knew to be the living room.

Retracing his steps, Harry found the window that best afforded him a view of the living room's interiors. Lyle was sitting down at his father's direction, face expressing an eagerness to see what his father had brought him. After a couple of apparent teases, Jay-Jay produced the thing he concealed from his son. Up to now, it had been a loose, leathery thing to Harry's senses. That didn't change now as the father dropped it on the nearest surface, like a cat offering the catch of a mouse to its masters. Indeed, there was a fleshiness about the saggy bundle, skinny as it was, that made the comparison not too far-fetched. But it wasn't until the boy lifted it up, now taking it in both hands and stretching it with his widening fingers, that Harry realized just how close to target he'd been, in various senses.

The thing splayed on the boy's fingers was a human face, with holes where the eye sockets should have—or potentially once *had*—been. For there was no denying the thing's *quality*, its sensual power. No mask Harry had ever seen conveyed what this particular sack of material did, especially when taken in context with the boy's expression.

But these were Harry's senses responding. Intellectually, he had to check himself. Without words to support it, Lyle's bewondered look was incomplete. Harry couldn't *know* for a certainty that what he was looking at from his distance wasn't an awfully realistic mask until he could hear the interplay going on the room. So he chanced, with all its risks, testing the security of the window. To his simultaneous satisfaction and terror, he felt the unlocked frame respond to the gentle force of his pull. He let the window up very slowly but very deliberately, leaning close with his best ear.

"But how did you get it through customs?" Lyle was asking.

"You'd be surprised at the organic food stuff they'll let through if you put forth the appearance of being honest about it. They could have brought in dogs and they'd have gotten nowhere."

"Where'd you get it? Amsterdam? It seems so…fresh."

"No, no. It has to have time to absorb the salt, to dry out, season in the sunlight. This was the first European one, in Paris. She was no older than you, son. Little mouse of a working girl. I was doing the degradation on her when I thought no, this face must absolutely be preserved. What's with all the damn questions anyway? Accept it for what it is, boy—a gift to you."

"It's exciting," Harry heard the boy say before he sank into a puddle along the wall, fresh out of shock, fresh out of faith in the whole human charade.

He would stay like that, slumped against the wall remembering other horrors from other times and more remote parts of the world. Whether sleep came before or after one dead human mask had turned into another that he'd profaned back when he was a captain on his first tour in the desert, he could not know.

* * *

A light in his eyes woke him from his nightmares. His lids fluttered against it as the force at the other end of the optic nerve eventually resolved the source into a cell phone's flashlight.

"You're here why?" its owner demanded.

"Billie. Maybe you know…it's your husband…he's back."

"*What?*" She struck his shoulder. "What are you saying?"

"I was only looking after Lyle. God, what kind of people are you?"

She struck him again, this time in the face. "I find you slumped by my living room window, sleeping or unconscious or god knows what, and you're asking me what kind of people *we* are?"

"What?" He looked around him. "How did I…I swear, Billie—"

"Shh. Quiet okay? We can't talk about it here."

"But he's got Lyle."

"He's always had Lyle," she whispered. "Now shut up and let's get to your house."

"But—"

"But nothing!" she hissed. "Former military man? Better get yourself back in the fucking game. And quick. Together, they'll wipe you out without a second thought. It's just like that. Mark my words."

"Okay," he said feebly. "Lead on."

They crossed the street silently, entering by the way he'd exited his home— the garage. At her prompting he took her into the deeper interiors of the dark house where they could not be seen by a snooper of his brazen kind. He motioned for her to sit on the sofa in the den, then returned to the kitchen where the control for the garage door was. Engaging it, he ticked off the seconds in his mind until he heard the motor quit. He then locked the interior door to the garage, doubling its security with the chain, and returned to the den, where she'd turned on a lamp by the sofa. She was watching him, the light of the lamp igniting her eyes.

"What in the hell is going on?" he said. "Wait. Let me get us a drink first."

"That would be nice," she replied as he went to a makeshift bar between two bookcases, where he kept ice, liquor, and glasses, though he rarely entertained anyone but himself.

"This is your study?" she said as he returned with the Crown on rocks.

"It's like that, yeah," Harry said as he placed the drinks on a coffee table and seated himself in an adjacent armchair. "But the term always seemed presumptuous to me when my ex flaunted it. So I go with my parents' description that the den is for privacy or friends while the living room is for formal company. This is the den. I read here. I watch TV here. This is my main space."

"Yes," she smiled. "I do the same. I wonder, is it a southern thing? Can't say I ever thought about it until now."

"Billie, please. What's going on?"

She sipped her whisky, grimacing slightly as it went down. "I feel like I'm always explaining something about my life to you, and yet, who are you exactly? It is against every safeguard I've established talking to strangers who would pry into my business."

"You know it's not like that."

"I do?"

"Yes."

She sighed. "You're dealing with something you want no part of. It's a dangerous, dangerous game, Harry. I can't stress this enough. You come snooping around my house when Jay-Jay's back and you're asking to die. It's that simple."

"But it's Lyle I'm concerned about. I was watching from my kitchen window when the cab pulled up, and I saw him literally leap into his father's arms. This contradicts everything you told me."

She stared at Harry a moment, then shook her head. "You don't understand. What I told you is how I *must* see it. Lyle's the victim. He's a boy. He's susceptible. He's under his father's spell."

Harry partook of his own drink now. "Look. I went to your house to sneak a peek through the window to make sure he was okay. Know what I witnessed? Your Jay-Jay giving him a gift he brought back from Paris."

"He's not *my* Jay-Jay. Choose your words better."

"Fine. But I'm telling you, what he brought for Lyle wasn't some tame something like a trinket from the airport. It was a *human face*. He talked about it. About where it had come from, and how he'd dried it out in the sun."

She'd stiffened, almost seized up at the words "human face," as anyone in their sane mind would have. But it was the reaction that followed the reaction that impressed Harry. For it was almost with resignation that she said, "Yes. Yes, that would follow form."

"Follow *form*? He's a psychotic killer dragging around trophies of his exploits and Lyle's at the fucking bad end of it, Billie! I feel more for him than the owner of the face, for god's sake. At least she's dead."

"She?"

Harry was startled slightly by her focusing on this technicality, but proceeded without pause. "Yeah, *she*. I believe his exact words were, 'She was no older than you, son. Little mouse of a working girl.'"

"What else?" Billie asked, her eyes in the light of the lamp assuming the bloodshot, diabolic hue that he'd encountered on their last sit-down.

"What *else*? Let's see…oh yes, how about him telling your son that while he was doing the …let me remember the word…*degradation* on the girl, he decided hers was a face that absolutely must be preserved."

Billie closed her eyes. Slow, protracted moments passed. Finally, eyes still closed, she said, "Then he's brought the rituals back. It's when the experiments turned ritualistic that things got so much worse. It's going to all start again. Unless…" She suddenly opened strangely clear eyes. "Unless he's shown up again to end it in one night."

"Would he harm Lyle in the process?"

"You mean more than he already has? Oh, yes. It's always been only a matter of time before his son's usefulness, like his wife's, wears out."

"We have to stop him," Harry said. "We must get Lyle out of the house."

"How do you presume to do that?"

"Well, there's the police for one."

"The police? You must be joking, right? *Bah*."

As Harry drank again, considering the situation, he experienced a feeling he hadn't known since combat. It was a part of him that perhaps he didn't like, but it was a part of him that put the victims, at all costs, first. "Then we'll do it ourselves."

If the words gave him courage, that courage was as quickly taken away by the sudden laughter with which she responded to his proposition. "Harry, forgive me, but when I say you *don't know what you're dealing with*, I mean you really don't know what you're dealing with. He will cut ribbons out of your flesh and strangle you with them if only to prove to his son what the both of them are capable of. Moreover, this is a thing that very possibly…are you ready for this, Harry?"

"Ready for what? What could be worse than this psychopath you describe?"

She smirked. Not snidely, but rather with a certain sad resolve. "Go on thinking like that, Harry, at your own peril. To finish my statement: this is a thing that very possibly transcends not only human measures of decency and justice, but the human realm itself."

Harry's mouth dropped. "*What?*"

"I know that's shocking. But morality simply doesn't come into play when you're playing outside the mortal…structure."

"What in the fuck are you trying to say, Billie?"

"I'm saying that Jay-Jay—and I don't mean to be simplistic or base—has friends you can't possibly prepare for."

"What friends, Billie? Demons? Ghouls from beyond the grave?"

"Something on that order, yes."

"Bull. Fucking. Shit."

She was silent.

"He's a freak like all the rest of them we have to deal with in this world."

She nodded. "That's true. There's no denying he's a freak. Or that he must be dealt with. But I assure you he's not like the rest of them. I can't explain the whys or the whats, but his DNA isn't configured like yours."

"And that makes him some—"

"I didn't say it made *him* anything. I simply said he had friends. He has his weaknesses like all the rest of us. But when it comes to his work—that's a different matter. Entities greater than him or his imagination are involved. It's fantastic, I realize. But it's what my experience has led me to conclude."

"And you haven't stopped to consider that you yourself might be insane?"

"I have and I'm not. Quit deferring. He will feed you your own soul while you're not looking. He serves these others, and they in turn serve him. "

"To what purpose do they serve him?" Harry demanded.

"Gaining access."

"To what exactly?"

"To humanity. Mortality. What else? I used to think, why would our religion-based monsters want in? Just for physical sensation? Is physical sensation that great a thing? So you have a body and you have sex and you kill to spill blood over your eager face? So what? Can't you do that vicariously? No, I think it's the affront to God they're after. In my life I've believed in God about as much as you believe in the Easter Bunny or the Tooth Fairy. But what other explanation? There must be something out there, some kind of quirk in the balance that compels or enthralls those who are not creatures of flesh. It's as though they want to feel the slaughter from every imaginable angle. Pig victim. Man slaughterer. Man victim. Pig slaughterer. Looking for anything that might wake up an uncaring God-Universe."

She paused to finish her drink in a single gulp. "I tell you, Harry. You can't hope to stop a career and heartbeat at the end of a cul-de-sac. They're always there, just in different forms. Maybe it's in the ones you let live. Maybe it's in the ones you let die. But the present moment? It's always Judgment Day, whatever your noble intentions. I know, believe me. I'm a mother."

It was several moments before Harry spoke. When he did, he did so carefully, sensitive to the barely comprehensible delusion she attempted to impose on him. "We can go back over there tonight or we can wait until tomorrow. We can do it together or I'll do it alone. I've a few weapons at my disposal either way. Understand me, Billie, in the army I've done multiple combat tours in some pretty unforgiving places. I should have died at least three times in the past. What's this current situation to me when it comes to saving a boy? *Your* boy, Billie."

She sighed. "You've been warned, okay?"

"Duly noted."

"These weapons?"

"Oh, there's no shortage of them. Can you handle a semi-automatic rifle?"

"Dynamite might make me feel a little better."

"Fresh out, sorry," he said. "But what about these rituals? Were you ever by chance a participant? Wouldn't happen to have any spells of your own at your disposal, would you?"

He regretted saying it as soon as it came out. Levity in the face of such grim circumstances was less than in poor taste.

It didn't seem to bother Billie, who replied, "Might at that," as her eyes flashed red again before being sucked away by the broader darkness.

6: Kisses That Last, While They Do

He liked the programs, the shows. News was number one for him, but he also liked the cable TV presentations of the world in a state of alert—never mind the cause. They fed his ambition of being a significant source of real-time emergency conditions while at the same time alerted him, via the people who wrote such rubbish, of the failures of the stupid human mind. They passed off their aliens and their comets because such things appealed to the average imagination, but they never seemed to get the human culprit right. When, pray, had the home-bred deliverers of mayhem ceased being what they were in favor of some stylized puzzle? Did chaos know algorithms? Did blood know from the vein it ran through and the ground upon which it was spilt? Oh, there was an internal logic all right, but it could not be expressed by any medium other than itself.

Still, there was a reason for watching, as Jason did now while Lyle slept on the couch beside him, legs across his lap. Watching fictionalized realizations of the Super-Id at work bridged a gap that otherwise separated him infinitely from other men. He found hope in such expressions, be they artistic or exploitative. He found a light burning in some small corner of the human imagination. A season or two and his fellow species members, particularly this expressive set, might come to (be) something worthwhile. Using himself as a model, they might find themselves deriving pleasure from breaking down the various human structures, not least morality. Might in fact find themselves reliving moments they were prone to forget during the intervals, having buried them deeply enough that a specialist or officer of the law, for instance, couldn't conjure them up, no matter how many sessions the subject was put through. In the end they could never be what Jason was—no one save God Himself could accomplish that feat—but they could certainly transcend their norms and begin to believe, at last, in the apocalypse they dashed across their screens.

He looked forward to that day as Lyle stirred beside him.

"Dad?"

"I'm here, son."

"What are you doing?" Lyle murmured, having only momentarily awakened as he shifted to a more comfortable position.

"Just thinking of your mother. Say she might be doing a double shift tonight?"

When Lyle said nothing, Jason wished him safe dreams for the short time that remained before the appropriate hour, and clicked off the TV. Placing the face he'd brought home for his son over his own, he closed his eyes and slipped back into those memories that only the choicest moments could bring.

*   *   *

Billie had seemed so small when he'd brought her into it. A nothing of a thing to them, the ones he would summon into his world. On the drugs, she lacked even more vitality than she did when carrying along with her miserable life through her normal routines. She was unworthy of them as surely as she was unworthy of him, or even herself. Indeed she'd nothing to offer anyone other than her weaknesses, in which the others seemed to find some strange and disproportionate value, considering their own powers. At the time, Jason was still a baby at the game. While his intellect was far beyond his years, his imagination had yet to catch up to the program. Billie was a lamb to him, to be offered in that particular service. While he understood she was a tool toward both his and their rewards, he could not clearly see how she might be used by them other than as a slave in some masturbatory way on their part. That she could be a gateway might have crossed his mind, but he was still coming to terms with the basic interconnectivity of the universe's elements at that time.

Not that he would have hesitated to offer her up even knowing the true circumstances. She'd been nothing to him since she decided to resist him. Any reward , at the hands of his guests, was a reasonable one in the aftermath of that day when she'd said no to him while in the process of feeding their suckling babe. That she'd been willing to forcefully do so while being aware of potential consequences said something to her character, perhaps, but not to her worth to Jason, who by now regarded character, like dignity and nobility, as a purely human invention and not worth the milk produced for it. She'd sealed her fate on that day. It was only the fate that remained in question when he presented her as the sacrifice to the beings that existed outside the polluted mortal realm.

The way she'd flung about during the thing had reminded him of the exorcisms that the TV had brought to the conscious mind. As far as he could tell from his extensive readings, not even the grandfathers of the Great Psychic Dance had allowed for that kind of dramatic reaction to external stimuli—even in the most psychotic episodes. The church, in all its various interpretations and incarnations, was the only thing that could theoretically touch the matter. And even that line of thinking failed in the end, as she succumbed where the cross-beaten, holy-water-doused victims of the good versus evil cases seemed to always magically, miraculously prevail.

Within a few hours of the sacrifice being made, Billie Sully was not Billie Sully anymore.

That the entity came to live within its human self in the most benignly human way was the only miraculous part about it, in that it left her in a state that her fellow spirits could do little more than rage against for its defilement of their goals. While it was a circumstance no party involved could have seen coming, Jason managed to find a certain amusement in it. Being the resourceful and resilient student of chaos that he was, he was able to look past the setback in favor of appreciating the irony and contradiction in it. Not that he didn't equally despise what he'd made out of the mud as he waged his war in the name of man's primeval nature. Reconciling the matter with himself boiled down to a single, perfect example in which he'd kissed her as he brought her to them, then been kissed by her after it was finished. That was delicious.

One day, he might even consider offering himself if they'd leave sufficient residue of his own identity to prevent this disgusting humaneness from happening again.

*　　*　　*

Billie Sullivan, once Billie Sully, crossed the street with an assault rifle in her hands. Harry Hinterlove, with a shotgun in his own, followed behind. There was no skipping from hiding place to hiding place as they did in the movies. The streetlamps precluded that. Instead, they made their way with a raw determination that both of them were accustomed to. Billie, for her part, had promised as they left the house to deliver upon Jason what he had delivered upon humankind. While Harry wasn't sure about his race in general, he was in agreement with the sentiment. And locked in now. The worst that could come of it, as was always the case, was defeat. But he'd damn sure make himself known in the process.

"Back door," she said before he could even phrase the question. "It has a single lock, which might not even *be* locked."

"But you have the key?"

"I do."

"Are you scared?"

"A little. But not how you think."

"How do I think?"

209

"Like a military man. A tactician. I have other concerns."

"Your son. I know." They were moving across the lawn now toward the rear of the house.

"Not like that. That goes without saying."

"Then?"

"This can't be accomplished like you think. Neither Jay-Jay nor myself are what you think we are."

"It's, what, a battle between light and darkness fought on the most available plane? Please, Billie."

"Shut up and be ready. He'll not sleep through it, I promise you."

Harry did. And with the sudden feeling that this was indeed a thing outside his grasp, and that his motions, resultantly, were of no consequence to the end result. As they came around to the rear door, she waved him back, and he obeyed. An outer screen door stood before the real thing, Harry imagining it screeching on its springs as she opened it. To his relief, it barely squeaked in her patient, delicate handling of it. She motioned that he hold it back for her before she tried the knob of the main door. He did, and the knob easily turned in her grasp.

So far, so good, he thought as he followed her into the dark room.

"Touch nothing," she whispered. "Let your eyes adjust and tell me when you're ready to proceed."

"I'm ready now."

"Keep the shotgun up at all times."

"Jesus, Billie, I made a career of this, remember?"

"*Silence*," she hissed. "*Be ready.*"

On those words a shadow fell across the spaces they moved through. It might have been nothing to Harry but for his honed-by-practice senses. Even as Billie ducked, so did he, dodging a wave of blackness so utter it might have consumed them where they'd stood.

"Billie Bee," said the voice of the presumable deliverer. "Is that you creeping about my house?"

She kept silent, and Harry followed suit, hugging the shadows of the wall along which he'd dropped. *Don't want no trouble*, he thought crazily, knowing he'd entered a realm in which he was not welcome, much less belonged. Clinging to the shotgun, he waited for her to make the next move, whatever it was. When she did, it wasn't as he'd have expected. Indeed, far from it as the hissing incoherency of words issued from her. The blackness at first seemed to recede from her assault, only to regather into an even more intense pulse, which this time literally passed through Harry's body, bringing images that he'd thought successfully lost after the years that had passed since his confrontation with a whole other, but no less determined enemy.

One series of frames bred another until the flashbacks came in on him in a barrage. His mind fragmented beneath the onslaught, shattered into as many pieces as were being remembered to him. But the chaos—as he grabbed at his head, his heart, anything that might hold the answer—as suddenly resolved itself into a single, burning focus. *These people*, he could hear himself shouting, *cannot be held accountable for the actions of the head of the household.*

"You put your *body* in front of theirs, officer? You risk even *that* for these slugs?"

"It has to end somewhere! *For god's sake.*"

"It ends somewhere all right. It ends right here and now. Remove yourself or be removed."

"Fuck you, major. You are subordinate to me and you will obey my goddamn command."

"While I have the colonel on the line with direct orders? I think not."

"Then do what you have to do. You know as well as I do what the intelligence said. I'll not let you take them."

"You'll be pushed out for this."

"With retirement? Good goddamn riddance of this senseless fucking war."

At that moment the woman that Lieutenant Colonel Hinterlove was protecting, the mother and wife of this clan within the clan charged past him, crying *Allahu Akbar!* as she lit up the area with a bomb tucked up in folds the naked eye nor any other polite inspection could have penetrated.

His second officer and the soldiers in the immediate vicinity dissolved as the blast, shocking Harry back to the present, blew out the surrounding windows of the house where he was now, in real time. *This* moment, the moment occurring in the here and now, could be controlled if he but followed through with his mission rather than let circumstances pass him along from hand to hand through a process in which he was a lost servant. By whatever magic or method, Billie, he sensed, had opened the doorway, and he was free to move through it now, at least temporarily, without resistance.

He'd no idea where she was as he pushed through the darkness into the deeper interiors of the house without regard for anything that didn't directly pertain to the boy or the danger the boy was in by virtue of being his father's son. There was a strange, blood-like light now permeating the house. And maybe that's what Billie had meant when she'd indicated she might indeed have her own spell in her quiver. As Harry passed through the glow, it was as though the burst she must have produced had neutralized the equally preternatural blackness. Or so his mind was telling him as he followed the corridors that had been laid before him, deliberately ignoring the fact that the house had become a labyrinth greater than its size should have accommodated.

Silence! Stay ready! he heard from her again, though she remained nowhere to be found in this infrared, surreal trap into which he'd invited himself.

"Looking for your neighbor, Harry?" came a voice from everywhere. "Lyle's told me all about how you rescued him in your civilian clothes. Do they give medals for that, I wonder. Being on duty when you're dead?"

Don't listen to him! Be calm, Harry. I am in control. You must trust me.

A series of strong, even thunderous reports sounded from a room somewhere to his right. A room doubling as an echo chamber apparently, as Harry tried to reconcile the powerful sounds his brain had processed from the more lean and metallic tat-tat that should have erupted from Billie's rifle.

If only the fruits of the thing would now present themselves, he thought as he cautiously made his way in that direction.

When they didn't, he checked his belt to make sure the nine millimeter he'd brought as backup was still in its place, safety off. It was only a complement to the single-load but nasty weapon he held against his shoulder, though it certainly gave him more flexibility should he find himself needing such. Not that he'd ever have imagined a firefight, unstable as the situation was. While the objective hadn't been clearly defined at the outset, he'd seen the task as a mission to extract one individual from the grip of a dangerous yet unsuspecting, unarmed other. But then again, there were a lot of things he wouldn't have imagined out of a set of circumstances that had begun its spiraling progress in the blades of a lawnmower.

Holding the shotgun firmly against his shoulder, he felt as if the whole thing had been drawn up and played out already, to his detriment. There was no denying the situation was still live, if only by his partner's silence after the firing off of the series of rounds. What could he achieve, after all, that a semi-automatic rifle hadn't?

Assuming of course it had ever been fired.

I'm going to die, he thought. *I'm going to die protecting a boy who doesn't want to be protected and a serial killer who won't be stopped. Should have taken that law enforcement job after they let me out of the military in good standing. I'd have been a world better prepared for this kind of localized shit.*

"You're still not getting it, are you?" said a voice that could only be its owner's as Lyle appeared in the hallway in front of Harry, mask over his face and what was clearly a .357 magnum revolver in his hand.

Harry barely flinched as training, practice, experience enabled him to suppress the initial surprise and maintain focus and composure. "Put the gun down, Lyle. We have to get you out of here. Remember you are your mother's son. Your father can only bring the worst for you."

"And you know this how?"

"I only want to help you, son. I repeat, put the gun down. You don't want some reflex action on my part landing a slug in your chest. Trust me, it can easily happen when a man is faced with his own potential death." He measured his words. "We're both holding powerful weapons here. I know what yours can do. Do you know what mine can? When the slug hits from this distance, when all the little 12-gauge pellets have dispersed only enough to form this narrow, closely grouped body upon impact, your ribs are going to shatter, your heart will burst, a hole the size of your fist will be blown through your back. There will be no more games to play then."

The boy smiled. "I'm liking the sound of it."

"Are you?" came a voice behind him. Billie appeared, with a face of her own. "Turn and look at me, son."

"No. I know about you and I'll not be mesmerized."

"Your father is gone, Lyle. If he'd loved you, he would not have come back. Remove the mask and return to being my son."

The boy turned, very slowly and very deliberately. "Father? You mean the dude I left lying in his blood in the other room? Love? Like the kind of love only you can give? Mask? If this was a mask, I might do as you ask and take it off. Since it's not—"

The sound that came next was deafening.

I discharged my own weapon and when the smoke cleared, the boy was gone, Harry would tell authorities later. *The thing had taken a whole different turn now, the family element having been exposed for the one-sided monstrosity Lyle was. What was I to think? That it hadn't been the boy all along?*

213

7: For the Love of God, It's *Profane*

"For the umpteenth time, Mr. Hinterlove, there *is* and *was* no boy. We've a dead husband and wife and your prints all over the weapons that killed them and that's all there is to that. What we want to know now is *motive*."

Harry shook his head, an exercise he'd been repeating for what seemed hours. "No, no, again *no*! What motive would I have, for god's sake?"

"Any history of PTSD, Hinterlove? They make allowances for such things these days. All we want you to do is—"

"Lawyer. I want my goddamn lawyer."

"And as you've been told, he's on his goddamn way."

"And I continue to demand, how can he be on his goddamn way when you haven't allowed me to goddamn call him?"

Just then the door to the interview room opened and in stepped the suit that had served the Hinterlove family through the last nightmare. "Hello, Harry."

"Don. Thank goodness you're here."

"I need to talk to my client alone," the bearded, well-dressed, Orson Wells of a parody told Harry's interrogator.

After the detective, or whatever he was in this slice of rural America, had led them to a separate room, Harry's attorney looked at his client gravely. "Again I find myself in a criminal law situation when you know that's not my area. What's going on this time, Harry?"

Harry found his balance, said, "They're accusing me of double murder, Don. As if I could even—"

"I know what they're accusing you of, Harry. Tell me what happened."

"Right," Harry said, smiling sardonically. "Because we've been through all this before, yeah?"

"Because they're obligated to tell me. Now what did you do?"

"Nothing! What the fuck kind of question is that? I did what I did in the defense of the boy who lives across the street from me. I don't know where he's gone. But he was there, and needed saving. His mother…she could tell you…" He broke down in tears as he tried to put it into some kind of sense. But the weight of it all was simply too much.

"Get a grip on yourself, Harry. This is doing you no favors."

"You don't understand, Don. All of this...I realize now it's to do with Whitewash Drive itself—there's some sort of activity on our street, from my parents' place on down to the end of the cul-de-sac, that I can't—"

"Okay, that's enough. I've heard all I need to hear."

"What does that mean?" Harry demanded. "What does that *mean*, Don?"

"It means, if I'm to be your representation we're going with insanity this time, to be settled in advance, out of court. I'll not go to trial with you again. It's...for the love of god, Harry, it's *profane*."

*   *   *

It should have been a routine mission. Question the villagers about possible rebel activity in the area. Sure, the circumstances that had led up to the need to interrogate civilians had been all but routine. But weren't there always such operations going on now that IEDs were killing soldiers every time you turned around? Whatever god was the one true god, Captain Hinterlove hoped they reserved a special place for the cowards responsible for such faceless attacks.

Yes, it should have been a routine mission. Talk to some of the villagers privately before rounding them up, if need be, to see if they might respond better that way. You never knew for certain where allegiances lay, but if a given village's inhabitants did not support the rebels, as intelligence suggested was the case here, they might find the strength in numbers to assist the foreign presence. It rarely worked out according to this simplistic model, but that's the way Hinterlove, like his commander before him, ran things. Structure first, improvisation when things broke down.

Unfortunately, this particular mission reached the breakdown stage long before steps in a process could be seen through. Always in there with his men, the captain sparked the sequence of events by ordering two of his men, after a tip, to forcibly drag a man out of a ramshackle stable in which he hid among his animals. Hinterlove wasn't in the habit of pulling subjects of interest out into the blazing sun, but norms had already been broken by one villager snitching on another and he thought a public message ought to be sent.

This had not gone well, as such situations rarely did. The goats had bleated the entire time. The wives had screamed. A separate party who'd been in the stable with the man had fled out the back door where things were at their most chaotic. Still, Hinterlove's men, on his silent okay, had worked the villager like he himself had planted the explosive that had led to the unit being here in the first place. All this happened in only a few minutes' time before an NCO by the name of Kwai put in the captain's ear that a boy of twelve or so, conspicuously appearing more alarmed than scared, had holed himself up in a smaller, sand-brick building behind the stable.

Alarmed? Scared? What difference did it make, Hinterlove thought as he followed the sergeant to the shed, where two other soldiers were already positioned by the locked door. Was the kid hiding explosive devices or their makings in the shed? He hardly thought so. He nodded to one of his men. *Break the door down.*

It was as easy a task as using the butt of a rifle. On the second strike the lock failed and the door swung inward. The spaces were lit by sunlight spilling through cracks in the planks. While the boy was nowhere to be seen, there were places where he could hide. Like the—

Hayloft.

I know you're here, boy. Show your ass now, Harry, or be whipped to within an inch of your life. What? No 'haven't done nuthin' for your pop? Yeah, I s'pose not when your mother caught you red-handed burnin' yerself on the stove while lost in one of yer daydreams. Show your ass now and maybe I won't wear your hide out till you're bleedin'.

Harry huddled in his hiding place, smelling the cut hay, praying that it protected him from his liquor-crazed, war-wrecked casualty of a father. He knew his prayers were futile, but what else did he have? The forces were overwhelmingly against him. The last time he'd been hospitalized, it hadn't been his father's punishment that had put him there, but the bite of an unknown spider that Harry couldn't help but think the elder Hinterlove had put in the hay out of spite. The son of these tides squeezed his face shut, daring not to breathe, to think, to remember. This time, if only, let him be left alone. What was war to him, a twelve-year-old boy? Why must he suffer because his father got a bad draw?

"Captain? Cap'n H?"

"Yeah, for fuck's sake. *What?*"

"If the boy's still here, he has to be behind that clutter in the back. Should we proceed?"

"Christ, Staff Sergeant Kwai. These are your men. *Move* already."

"It's just that…"

"What?"

"Funny feeling things aren't right. Door at the back appears to have a chain on it. Meaning he's here, and on purpose—"

"Fire into the clutter."

"Sir?"

"Fire into the fucking clutter."

"But sir—"

Hinterlove drew his own sidearm, opening up on the whatnot.

"See?" he said. "Easy, right? Now proceed."

"Sir, I'm just not feeling good—"

"Goddamnit, Kwai," the captain said, pushing forward on his own.

He glanced back once to see the sergeant motioning his men forward, all rifles training upon that one place. Then the unexpected happened. No one could have seen it coming. No one could have anticipated the boy dropping from a perch above the front door, some nasty implement of destruction in his hand. That's what they first saw—this arched metallic blade—not the more recognizable something the kid let fall into their midst.

"Grenade!" cried the sergeant while his captain looked on stupefied.

But it was already too late. The legs of both Kwai and the soldier nearest him were blown out from under them. A third soldier, catching the impact of shrapnel in his torso was thrown backwards and through the body of the one who'd delivered the destruction, landing beyond him but having protected him in the process. It was seconds before any additional noise pierced the general soundlessness. When it came, it came in the form of a laugh.

A boy's laugh.

Hinterlove didn't wait until his senses returned to him. He was on top of the kid in a flash, securing him with his knees before bashing in his teeth with the butt of his weapon. Inserting the gun's barrel into the jagged and bloody hole, he blew the back of his skull into the desert floor. Regarding the end product satisfactorily, he then stood, undid his fatigues, and in an action that received more shock than support from the contingent of men that had rushed in behind their fallen comrades, pissed on the boy's face.

"Kisses to you, son. May all your dreams be realized."

8: Licking Up the Spill

Harry woke sitting up in his bed, sweating like a pig. Oh thank god, he thought. Oh thank god it's not like that...

Before stretching or relieving himself or anything else, he went to his kitchen window to look across the street. There was Lyle, right where he should have been, mowing the grass with his long shoelace dangling dangerously in front of him, mind on anything and everything but the chore itself. Harry immediately opened the window, yelling across the space that separated them, though futilely so over the sound of the motor. In his shorts, Harry rushed out of the house and across the street, panting as he arrived before any damage had been done.

"Cut it off!" he said at the boy's look. "Cut the engine off." He drew the gesture across his throat.

The boy shut the machine down. "Got it before, Mr. Hinterlove, okay? I learned my lesson last week when you took me to the hospital."

Harry collected himself. "And yet you're still wearing your shoelaces un—"

But he saw that they weren't. Not really. They were long and kind of sprawling in the loose bow Lyle had made of them, but at least they were tied and well out of reach of the lawnmower blades.

"Sorry, son. Being a bit overprotective after the accident, I guess. You okay?"

Lyle looked at him oddly. "Shouldn't I be?"

"I don't know. Just checking in on you, that's all."

"You don't have to worry. Like I said, I learned my lesson."

"Good for you, son. Your mom's okay too?"

"Yeah. Why?"

"Nothing, just asking." *And while we're at it, would you by chance know what happened to the last week of my life?*

"You okay, Mr. Hinterlove?"

"Yup. I'll be out of your hair now. I mean unless you want to tell me…"

Harry had lived a life of control mixed with the fractures that finger-crawled down the surface of his personal glass dome. He hadn't asked for any of it. If anything he'd been a victim of his heart—in romance, in love, in commitment. If there were three noble things left in the world, then those were they. Compassion, mercy, tenderness, sympathy, tolerance…these emotions, these virtual human imperatives hung around too. But they failed to capture the condition as it should be captured; the dome would simply have shattered trying to contain the force of so much emotion. No, the rewards, however ephemeral, were in the simple things. Harry had learned that the hard way. And maybe the easy way too.

"Tell you what, Mr. Hinterlove?"

"Where your mom is. Can you do that?"

"She's at the factory. She's always at the factory. Don't worry, okay? I'll do better taking care of myself." He looked up. "Shit. I feel like I'm being watched now."

"No, no, carry on," Harry said. "I didn't mean to make you feel that way. Get back to your mowing and tell your mom hi from me."

Lyle's eyes, behind a boy's slightly puzzled, slightly amused look, followed Harry back to his house. Harry could not only feel them on his back—he could see them. Some things, those eyes conveyed, were best left to lie. No one would come rolling up in a taxi tonight. No phantoms would appear to fulfill the phantasms of anyone's mind. It had all been a thing of misinterpretations and misjudgments. Like such things always were. Better the wonders merely be wondered over, not further inspected, as surely war has taught the warrior.

Has it? Harry thought, sitting at his kitchen table. *Did I learn anything other than the horrors of which we're capable as a species? I'd not deflect anything that proved me wrong, would I?*

He thought of his mother and father, of living rooms and dens, and decided that somewhere there must be some dripping sack of humanity remaining. As long as there was a dog there to lick up the sticky spill, there were still such things as American kisses, weren't there?

*   *   *

" Get out of the tree, kid. You're going to kill yourself."

"Who are you talking to, Colonel?"

"What? Oh, it's you, Billie. Look at your son out there—he's going to cut himself to pieces. Can you talk to him?"

"Colonel, they're just trees. We've been through this again and again. My son is in school, you're not at your old home, there are no chainsaws outside your window."

"You're working for them, aren't you?"

"Working for whom, Colonel? I'm just an orderly assigned to you."

"No, you are one of them! I remember now, you're the one with the secret weapons—they call you the spider, isn't that right?"

Laughter. *If it were only that simple, Colonel.*

"Who? What? Laugh all you want."

"Calm down, Colonel, or I'll have no choice but to call the nurse, or even Doctor J again."

"Good! Do it! I'm tired of being flung around like a sack of skin in your nest of demons. I know what you want and you'll never, in a goddamn million lifetimes, have it. I was there, I saw it! I saw it as all the players were reduced to remnants of themselves, including the lamb. So I'm the only one left…so what? You can manipulate me like you did him? Reduce my smile to a bloody hole among scattered teeth? Didn't you consider the motherfucking consequences—"

Not like this, sir. Never like this.

"Where are you, goddamnit?"

"I'm here, Colonel. Doctor J at your every service."

"Can you explain to this woman that she doesn't know from the victims and the victimized?"

"There's a difference?"

"If you consider the teeth in your head first, yes, there's a difference."

"How so?"

"You can't put them back in, that's how so. Factor in the way the face dissolves in the acid of your piss and there's nothing left to extend the misery. For god's sake, can't we find an end to it?"

"That's what we're trying to do here every day, Colonel. Bring an end to what ails the patients in our hospital."

"What hospital? You call this detention facility a hospital? What's to make us trust people like you?"

Us, Hinterlove?

"I mean the survivors. The ones who come back."

You're one of those, are you?

"If you could give me a moment, the merest moment, to collect myself…"

Sadly, the moments are done. There's the going back if you so desire, other than that…

"Going back where? And for what?"

Corrections, perhaps? A tweak here or there?

"But where to begin?"

A boy in the angry grip of a machine might do.

"That seems so beneath the real story…"

Then write something better, Colonel. A long sentence lies in front you. Give it the spin that seems best for you.

"Kisses. That's what's missing from the tale. A mother kissed me once. So did a father, later. Let's dedicate this to them then, understanding I can only tell you where their bones are, not their souls."

Fair enough. We require only the residue.

9: An Epilogue of Sorts

Detective Moore was sitting at the bar with a Manhattan when his partner Lambert entered their favorite local Chattanooga pub, the *Chu-Chu Chumba*, which tonight was otherwise empty. At the ring of the bell hanging from the door, Moore looked over his shoulder. He'd been anticipating his partner and the "bizarre news" the other had mentioned when he'd phoned an hour earlier, interrupting Moore's enjoyment of his son's scrimmage.

Ordering a beer, Lambert looked at his mate. "Got a good grip on your whisky, Jimmy? You ain't gonna believe this shit."

"Must be something special. You sounded downright reverent on the phone."

Lam knitted his brows. "Reverent, eh? That's a damn close approximation to the way it felt when the geeks uncovered the shit buried deep in the dude's laptop."

"Dude being the male victim in the Sully case if I got you right. There was a lot of noise in the bleachers. Bye week scrimmage might as well have been a game itself, with everybody's hopes up for the state championship."

"Yeah, g'luck on that by the way. Didn't even know high school football had bye weeks."

"Just the one."

"Ought to do it later in the season," Lam said. "Heal the bruises before postseason play."

"Oh? You have an opinion after already demonstrating you know nothing about high school football?"

"Just sayin'."

"Will you come out with it already? You had my interest piqued, now you're just annoying me. What the fuck did the techs uncover?"

Lam thanked the bartender as his beer was placed in front of him. "Keep the change. A little something for Liz and the kids."

The bartender crooked a grin. "You always say that, Lam."

"And I always mean it."

"For God's sake," Moore said.

"Okay, okay, partner, here's the dirt. Remember how the Hinterlove character—still can't bring myself to call him Colonel as it just don't fit—remember how he kept maintaining there was a boy involved?"

"Yeah?"

"Well, they found what I guess you'd call a memoir buried deep in his laptop. It was in manuscript form as if he was preparing it for possible publication. It's short—he claims to have written it while flying back to the States—but it's a motherfucker of an engaging read. Slow a reader as I am, I sucked it up in less than an hour, even with the backovers. He gave the thing a name. Called it *The Tennessean*, with the subtitle *Utter Destruction*, if you can fucking dig that. If I hadn't already been warned, the title would have made me think I was about to read either a manifesto or a work of fiction. Still could be the latter, but I—"

"Jesus Christ, Lam. What did the damn thing say?"

"Yeah," chimed in the bartender from where he was washing mugs. "Spill it already."

Moore marked the bartender with a finger. "Get me another Manhattan, Felix, and stay away from this conversion or the next tip Liz and the kids are going to get is that you're in Mercy General recovering from me pulling out a fistful of that long-ass hippy hair of yours. Get on with it, Lam."

Lam drank deeply of his beer before looking squarely at his partner. "If his memoirs are to be believed, Hinterlove is an all-out serial killer. He described in detail doing several slayings in various European cities before coming back to the States—get this—in the company of a boy he picked up in Amsterdam."

"You have got to be fucking kidding me."

"Shit you not. But wait, there's more. These apparent confessions are only a precursor for the really weird shit."

"Which is?"

"Geeks found an email sent to Hinterlove, with the relevant document attached."

"I don't get you. What document? We were talking about the colonel's memoirs—"

"Exactly. Attached to the email was the same file Hinterlove claimed to have written on the flight. Only without the introductory comments."

"You're confusing the shit out of me."

"You and me both," said Felix, placing Detective Moore's drink before him.

"Shut up, Felix," said Detective Moore. Looking at Lambert, he said, "Where did this email come from? Was it possibly a reply to one Hinterlove sent?"

"That's just it. It was an original email, dated the same day Hinterlove downloaded the file. The times confirm that the email actually predated the Word document on Hinterlove's computer. Apparently the colonel—your title, not mine—downloaded the file, read it, then a day later added an introduction to it that explained when and why he wrote the thing."

"You said the 'when' was when he was on the airplane. You didn't mention the 'why'?"

"What's to mention? He said something to the effect that the purity in the boy's face brought him to realize the truth of his actions. Or some such psychopathic garbage. It's irrelevant if the email that preceded this addition to the document is in fact—"

"But where did this email come from? He could have sent it himself if he's a head case."

"The account was opened under the name of Billie Sullivan. Recognize that name?"

Moore had been in the process of sipping his drink before pausing to stare at his partner. "Are you telling me one of the victims sent the email?"

Lam abandoned his own drink. "Remember Hinterlove's account of events after we nailed him? Of being lured into the web of this dysfunctional family, of being seduced into this world of..."

Moore cocked his head. "Otherworldy entities? Demons? Is that what you're talking about, Lam? Because if that's it, I have to tell you you've been on the job just a little too long."

"I know it's a reach—"

"A *reach*? Are you fucking with me? It's bad Twilight Zone episodes. What the fuck have you been into? Felix here supplying you with acid or something?"

"Dude, the woman sent the email. The boy was in the document. Hinterlove talked about a boy. This came *before* the events of that morning, *before* the system deemed him crazy and sent him off to the farm."

"Yet how quickly that happened."

"His lawyer betrayed him. It happens."

Moore sighed. Drank. Sighed again. "Emails from people now dead. Boys who don't exist. A suspect convicted and locked up. Where's the 'bizarre news' you were so proud of on the phone? It's a day at the fucking office, Lam. That's all."

Lam pursed his lips, nodding. "But you never let me get to the last thing."

"What last thing, Lambert? Christ on a spaceship?"

"While the email account was registered under her name, it originated in Amsterdam where Jason Sully happened to be travelling at the time. *He* was the one at the heart of it, according to Hinterlove."

"Yet another resonsible victim? Why don't we just lay it on the devil himself and let the colonels go scapegoating into the sunset? That would be true justice, I think. What do you think, Felix?"

Felix suavely tossed his hair out of his eyes. "I think you're all missing the point. Which is that *nobody* writes memoirs from hell. They were all damned to start with, obviously. What's there to investigate other than another nest of what we are? God bless 'em, I say."

About the Author

Darren Speegle is the author of six books, including his recently released debut novel *The Third Twin* (Crystal Lake Publishing). His second novel, *Artifacts*, is due in 2018, while a third, *The World Is My Oyster*, has recently been completed. The latest of his five short story collections, *A Haunting in Germany and Other Stories*, was released in 2016 by PS Publishing. His short fiction has appeared in numerous venues, including *Subterranean*, *Cemetery Dance*, *Clarkesworld*, *Postscripts*, *ChiZine*, *Crimewave*, *The Third Alternative* (now *Black Static*), *Fantasy*, *Dark Discoveries*, and *Subterranean: Tales of Dark Fantasy*. He has recently become interested in editing, and his human-evolution-themed anthology *Adam's Ladder* (co-edited with Michael Bailey) will be a late 2017 Dark Regions Press title. A widely traveled American, Darren often sets his stories in exotic or interesting places where he has lived (Germany, Alaska, Southeast Asia) or otherwise explored (broader Europe). Between gigs as a federal contractor in the Middle East, Darren resides in Thailand. When not writing, he enjoys outdoor activities like hiking and biking.

CPSIA information can be obtained
at www.ICGtesting.com
Printed in the USA
FSHW022002120122
87624FS